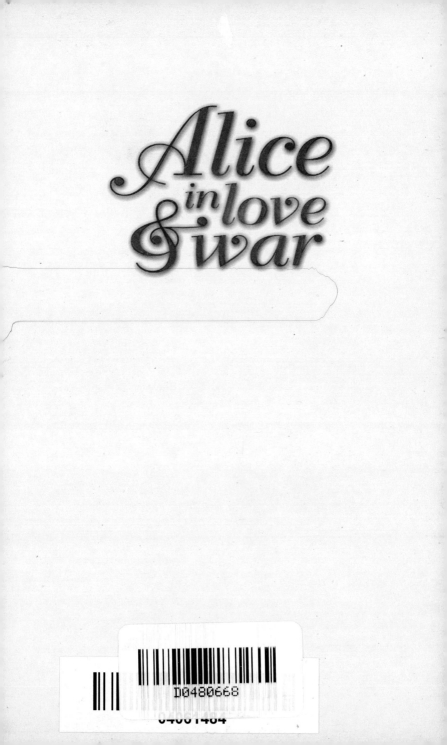

Alice in love & war

Alice in love & war

Ann Turnbull

WALKER
BOOKS

I would like to thank everyone who helped me with research for this book, in particular Catherine Johnson, Sara Read, Tony Rowland and Katherine Langrish. Thanks also to my editor, Mara Bergman, and to my family and writer friends for all their support and encouragement.

First published in Great Britain 2009 by Walker Books Ltd
87 Vauxhall Walk, London SE11 5HJ

2 4 6 8 10 9 7 5 3 1

Text © 2009 by Ann Turnbull
Cover photograph © Ebby May / Photodisc / Getty Images

This book has been typeset in Bembo.

Printed and bound in Great Britain by Clays Ltd, St Ives plc

British Library Cataloguing in Publication Data:
a catalogue record for this book is
available from the British Library

ISBN 978-1-4063-0244-8

www.walker.co.uk

To the memory of Faye, with love

Prologue

Prologue

In the name of God, Amen. I, WILLIAM NEWCOMBE of Bideford in the County of Devon, being sick in body but well in mind, make this my last Will and Testament the eighteenth day of August 1639. I give all my goods and chattels to my brother HUMPHREY NEWCOMBE of Tor Farm near Tavistock in the County of Devon, and desire that he will take in my daughter, ALICE NEWCOMBE, and care for her as his own.

In the dispensing room, men were packing the oils and potions into boxes, cramming in bottles carelessly, wherever there was space.

"No!" Alice exclaimed. "They must be stored like with like."

Her father's work, her home, her life – all were in disarray. She ran and tried to intervene, but the men only put her gently to one side and continued their activity.

A dried turtle hung from the ceiling on strings. They cut it down, and dust flew about and glinted in the thin shaft of light from the window. Hanging bunches of dried herbs scented the air with a warm, sweet aroma. These were not dusty; her father would renew them and always kept fresh supplies. She remembered going out with him to gather them in the meadows and woodland: heart's-ease, lovage, comfrey, rue. Now the neighbours would take the herbs away; but the medicines would be sold and the money given to her uncle towards her keep.

Tossed aside on a stool was her father's book: the one in which he had kept his lists of medicines and herbs, and their uses – all in the small, neat handwriting that he had made sure also to teach her. "Always write clearly," he'd said. "Mistakes can be dangerous." Alice picked up the book and pushed it quickly down the front of her gown, between her bodice and stays. This was hers now, she thought; no one else should have it.

Behind the half-closed door of the kitchen she heard women gossiping. They were neighbours, come to help clear the rooms. Their voices were hushed, reproachful.

"…should have made better provision…"

"…too kind to poor folk; never earned much…"

"…child to go to strangers…"

"He's her uncle!"

"But a stranger to her*. And she doesn't come with money. Why would he want her?"*

Alice's grief and fear rose up, overwhelming. She burst into the room and threw herself at Goody Chammings, clinging to

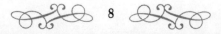

her. "Take me in, please! Don't let them send me away. Please take me! I'll be good, I promise."

The woman held her close; her bodice smelt comfortingly of sweat and lavender. "I wish I could, my pigeon. But it's a family matter. Not for neighbours to decide."

"This is the child," the Reverend Master Morton told the man and his wife. "Alice. Eleven years of age." His glance down at her was kind and regretful. "A virtuous child, tenderly reared."

Humphrey Newcombe, yeoman farmer of Tavistock, had a look of her father, Alice thought, but with a face set in discontented lines. She curtseyed, and he acknowledged her with a nod. He took a step forward, awkwardly, as if to embrace or kiss her, then seemed to change his mind. His wife remained still. She looked Alice up and down with a cold eye.

Master Morton withdrew, leaving the three of them together.

Humphrey Newcombe turned to his wife. "It is our duty to take the child in." He was the master, but he sounded almost apologetic.

The woman was full of suppressed resentment. Alice could see it in the rigid set of her head and body. She knew she would not be welcome at Tor Farm.

1644

One

Alice was upstairs stripping beds, the windows flung open to sweeten the air, when she heard the drums.

Soldiers! The king's army, it must be, hotfoot from their victory at Lostwithiel. News of that battle had been all around the village yesterday. She ran to the window and looked out at the valley below. They came through steadily falling rain along the road from Tavistock; she saw the glint of metal, the colours raised aloft, the cavalry; and behind them a ripple of movement, countless men marching.

Alice felt a charge of excitement. It was a brave sight, joyous, no matter which side you favoured. Like many people, her aunt and uncle cared for neither. Their two sons, Tom and Ned, who had always been rivals, had joined up with opposing sides. Ned, who had fought for the king, had been killed in a skirmish last year. Tom was off somewhere with General Waller's army – the further

away the better, to Alice's mind. She only wished his father had gone too.

Her aunt came into the room behind her and pulled her back from the window. Her fingers dug into Alice's upper arms. "Don't stand gaping!" Yet she stared out herself. "Jenefer said a quartermaster was going around the village yesterday. Pray God they leave us be."

Alice knew that her aunt, prudent as always, had begun to store what she could against the coming winter. It was early September, and followed such a cold, wet August as no one could recall: the roads awash with water, the crops rotting in the fields. There was hunger in the country, for last summer's harvest had also been bad. Her aunt believed that the succession of ruined harvests was a punishment from God for the civil war that had begun two years ago. The armies lived off the land, demanding food, bedding, stabling, even livestock; people went in dread of them. Humphrey Newcombe had been lucky so far; Tor Farm was up a steep track, a mile and a half from the village.

Let them come, thought Alice. She wanted them to come, even though it would mean more work for her. She longed for change. And why should she care if her aunt was distressed? Alice had no interest in the king's war with Parliament, but she had been conducting her own war with Mary Newcombe for the last five years: a war of small disobediences and unwilling submission that had recently taken on a new intensity.

* * *

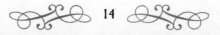

She was not disappointed. An hour later a detachment of soldiers could be seen tramping up towards the farm. Alice ran outside as they marched into the yard. They looked tired: wet hair hanging lank on their shoulders, their boots and breeches spattered with mire. One of their leaders – young, dark, a band of powder charges slung across his body – caught her eye and winked. She looked away, feeling her face grow hot – then flicked a glance back. He was still watching her. Her heartbeat quickened.

Mary Newcombe was in dispute with the sergeant. "Twenty men! We have not the beds!"

"You have barns? Outhouses?"

She nodded. Alice knew she would have to let them in. If she didn't, they would take what they wanted by force.

The servants had gathered in the yard: the maids, Jenefer and Sarah; the cowman, Jacob. Young Matt had already set off at a run for the high moor to fetch the master. Her aunt gave orders.

"Sarah! Off to the kitchen! Help Jenefer with beer and meat. Alice, come with me."

Alice stole a quick glance backwards at the soldier who had winked at her, before following her aunt upstairs. She saw that he had caught her name.

The rooms on the upper floor led one off another. Alice slept in a small chamber of her own, but her aunt and uncle had to pass through it on their way to their bedroom. These days Alice kept her bed curtains tied tightly closed and her knife near at hand.

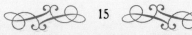

"We'll put one of them here," her aunt said. "You can sleep in our room – and don't give me that face!" Her own complexion had darkened. "I'll hear no more of your lies. We'll all share the one chamber – the maids too. Better that way. I can keep an eye on you and Sarah. Can't trust you girls around men."

Alice seethed inwardly, furious at being linked with the kitchen maid, whom she despised, and even more at the accusation that she'd lied about her uncle.

He had begun pestering her two years ago, but lately it had got worse. He would waylay her in the barn, the sheep sheds, even the kitchen. Last week it had taken all her strength to fight him off; she had bitten his hand and kneed him where it hurt and cursed him for trying to commit a sin against nature. She had run, trembling, into the house, found her aunt alone upstairs, and shouted and sobbed out the truth to her.

Foolishly, she had expected her aunt to take her side; after all, there seemed little love lost between husband and wife. But Mary Newcombe had screeched at her, calling her a lying slut. She slapped Alice's face so hard that her head rang; then she seized a broom and beat her across her back, shoulders and ribs till she begged for mercy. Alice hadn't dared speak out again.

Now, her aunt lifted the lid of the linen chest and the scent of lavender wafted into the room. She began pulling out sheets, her mouth set tight in resignation. From below came a crash of breaking crockery, a shriek from Sarah, and male laughter. Mary Newcombe stiffened, and Alice felt a brief moment of kinship, almost

of sympathy. A liking for order – for a clean dairy, herb-scented linen, jars and bottles all in their right places – was the one thing the two of them had in common.

Her aunt thrust a pile of linen into Alice's arms. "Take those and make up beds in the stair room. And when you've done that you can go down and help in the kitchen. But keep away from the soldiers." She glanced out of the window. "Here's your uncle at last." She spoke of him, as always, with mild contempt.

She went downstairs, and Alice heard a clamour of men's voices, over which her aunt's was raised in complaint.

Left alone, she took her father's book from the shelf in her chamber and hid it for safe-keeping above the lintel in the room she was now to share. Then she made up beds, smoothing the sheets, her mind on the soldier who had caught her eye. She met few young men. Two years ago she had formed a shy friendship with a boy in the village: the baker's apprentice, a lad of fifteen. That summer they had exchanged smiles and glances, a few words. She had liked him, but it had come to nothing, for that winter he fell ill with a fever and died. There had been no one since. Her aunt kept her hard at work, close to home and farmyard; it was only on market days at Tavistock that she had a chance to look around. Of course, it was expected that one day she would marry. Her aunt complained from time to time of the inevitable loss of labour this would cause and of the cost of a dowry – pointing out that Alice was ill-tempered and without beauty, and that it was unlikely any man

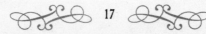

would choose her unless the dowry was worth having.

And yet, thought Alice, it was not Sarah the soldier had winked at.

When she went downstairs the sergeant was sprawled in her uncle's chair, leaning back – his feet, in dirty boots, on the table. Three others sat on the stools, and all were drinking beer. There were pies, meat, bread and cheese on the table: everything Jenefer had been able to find. The master and mistress were not in sight. Alice knew they would have gone to hide away their money and good clothes and any other valuables. Jenefer, red-faced from the flames, was roasting beef on a spit; a cauldron of water for washing was heating to one side. Sarah was red-faced too. Blonde curls had escaped from her cap and now hung on her rosy forehead. She stood close to the sergeant, and Alice saw that he had his hand up her skirt. Quickly she looked away, at the other men.

Close to, she became aware of how dirty they were. They smelt bad, almost rotten; and she thought of the waterlogged roads and the boots no doubt in need of re-pair. Their linen, where it showed, was grimy and torn, their blue coats stained, their hair matted and moustaches untrimmed. And yet they excited her. They brought with them an air of danger and freedom. They moved in the greater world. They were passing through – not trapped, as she was, in this cold-hearted house on the edge of the moor.

Her gaze settled on the one who had winked at her. She began to rearrange some plates on the table, drawing gradually closer to him.

"Alice, isn't it?" He spoke softly, with an accent she didn't know. "Are you chambermaid or daughter?"

"Neither. I am Master Newcombe's niece."

"And how old are you, Alice?"

"Sixteen."

She knew she must be blushing. He looked older than she was – twenty or more – and she thought him handsome, despite the dirt: a "proper man", as folk would say. He was tall and lithe, his hair and eyes dark and his face tanned from being out in all weathers. She wanted to ask *his* name, but did not dare.

As if he guessed her wish, he smiled and said, "Corporal Robin Hillier, of Sir John Agnew's Regiment of Foot."

She found her courage. "You're not from around here?"

"No. From Oxford."

Oxford: where the king now kept state, since Parliament had forced him out of London. Alice had only the vaguest idea of where Oxford was, or how far away, though she knew it was to the north. Most places were north of Tavistock.

"We've been on the road five months," he said. "Makes you long for home comforts."

Alice did not know what to say to this. She was almost relieved when her aunt reappeared and said, "Alice! Sarah! Be about your work!" Her sharp gaze would have taken everything in.

The sergeant called for a tub of hot water "and a maid to pour it over me!" Sarah gasped and giggled, but

Mary Newcombe assigned this task to Jenefer, who was forty and had – so she muttered on her way to fetch the tub – "seen it all before, and it's nothing much". Alice was set to tearing up rags for bandages. It seemed that some of the soldiers had been wounded at Lostwithiel and the wounds required dressing.

"You'll be more use to me than Sarah," Mary Newcombe admitted grudgingly. "Come out to the barn and help."

They took cloths, clean water in a leather bucket, and a pot of salve that Alice had made from one of her father's recipes. The hens were all in the yard, clucking and grumbling at being evicted from the barn. Their place had been taken by a crowd of men, most of them eating and drinking, a few lying exhausted on straw bales.

The first man they dealt with had a sword cut in his upper arm. When her aunt removed the bandages Alice saw that the wound was oozing foul-smelling pus, the flesh around it red and swollen.

"You need a surgeon," Mary Newcombe said, and the man looked at her in terror. "There are surgeons with the regiment?"

He nodded, his teeth knocking together as she swabbed the wound, smeared on salve, and got Alice to help her re-bandage it.

"I'll tell your sergeant. It must be seen to, soon."

Afterwards she said to Alice, "He will die, no matter what. It's infected."

With brusque hands she set about attending to the

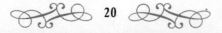

next one. Alice went to help a red-haired lad, greenish-pale under his freckles. He had a thigh wound, still bleeding after four days. She washed it gently, trying not to hurt him, but she saw that he was frightened by the fresh gush of blood that ensued.

"It will stop," she reassured him. "And this salve will ease the pain and help healing." She laid a piece of lint on the wound and bandaged it carefully.

"Thank you, mistress," he said when she was finished. He was a mere boy, no more than eighteen. She hoped she was right, that his wound would heal.

When they were done, Mary Newcombe burned the soiled bandages and they both washed themselves in clean water from the well. Alice looked down the hillside and saw large movements of soldiers, horses and wagons all around. It seemed that the entire army was settling in the village and the surrounding farms.

"How long will they stay?" she asked her aunt, thinking of Robin Hillier and his warm gaze.

"Why ask me? The sooner they go the better. They'll be all over the village, making whores of folks' maids and daughters, drinking a month's brewing in a day." She looked keenly at Alice. "You keep away from them! I know you and your sluttish ways."

You know nothing about me, thought Alice. Nor care. She remembered how she had tried, at first, to please this woman who so clearly did not want her. Alice had come from a loving home, a place where she was never beaten, but praised and cared for; where there were streets full of friends, neighbours, customers. Here

there was nothing: no life, no love. And now her aunt called her a slut because she had grown into a woman and her uncle had laid hands on her. As often before, she thought, Why did my father send me here, to a brother he hadn't seen for years?

She knew the answer, of course: it was that or the orphanage and a life of servitude. He'd put his trust in his brother.

When Alice and her aunt returned to the yard they found Robin Hillier there, alone except for the guard dog, Watch, who lolled against him, allowing the man to pull his ears and fondle his muzzle. Robin had shed his stained blue coat and wore fresh linen. The shirt hung loose on his lean frame.

He stepped forward with an easy grace and acknowledged them. Alice dared not catch his eye with her aunt there. He smelt of her aunt's wash-ball of best lavender soap, and she recognized the shirt, from a darn on the sleeve, as one of her uncle's.

Mary Newcombe also recognized it. "I see you have found my linen chest," she remarked.

"Indeed. And we are most grateful. Your generosity, mistress, prospers the cause of his sacred majesty."

Was he mocking her aunt, Alice wondered? If he was, Mary Newcombe did not see it. She appeared quite disarmed.

"That one has better manners than his sergeant," she said as they went indoors. She told the sergeant about the badly wounded soldier. "If your surgeon is in the village, the man must be taken down there."

While they were discussing this, Alice slipped outside. There was always work to do on the farm – and many places to be busy yet away from her aunt's eye.

The barn was a good place to hide, and there was often the excuse of eggs to be searched for. But the barn had now been taken over by soldiers. Instead she chose the dairy, deliberately passing Robin Hillier without a glance as she walked across the yard.

The dairy was a favourite haunt of hers: cool, fresh and orderly, with a faint pleasant sour-milk smell. There were stone sinks and tables and pewter dishes all scrubbed clean; linen aprons hanging on a hook; butter shapers with the Tor Farm mark on them; curds tied in a linen cloth and hung up for the whey to drip into a bowl; bunches of parsley and chervil. This morning there had also been a great round yellow cheese. That was gone – taken by Jenefer to feed the soldiers.

She busied herself chopping herbs for the curd cheese. It was not long before Robin Hillier's figure darkened the doorway. She glanced up, nervous now, even though she had hoped for this.

He looked about in approval. "Your uncle has a fine house and farm."

"He keeps sheep, mostly," said Alice. "They run free on the moor."

"He'll be taking some to market soon."

"Yes."

They were talking of nothing, and both knew it. Her hands trembled; she struggled to chop the herbs finely.

"Has he children?"

"Two sons. One dead, last year, fighting for the king."

"I'm sorry to hear it. He died in a noble cause."

"The other is with the Parliament army. They had always fought each other, even as boys. There is no love in this house." She blushed and looked down as she said the word "love".

"And how came *you* here? An orphan?"

"Yes. My mother died when I was five; I scarcely remember her. My father did not marry again. He brought me up himself, with the help of neighbours, and I was always with him in his shop."

"His shop?"

"He was an apothecary. We lived in Bideford. It's a big port – do you know it?"

"No." He leant back against the table, settled himself to listen. "Tell me."

So she told him about Bideford, with its quay where ships unloaded cargoes from all over the world: tobacco, wine, spices. She told him about the long bridge – "twenty-four spans" – across the River Torridge. "Our shop was at the top of one of the drangs—"

"Drangs?" He was teasing her, and she laughed.

"Alleyways. They lead up from the quay into the town. My father was always busy. We'd get sailors as well as townsfolk. And sailors' wives…"

She thought of the sailors' wives, those women, often desperate, wanting remedies for whispered "women's troubles". She'd been too young then to understand

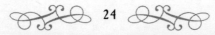

what some of these troubles might be. But of course no woman wanted a new baby at the breast when her husband came home after a voyage of a year or more.

"I became my father's assistant. Helped him make medicines, keep records and accounts."

His eyes widened. "You can write?"

"Yes, indeed."

He questioned her more, and seemed to listen to her answers; and she found herself telling him how much she had loved her father, her grief at his death, the coldness of her reception at her uncle's farm, how her aunt resented her. "My uncle was not so bad, at first. But he's a weak man." She could not tell this young man about her uncle's advances; that would be too shaming. Instead she asked, "And you?"

"I am lucky. My parents are both still living and have always been indulgent." He smiled, and Alice felt that she too would want to indulge him.

He told her his father had a farm in a hamlet near Oxford; he himself was twenty-one, the youngest of three sons. He had worked there with his family, but had been glad enough, when the chance came, to join up and serve the king. His eyes lit with enthusiasm when he spoke of the king, and he described with shock and anger how the rebels were in contempt of both king and church, stealing silver plate from a bishop's tomb near Exeter, riding their horses into the nave. "And in Lostwithiel church," he said, "they made play of christening a horse in the font, calling it Charles in mockery of his sacred majesty. They are rough fellows,

many of them, apprentice boys from London; and their leaders psalm-singing hypocrites. But we humbled them at Lostwithiel."

Alice, who until then had thought little about it, felt herself drawn to the campaign, to him, to his loyalty to the king.

"Oh, I envy you!" she exclaimed. "To have such a cause! I long to leave this place."

"But you'll leave in time. You'll marry, won't you?" And he moved closer. "You must be spoken for, a pretty girl like you?"

A pretty girl? She shook her head in denial that she was promised to anyone, and considered these words with hope but some mistrust. Her aunt had told her frequently that she had no beauty, no pleasing ways. But there was no man hereabouts whom she wished to please. It was true that Sim Braund, from Upper Farm, had called her pretty when she encountered him at Tavistock sheep fair. But he had been drunk, with hands that had constantly to be slapped away. She flinched at the memory. He disgusted her. She knew well what he was after.

This one made it sound true. And marry? Oh, if only one such as he—

"Alice? Where are you?" Her aunt's voice came from the kitchen doorway.

"Stay here!" Alice whispered, and put out a hand, almost touched him. "I'll go out to her."

But he seized her hand, making her shiver with excitement and alarm. "Alice—"

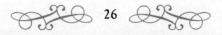

"Alice!" came from the yard, loud and irritable.

"She must not see me with you!" She broke away and ran out, breathless. "I'm here, Aunt. I was chopping herbs for the curd cheese."

Mary Newcombe was no fool. She looked suspicious and glanced towards the dairy, but at that moment her husband came tired and hungry into the yard, and her attention was turned to him and the forthcoming supper as well as food for the men in the barn.

Later, Alice was kept busy hurrying back and forth between barn and kitchen with Jenefer, taking meat and beer out to the soldiers. ("For if we don't, they'll seize what they want themselves, and make havoc," said her aunt.) Mary Newcombe and Sarah waited on the officers indoors. There was no time for Alice to talk to Robin Hillier, though once he brushed his hand against hers as she passed by. The sergeant, however, was grappling with Sarah as openly as with his meat; she made only token resistance.

Jenefer, crossing the yard with Alice, said, "If he gets that foolish slut with child the missus'll throw her out."

That night, Alice could not sleep. The room was full: Sarah, Jenefer and herself all sharing it with her uncle and aunt, all breathing with different sighs and rhythms. Alice had been given a mattress near the foot of her aunt and uncle's bed, and was disturbed not only by these sounds and by wariness of her uncle – though she was sure he'd try nothing here, and he soon fell to snoring – but by thoughts of Robin Hillier and where in the house

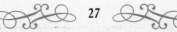

he might be lodged. In her mind she went over and over their encounter in the dairy, and imagined what might have happened if her aunt had not called for her; and what might happen tomorrow. She longed to be loved. She imagined kissing him, lying down with him, and was shocked at her own thoughts about a man she had only just met.

There was no chance of leaving the room during the night, for Jenefer's mattress was laid across the doorway. Before daylight Jenefer went downstairs to start the kitchen fire. Mary Newcombe followed, after prodding Sarah and Alice to encourage them to get up. Sarah groaned and pulled the blanket over her head, but Alice rose promptly and went out. In what had been her own room, the bed curtains were drawn and she heard snoring. The sergeant, she guessed. She shuddered at the thought of him there, in her bed.

The stair room was an annexe screened only by a curtain. Alice started when she heard Robin's voice from behind it. "Alice?" The curtain was twitched aside, and he was there, kneeling up in his shirt on the bed she'd made yesterday. "Alice!"

He caught her hand, pulling her down to sit beside him. His hair was tousled, his shirt untied and open at the neck. She smelt the bed warmth coming from him, and trembled.

"I must go! My aunt—"

"Where can we meet? Away from your aunt."

Alice knew that either Mary Newcombe or Sarah might appear at any moment. And now, to her alarm, she

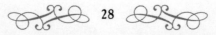

heard a sigh and movement close at hand in the shadowy room, and realized that at least one other soldier was lodged there.

"Let me go, for shame!" she whispered.

He released her, but persisted. "Where, Alice?"

"Up on the tor. The high rocks, at the top. I don't know when."

Two

As she went about her morning's work, fetching water from the well, looking for eggs, scouring the plates, Alice thought about what she had proposed. Had she demeaned herself? Would Robin think she was like Sarah? She asked herself, over and over, whether she should go. But the desire to spend more time with him was so strong that she knew she would.

Her heart was racing with more than the exertion of the climb as she set off at mid-morning, after slipping away from the farm. The tor was her special place, where she came to be alone, to weep, or think, or simply sit and gaze into the distance. It was over half a mile from the farm, and she took the long route, skirting the edge of the circle of old stone houses rather than crossing it. These houses were foundations only: hut-sized rings of flattish stones enclosed in a larger circle. They were ancient, perhaps not built by humans. The pixie rings,

people called them, and were wary of entering the enclosure.

Robin had the sense to climb from the other side and not be seen following her up the open hillside. When she saw him approach she wondered again what she had set in motion, what he would expect of her. Fearful of being observed from the farm, she sat down out of view with her back against a large stone.

He dropped down beside her, breathless from his climb. "What a place you've chosen! Windy, wet and in view of everyone!"

"Not if you stay low." And then she blushed, wondering what he'd make of that remark. But it was true that although it had stopped raining, the ground was wet and she could feel the damp through her skirts already.

He took off his coat and spread it out. "We can sit on this."

It obliged them to sit close together, touching. He put his arm round her. Alice felt breathless, intensely aware of his body next to hers, of the feel of his arm encircling her.

"That's a fine view," he said.

The moor stretched out before them: green turf and grey rock, sheep calling, a wide, pale sky.

Alice drew breath, found her voice. "It's misty. On a good day you can see for miles."

"Which way is Plymouth?"

She pointed.

"We might be going there. I heard talk."

She tensed, and his arm tightened around her.

"How long will you stay here?" she asked.

"I don't know. Till the king and Prince Maurice and their generals come to a decision. It won't be long, I fear."

They turned towards each other, their faces close; and then both his arms went around her and he began to kiss her in a way that was gentle and exciting, and as different as could be imagined from her uncle with his wet, eager mouth and bristly chin.

Robin must have untied the strings of her bodice for she felt his hands, warm and sudden, on her flesh. The pleasure she felt was mixed with a fear that things were going too fast, that she should not be here, alone with him: and she tried to cover herself and said, "I can't stay long … my aunt will miss me—" but he interrupted her with kisses.

"Truly," she said, "I must go back."

"In a while."

And he drew her down with him on the coat and they lay close together and kissed. She liked that, and the feel of the breeze on her bare shoulders; but when he began to reach under her skirts she stopped his hand. He laughed, and his breath tickled her ear; he did not try again.

When they sat up he brushed earth and twigs of gorse from her hair, and set her cap back on her head. "There! A modest maid!" She giggled. He kissed her once more. "Come here again? Please?"

"My aunt will have her eye on me…"

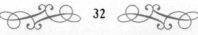

And yet she knew she would contrive a meeting, somehow. There was so much excitement in being desired by this man, and the longing to be with him – to escape, to be loved – was so strong. She had never felt like this before, and was amazed at her own boldness. "I don't know when," she said. "You'll have to watch me."

"I will." And he grinned, making her laugh.

She had no chance to be with him again that day, but the next morning her aunt sent her down to the village on an errand. The village was now the centre of the encampment. There were soldiers all around the streets and byways, and among them she glimpsed Robin, along with others from Tor Farm.

She saw women too: the women who followed the army. Some, with painted faces and dresses cut low almost to show their nipples, she knew at once to be whores. But there were also homely looking women there, one holding a small child by the hand. She wondered, uneasily, if Robin knew any of these women; if he used the whores. Surely, she thought, he would not?

And, indeed, he took no heed of the women, and when he saw her he smiled and came straight towards her. He walked back with her to the farm, taking her hand as soon as they were out of the village. Some of his friends overtook them and called out, chaffing him; but he only laughed and kept hold of her, and swung their joined hands. Alice felt a rush of happiness to be out with him like this, acknowledged by him in sight of his companions.

As they walked he talked to her about his time in the army: shocking stories of men hanged for pillaging, of duels between officers, accidents with muskets – men's fingers blown off – and he made her laugh with tales of townsmen chasing chickens in a farmyard, his own attempts to build a waterproof shelter. Once, they stopped and chatted with a group of soldiers, and he stood with his arm round her, drawing her into their circle. She felt admired, approved of, as she never did at Tor Farm, and proud to be seen with such a handsome man.

When they came in sight of the farm he let go her hand and she ran on ahead, and so arrived alone.

That evening, after supper, they met briefly behind the dairy. He pressed her against the rough stone wall and kissed her with a passion that startled her. She felt him grow hard, and he whispered, "Alice, please… I'll be going away soon…"

And his hand went again to her skirts, but again she caught it and said, frightened, "No, I can't, not—"

And then they heard someone coming, and sprang apart.

The next day, Sunday, Alice was miserable. In the morning the soldiers went down to the village for a service led by the army chaplain. Alice had hoped to go to church, so that she might meet Robin afterwards, but her aunt saw through her plans and said she would not allow Alice and Sarah loose in the village on a Sunday, ogling soldiers; they could go to evensong later with

her. Mary Newcombe was angry because the soldiers had killed and eaten five of her chickens. She harried Alice and kept her constantly at work in the house. Alice found no chance to speak to Robin that day, and neither did he seem to seek her out. All through evensong she brooded on their last encounter, and thought, I told him no; I denied him; and now he thinks I don't love him. He'll reject me, find another girl...

On Monday morning he was nowhere to be seen. The soldiers' beds in the house were empty; there were no men in the kitchen. Alice had heard, at dawn, a distant drum tattoo from the village. Now, barely able to speak for dread, she asked Jenefer, "Have they gone? Struck camp?"

"Eh? No, young mistress." Jenefer glanced up from the ashes of last night's fire. "But a bunch of them took off to the village, early." She looked slyly at Alice. "Your lad among them. They'll be back, don't fear. They left their shirts and hose with me for washing."

Alice breathed again. And, indeed, Robin returned in the afternoon, but he was deep in conversation with his fellow soldiers. She knew something must be afoot. It was evening before she found out what.

She made her way up the tor, her desperation to speak to Robin overcoming any fear of passing the pixie rings at sunset. The afternoon had been fine, and the low sun lit the moor with a mellow golden light. It was too wet from yesterday's rain to sit on the earth, but she leant against a rock and watched the way he would come – if he came at all.

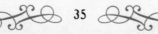

When she saw him she forgot all reserve and ran into his arms.

He kissed her eagerly. "Oh, Alice, I'll be sorry to leave you!"

She looked up at him, shaken. "You're going soon?"

"Tomorrow, early. Now, listen, Alice." He held her against him as tears sprang to her eyes. "We go to Plymouth. But the wounded will remain, and the baggage, and many of the men. So we won't strike camp here. We'll come back."

She wiped her eyes, and sniffed. "What will you do there?"

"We'll storm the defences. The town is in rebel hands."

"Cannon? Artillery?" The images terrified her.

"Yes."

She tightened her arms around him. He was perfect, unmarked, unhurt, alive. But tomorrow?

He said, his voice muffled by her hair, "There's a shepherd's hut I passed…"

Alice knew what he wanted. For her own part, she would have liked more courtship, more time, a promise of marriage. But the country was at war: there *was* no time; and soldiers, by their nature, were bound to be passing through. She wanted so much to please Robin, to be loved by him. If she agreed to this, then surely he would love her more, come back for her? And even if he did not … there was a fear always in her mind that one day soon her uncle would succeed in taking her by force. If I'm to lose my virginity, she thought, then let it be to Robin, who is

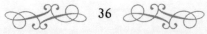

handsome and desirable and the man of my choosing.

She followed him into the small stone enclosure. It was almost dark inside. The roof was partially fallen in, and the hearth cold, but the earth floor was mostly dry. They lay down together on his coat, and in no time he had unfastened her bodice and she heard him loosening his own clothing. He kissed her, and she felt his hands on her breasts, and then under her skirts, between her legs. She put her arms around him, slid her hands beneath his shirt, strained closer to him. She felt a warmth and softening throughout her body as he moved to lie on top of her. It hurt a little when he pushed inside her, but she didn't mind; she knew she had pleased him. She clasped him in her arms and felt his heat and sweat and the weight of him and the pounding of his heart.

Afterwards, when they lay with their arms around each other, she thought about what she had done and felt both elated and scared. Would it show in her face, she wondered, when she went back to the farm?

"Did I hurt you?" he asked.

"No – not much."

"I tried not to. I knew you were a maid."

Were. She had given something of herself away to him; lowered her market value, her aunt would have said. But her aunt did not love her; whereas Robin... She asked, tentatively, "Do you love me?"

He drew her closer. "Of course. And I'll come back to you, never fear."

Three

The next morning, before dawn, Alice heard the distant drum again. She knew now what it meant. She sat up. Jenefer was lying, as before, across the doorway. On an impulse Alice rose, squeezed past her, opened the door and began to edge out through the narrow gap. Jenefer murmured and opened her eyes, but Alice thought, What does it matter? She knows already. And she ran barefoot to the stair room, where she could hear movement behind the curtain.

"Robin!"

He pulled back the curtain, seized her in his arms and kissed her hungrily. He was half dressed. She felt his heat through their two layers of linen: shirt and shift. As his hands went under her shift she realized, with shock, that the other man who slept there was awake and watching.

"Robin, don't…"

He released her – and at that moment, to her terror, the curtain was whisked open from outside and something tossed in. It was Alice's clothes and shoes.

"Get yourself dressed," Jenefer hissed. "Mistress is stirring."

The racing of Alice's heart subsided – but only a little. She pulled on skirt and bodice, provoking a soft whistle and laughter from the other man. She put her stockings in the pocket under her gown and pushed her bare feet into her shoes. One last kiss, and she ran downstairs, where Jenefer was stirring pottage over the fire.

"Thank you," she murmured.

Thanks were due, but she disliked being beholden to the maidservant. Nor did she like the way Jenefer smirked in response.

Afterwards Alice could not believe she had behaved so shamelessly with another man looking on. She had thought only of her longing to embrace Robin before he left. Now, she avoided catching the eye of any of the men as they came down to eat, and stayed in the scullery as much as possible. Robin gave her a brief smile once, when her aunt's back was turned, but when breakfast was over and the soldiers began to assemble in the yard his attention was elsewhere. They marched out, leaving behind two wounded men, an empty larder and a pile of dirty linen.

Before her aunt could involve her in washing linen, Alice climbed the tor and stood looking down on the village. Up here she could give vent to her tears. She saw manoeuvres of men, horses and gun carriages taking

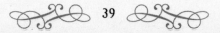

place, and heard drums and fifes. The colours fluttered in the wind. Soon the crowd formed itself into a marching column and began to move away.

Be safe, she prayed. Come back to me.

When they were gone she walked down the hill, and back into the old routine of life at Tor Farm. Only nothing was the same. *She* was not the same; and her existence there – which had once been like a familiar injury, to be rubbed and complained of, but borne with resignation – now seemed unendurable.

She thought all the time about Robin; tried to imagine Plymouth, its defences, the fighting that would be taking place there. How long would the king stay? Days? Weeks? She wondered too – a little cold fear – whether she might be with child. She'd heard it could happen the first time, if the girl had been willing. And I *was* willing, she thought. But he'd marry her, for sure, if she was with child. He'd said he loved her. And he'd talked about marriage. "You'll marry, won't you?" he'd said, the day they'd met in the dairy. She went over and over that conversation now, pondering the significance of it. All her knowledge of love came from romantic ballads or the gossip of Jenefer. Both sources were full of passion, betrayal and yearning. Love, it seemed, was never easy.

Sarah, bereft of her sergeant, had found consolation with a pikeman, one of the wounded soldiers who remained behind. Alice stepped into the barn one day and heard their grunts and gasps coming from the hayloft overhead. As she turned to leave, her way was blocked

by the bulky figure of her uncle. She dodged, trying to avoid him – "I'm looking for eggs" – but he pulled her into the shadows and forced his wet mouth on hers. She pushed at him in disgust.

"Alice," he pleaded, "be kind to me, eh?" He looked at her slyly. "You girls don't mind the soldiers, do you?" He seemed excited by the sounds from above.

Alice struggled, broke free, and yelled, "Aunt! Aunt!"

At once he let her go, and slipped away. The sounds from the hayloft abruptly ceased. Alice ran to the kitchen, where her aunt said, "What's to do? Did I hear you call?"

"No. Nothing," mumbled Alice. She did not want another beating. She kept her head down and glowered as she went about her work.

Her aunt made a sound of impatience. "I can do without moping wenches."

But Alice remained in low spirits. It was three long days since the army had left. She could not bear the waiting.

She went into the parlour and took up her sewing from the basket beside the settle. It was plain work, hemming sheets and pillow covers; work she could do while her mind was elsewhere. Often, when alone like this, she would daydream of escape from Tor Farm. Sometimes, in her imagination, she would find a ruined cottage on the moors, restore it and sweep it clean, hang lavender and rue from the beams. There she would try out remedies from her father's book, gather herbs, study

the movements of the moon and stars, become a wise woman – perhaps even, in time, an apothecary; for her father had told her that female apothecaries were not unknown.

That was one dream of escape. Another was love – a man who would marry her and take her away. Today she set down her sewing and opened the only other book in the house, the family Bible, and turned not to the New Testament but to the Song of Solomon.

"Let him kiss me with the kisses of his mouth: for thy love is better than wine…"

Oh, Robin! If only…

On Friday, the fourth day, she found an excuse to walk the mile and a half into the village. She hoped she might hear some news there.

She saw wagons and horses in the fields, and a few soldiers, but no sign of the army's return. The women were still about. A group of them were at the well with their pails, jabbering in some foreign language and taking over the space. A few village women waited impatiently and muttered together. One of them – the hefty maidservant from Hannaford's, the cobbler's – lost patience and snatched the leather pail from the hands of one of the strangers and flung it away, pushing the woman in the chest so hard that she stumbled back against her companions.

At once an affray broke out. A woman launched herself at Hannaford's servant, punched her and pulled off her cap. Others joined in from both sides. Soldiers

came at a run and separated the two groups. The village women reclaimed the area around the well, hands on hips, shouting complaints to the soldiers about being overrun by Welsh whores. Those from the camp began to move away; but one – a small sturdy girl with brown hair curling below her cap – hung back, and Alice recognized her as the one who had lost her pail. It lay on the other side of the street, and she could see that the girl did not want to pass the village women to retrieve it, let alone queue again for water.

Alice knew how it felt to be unwelcome. She ran and picked up the pail herself and took her turn at the well behind the last of the gossiping women. When it was full she walked across to the group of army women and offered it to the girl, who looked at her with gratitude and said, *"Diolch yn fawr,"* and then, in English, "Thank you." Her friends nodded to Alice and the group moved on.

The village women had watched this exchange with disapproval. Alice felt their eyes on her as she returned. No one challenged her, but Hannaford's servant said loudly, "Foreigners! Soldiers' whores!" And she spat.

Alice didn't think the women had looked like whores. They were not tricked out to display their charms like some of those she'd seen last time. Their clothes were plain and modest in style, and much mended, though far from clean. She wished she had asked the girl if she had news of the army. She'd wanted to, but the girl's foreignness had put a barrier between them. Later, in the village, she heard nothing but speculation, along with stories of plunder and of two young sisters raped by soldiers, which made her realize they had been lucky at Tor Farm.

The next day, the army returned. Alice heard the drums and ran outside, along with everyone else. They saw the distant column of men coming along the road from Tavistock.

Jenefer said, "Reckon they beat the rebels? Don't look defeated, do they?"

Mary Newcombe agreed. "But, God willing, they'll be gone for good soon."

Alice turned away, afraid her anxiety for Robin would betray her. It was hours later when at last the billeted men appeared at the gate of Tor Farm. And he was there! Uninjured, by the look of him. They exchanged a warm glance. She wanted to fly into his arms, but was forced to wait all through supper and after, when the men demanded beer, and their leaders – Robin among them – sat drinking by the fire.

But his eye was on her, and as she passed he caught her hand and whispered, "The shepherd's hut?"

And she nodded, trembling.

He left soon after. She waited a short while, then slipped out through the scullery door. The evening was mild, the air full of midges. Watch appeared and barked, wagging his tail.

"Hush!" She put a hand on his head, glanced around, then set off quickly up the tor.

Robin was waiting for her in the shadow of the hut wall. Their arms went around each other.

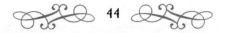

"I was so afraid you'd never come back," she said. "You're not injured? Not hurt at all?"

"No." His rough cheek scraped hers; he smelt of gunpowder. "Soldiering's mostly waiting about, wondering what they'll tell us to do next." His hands were on her body. "And wishing we were somewhere else. Lie down with me, love?"

They went into the hut and lay on his coat, kissing and straining close to each other. Alice felt as if she could never get close enough.

"Oh, I've missed you!" she said. She couldn't explain how much.

This time, when they made love, it did not hurt, but everything was overshadowed by her fear of losing him. She had never felt such intense happiness and misery before.

"They say we'll leave soon," said Robin. "I doubt it'll be tomorrow. Perhaps Monday."

Alice felt desperate. "What can we do?" She had a mad idea that they might run away, hide, find some wild place where only love mattered. "I shan't be able to bear it when you go," she said.

He stroked her hair, kissed away her tears. "I'll never forget you, Alice."

But that made it worse! She wanted to be loved, not remembered. She only cried the more, and nothing he said could comfort her.

The next morning the soldiers went out early and stayed in their encampment. Alice accompanied her aunt and

uncle to the village church. She saw great activity in the camp – a sign of change that made her fear Robin was right and the whole army would be gone tomorrow.

That afternoon she waited in increasing anxiety for him to arrive at the farm. But it was not until suppertime that the group of soldiers came trudging up the steep track. Once again she was obliged to serve food and beer to them, maddeningly close to Robin but watched by her aunt. After they had eaten, several of the men fell asleep, and Alice's uncle, ousted from his own chair, sat nodding on a bench, exhausted after a long day's work on the hill. Sarah slipped away, presumably to her pikeman in the barn.

Alice and her aunt lit candles. Alice thought she would never have another chance to be alone with Robin; never even say goodbye. It was dark – too late to go up to the tor, even if they could get away unnoticed. Once, he caught her eye and cast an enquiring glance upwards at the ceiling. Alice, shocked, gave a little shake of her head. She wouldn't dare! Not with her aunt here.

The sergeant told how they had stormed Plymouth's defences with little success, and had left the Devonshire general Sir Richard Grenville to continue the assault.

"The king moves on to Okehampton tomorrow," he said, confirming Alice's fears. He belched, and looked around at the attendant females. "Where's Sarah got to?" And then he announced loudly that he needed to piss, and went outside.

Soon after, a rumpus broke out in the yard: men's

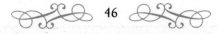

voices, loud and angry; Sarah screaming; Watch barking. Everyone ran to the door – except Alice and Robin, who turned to each other. He seized her hand and made for the stairs.

"No!"

Alice resisted, but only for a moment. This might be their one chance. She followed him up.

Behind the curtain, on his bed, they began to kiss. The darkness enfolded them in an illusion of safety. She heard the others come back in, Sarah sobbing and protesting, Mary Newcombe scolding. The men continued to argue, and Watch to bark.

Robin held her close. "I'll miss you."

And Alice thought how he'd be gone in the morning and she'd never see him again. Unless… "Take me with you!" she said.

He laughed, his mouth against her hair. "I wish I could."

"No! I mean it! I'll march along with you. There are women in the camp – soldiers' girls. I saw them. Take me with you, Robin."

Now he understood that she was serious. "No, Alice, no. That's impossible."

"Why?"

"You don't know what it's like, camp life. Those rough women… You'd hate it. It's not for the likes of you. You'd want to go home, and then what would I do with you?"

"I don't care how hard the life is! I'm not afraid of that. Robin…?"

He breathed out heavily, took her by the shoulders,

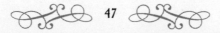

looked into her face. "Listen, sweet: I'll come back to you, when the war's over, when I can."

She felt her eyes brim with tears. She wanted to be with him *now*. "Don't you love me?"

"Of course. But … it's difficult." In the darkness she could not see his expression.

"There's nothing for me here!" she whispered passionately. "*Nothing!* My aunt and uncle don't want me. I hate this place. And I love you, Robin."

He made a sound between a sob and a sigh. "Alice, I can't—"

"Please!" She flung her arms around him, kissed his face and neck until she felt him respond, kiss her back and give in.

"Oh, Alice!" he said. "It won't be what you imagine."

But she didn't care. He would take her; that was enough.

"We leave soon after dawn," he said. "Can you get out without your aunt seeing?"

She met him halfway down the track into the village. She had brought a hessian bag with her, containing a spare skirt, bodice and linen, her red winter cloak, and her father's book. There was also a purse full of coins – her aunt's butter money. She felt guilty about that, but knew she might need it. She had never had any money of her own, and they owed her a dowry.

She was in terror of being pursued.

Robin said, "You could still go back if you've a

mind to – before you're missed."

"You don't want me to, do you?"

"No."

But she thought he looked uncertain. "Robin? You haven't changed *your* mind?" He must take her with him now; he *must*. She had burnt her boats.

He seemed to make a decision then; he took her hand and walked down to the camp with her while his friends joked and whistled. The camp was spread over several fields. Drums were beating and companies already forming up.

Robin led her to a field where there were wagons laden with officers' boxes and chests; with rolls of canvas, tents, cooking equipment and other supplies. This, she saw, was where the women were. And where Robin would leave her.

"I can't stay," he said. "You hear the tattoo. Mistress Erlam's here."

He brought her to a woman of Jenefer's age who was directing the packing of stores of beer and cheese. Mistress Erlam was broad and heavy-featured and looked formidable to Alice. It was clear that she knew Robin well; she exclaimed and smiled and clasped him in her arms. But she seemed astonished when he introduced Alice and explained why she was there. She looked at him disapprovingly, Alice thought; and he appeared somewhat hangdog. But she shrugged her shoulders and turned away while they said goodbye to each other.

It was brief enough: a quick kiss, and a promise to meet up when they made camp at Okehampton.

And then Alice was left standing in a field full of strangers.

"Get in this wagon and hide yourself," said Mistress Erlam. "If anyone asks, I haven't seen you."

Four

Alice hid inside the covered wagon, squeezed between damp-smelling bales of cloth, for several hours, while the army got under way. Robin had warned her it would be slow. The cavalry would go first, then the foot. There were sheep and cattle to be driven along, and the huge ox-drawn wagons of the artillery and ammunition trains laden with cannon, shot and casks of gunpowder; then the baggage train, full of provisions – food, medical supplies, tents and clothing – the officers' belongings and the closely guarded sumpter wagons containing the king's private possessions. The camp followers were always the last to leave.

Once, she heard a familiar voice, Matt's, from the farm, asking after her – "A girl of sixteen years, of middle height, fair complexion…" – and almost had a change of heart, for she was beginning to feel frightened at what she'd done; and she liked Matt, who had always been friendly.

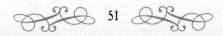

But then came Mistress Erlam's voice, dismissive. "Could be anyone." And Matt's, apologizing for troubling her. Alice thought of her life at the farm: her aunt's cold anger; her uncle; her constant fear of rape. Matt wouldn't be able to protect her from all that. She inched back, out of sight.

The boy was gone now. Alice felt afraid and yet excited. Robin had already left; through a slit in the canvas she'd watched the infantry move slowly out of the village. Robin! She pictured him on the march: his long agile stride, his dark looks, the bandolier across his body, his sword and musket at his side. And she imagined meeting him again that night. They'd be together, without fear, with no need to hide. Everything would be different. They would belong together.

"You can come out now," said Mistress Erlam.

Alice climbed down, and almost at once the train began to move. She became part of a column of people walking: women, farriers, armourers, sutlers, cooks. Dragoons – musketeers on horseback – rode alongside as guards. Alice kept close to her new protector. Some of the women around her were foreign; some were clearly whores; all seemed to move in their own groups, and she was not part of any of them.

"You might as well get used to walking," said Mistress Erlam, who wore big leather boots, like a man. "We keep the wagon space for those who can't." She looked narrowly at Alice. "Run away from home, have you? Taken a fancy to young Robin?"

"He was billeted on the farm."

"Ah. Well, you've netted yourself a proper man there. He's a charmer, is Robin. Always popular with the girls."

Alice was silent. She didn't like that "always". And she thought, He'll make me jealous. She was jealous already, of women he had not yet met. What have I done? she wondered. Can I trust him? Well, it was too late now.

Mistress Erlam, it seemed, was a wagon master's wife. She always travelled with her husband. Their dog, a scruffy, friendly mongrel, ran beside her. The train was her life, she said, and Alice saw that she had made herself indispensable. She oversaw the packing of much of the baggage, and took it upon herself to keep an eye on the groups of younger women and everything that went on in the train, and to give out advice.

"You need to tuck your hair away and keep your bosom covered," she told Alice. "There are some rough men in the ranks: convicts, imbeciles, beggars; they scoop up the dregs, take anyone, to fill their quota of conscripts. And some of the officers are not much better. You must have heard about Prince Rupert's men?"

Alice had heard. She remembered stories of how Prince Rupert's army had fallen upon a little Puritan town called Birmingham, where the people were metalworkers and made swords for Parliament. They had brought terror to that place: robbing, killing, dishonouring the women; and setting houses and workshops ablaze as they left.

"I'll have to get you a hat and some breeches," Mistress Erlam went on.

Alice, who'd been half listening to all her talk, was startled, and stared. Had she heard aright?

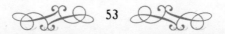

The older woman laughed. "It's often the safest way to dress, believe me. We all do it on occasion. Much safer to be taken for a man if you're away from the train, out foraging in the countryside."

Foraging. Alice hadn't thought about food, beyond the bit of bread and cheese she'd brought with her from the farm. She hadn't thought about much at all, except Robin, and love, and escape. How would she live? Would she need money? She'd supposed Robin would take care of her.

Her companion glanced at her and clicked her teeth. "I don't know what Robin was thinking of, bringing a young lass like you along. How old are you? Sixteen? Seventeen? The train's no place for such as you."

Alice said nothing. She was indeed frightened and amazed at what she had done – and it was I who did it, she thought, not Robin – and yet she would not for anything go back. She had escaped. The rain of the past week had blown itself out, and the day was mild, with blue sky showing. As they walked the track across country, skirting the edge of the moor and passing a few farmhouses and hamlets, she looked about her and breathed deeply and felt a great upsurge of freedom such as she had never experienced before. She was herself, in charge of her own destiny. Already she was seeing new places. The track led them along the edge of a deep wooded gorge where a waterfall plunged with a great rushing roar onto the rocky riverbed far below; and from there they came over a high bridge into a town with a castle on a steep spur – a place she suddenly recognized

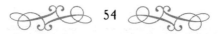

as one she used to see in the distance from the top of the tor – and then out again onto hilly land with farms here and there; and always the high open moor stretching up on their right.

In the late morning people began to bring out food from their packs. Alice finished most of her bread and cheese and drank small beer from a leather bottle. She wondered what she would eat in the evening; whether she'd share food with Robin; where it would come from. None of the women took any notice of her, so she stayed close to Mistress Erlam. Then Master Erlam joined them, and he and his wife talked of army matters together, and Alice sat alone, looking around her and thinking about Robin.

It was late afternoon when they reached the outskirts of Okehampton: a fair-sized town, though not as big as Tavistock.

"The king and his gentlemen will stay in town," said Mistress Erlam. "The army moves on."

"How much further?" Alice was tired. Her feet felt tender from walking along so many steep stony paths.

"About another five miles, I heard."

"Five miles!"

The woman smiled. "The last few miles are always the longest."

They were. Alice felt an ache spreading through her legs and hips as they trudged uphill and then along endless narrow lanes, past fields and farms that all looked the same. But at last Mistress Erlam pointed out to her a church steeple and what might have been a castle, and

they entered some fields on the edge of a small town and the wagons circled round and stopped. Alice sank down on the muddy grass and thought she would never have the strength to rise again.

But then she saw Robin coming towards her. Mistress Erlam laughed as she sprang up and ran to meet him.

Robin caught and held her close, and she clung to him and felt tears start to her eyes; she hadn't realized till then how lonely she had felt, among strangers all day.

"Are you tired, sweet?" he asked. "Hungry?"

She nodded, not trusting herself to speak.

"We'll go into the town."

They walked with their arms around each other. Most of the soldiers, except those left to guard the wagons, were heading into town. The Erlams were setting up a hearth for cooking. Alice supposed they lived in their wagon. It looked comfortable enough with its covered frame, the dog sitting up there watching all the coming and going. She waved to Mistress Erlam, then turned towards Robin as he led her away.

The quartermasters had evidently been into town ahead of the army and requisitioned billets. Many of the inhabitants were watching from doorways and windows; others had closed their shutters and presented a blank, unfriendly face to those they saw as invaders.

There were about a dozen men in Robin's charge. He led his group through the town, towards some cottages that straggled along a lane heading out to the fields on the other side. Alice knew the officers would have filled the town billets, leaving the common soldiers to lie in

whatever lofts, barns or stables could be found near by. Robin banged on several doors – farm labourers' homes, Alice guessed – placing two or three men at each cottage and handing a payment voucher to the householder.

Now there were only three other men remaining with him and Alice.

"We'll stop here," he said, approaching the last cottage.

The door was opened by a thin woman with children clinging to her skirts. Both woman and children backed away as the men strode in. Alice felt herself being observed in a way she had never experienced before. A whore, the woman's glance said; we must endure not only the Cavaliers but their whores. Alice could not meet her eye.

A girl of about ten years old was putting a meal on the table: cheese, bread, onions and some small beer. Alice saw the food and felt weak with hunger. But Robin demanded to see the sleeping quarters. The woman showed him the only bed: a box bed in the single room that she shared with the younger children. The men could sleep by the fire, she said; there were mats, and they could have the straw-stuffed pillows from the bed.

Robin turned to look at a ladder leading up to a hatch in the ceiling. "What's up there?"

"A loft. It's small, low. The older boys sleep there."

"Turn them out," said Robin. He glanced at Alice. "We'll have it."

Alice felt herself reddening and looked at the floor.

The woman and children watched them as they ate.

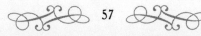

Alice wondered if the family had eaten, or if this was all they had. Their obvious poverty, and the imposition of the army's sudden demands, took away her own appetite, and although she was hungry she could not eat much. But she was thirsty and drank more beer than she was accustomed to.

"My husband died in the wars," the woman said. "They were quartered in the field in bad weather and he froze to death overnight. His comrade told me." She was holding the youngest child – pale, with blue shadows under its eyes – on her hip. "I have no way to live now."

Robin glanced at the food – he was eating heartily – and said, "A quartermaster will pay you later for our food and keep. Give him the voucher I wrote for you."

"The voucher…" The woman took out the piece of paper from a pocket under her skirt and looked at it, bemused, as if willing it to turn into coin.

"It will be redeemed," said Robin. He did not say when.

"I have nothing, sir. Nothing to live on."

"Don't fear. It *will* be redeemed, and soon." He touched her elbow. "I'll see to it myself."

The woman's face softened, and she smiled. "Oh, thank you, sir. You are good."

She believes him, Alice thought; she trusts him to help her. Yet what could he do? The Royalist armies, in particular, were notorious for not paying up. And if the army did not have the money, how could he see to it that she was paid?

But the woman looked happier now, and sent the

eldest girl out to draw water for washing; and Robin encouraged Alice to eat.

As soon as it began to get dark everyone went to bed. The three men had the mats by the fire; the boys squeezed into the box bed with the rest of the children.

The woman took a chamber pot and a pillow up to the loft. She came down apologizing. "It's small, sir. And the boys…"

"No matter," said Robin.

Alice went up ahead of him. The loft was low and dark, the straw not very fresh. An unpleasant smell came from the far corner. Either the boys had overshot the chamber pot or they hadn't been using one. Robin made a sound of disgust at the stink, and cursed when he banged his head on a beam. Even Alice could not stand upright.

Robin laughed. "Oh, Alice!" His arms went around her, and he drew her down beside him on the straw. "I've had worse lodgings," he said.

She felt his lips warm on hers, his hands under her shift. This time there was no hurry, and she felt relaxed; a little drunk, she supposed. She responded ardently to his kisses, and as they began to make love she wanted to lose herself entirely to the moment; but all the time she was aware of the open hatch near by and the men lying below. She hoped they were asleep, but feared they might be listening.

"Don't think of them," said Robin.

And later, when they lay still, their hearts beating fast

and arms wrapped around each other, she forgot them, and was happy. She fell asleep, curled against Robin for warmth.

She woke early. There were sparrows in the thatch, and patches of light where the roof needed renewing. She was lying close to Robin, her right arm partly under him. The arm was numb, but she didn't want to move. She studied his face as the light brightened. It looked soft in sleep, younger. His eyelashes lay like dark fans on his cheeks. She gazed at the line of his cheekbone, his roughly cut moustache and beard, the hollow of his throat.

I love him, she thought. And the thought was both a pleasure and a pain, for she saw how desirable he was; how other women must envy her.

His eyes opened. He smiled at her and said, "Good morning, sweet."

And then he stretched and stood up and went to use the chamber pot. Alice thought the sound would wake the dead. It certainly alerted those below. She heard voices, and caught the words "…now those two lovebirds be up and pissing…" She moved her numb arm; prickles of pain ran all along it.

Robin, stooping under the beams, pulled on his stockings and breeches. "Crediton today," he said. "And from there they are saying the king will ride in state to Exeter."

Five

Perhaps we'll be married in Exeter, Alice thought. She knew Exeter was a great city, and if the king was to arrive there in state then surely he would stay more than a night? She and Robin would have time together; time to find a priest.

There had been little enough time that morning after they left the cottage. Robin and the other men had gone off to rejoin their company, and she had walked back alone to the baggage train, where there was an air of comradeship among those who had slept in tents and shelters overnight and who were now stamping out their fires and packing up. She saw groups of women chatting, combing their hair, gathering their belongings. She also noticed how few had children with them.

They know what to do, she thought. She knew a little herself, from studying her father's book and from listening to Jenefer and Sarah. Mint leaves were good: a

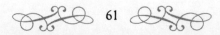

bunch pushed well up. Or fern, which might be readier to hand on moorland. Not that she'd done anything about it at all, yet. Some part of her didn't want to; wanted everything to be unspoiled, perfect, like Adam and Eve.

She'd felt a heaviness in her lower back and thighs all day yesterday, and had put it down to the unaccustomed walking. But it was not that. She recognized it now. Sure enough, when she went into the bushes to relieve herself, she found spots of blood on her shift. The slight anxiety that had hung over her ever since that first time with Robin instantly lifted. She had brought rags in her hessian bag. But how would she wash them, she wondered, while on the move like this? She would have to watch what others did.

She emerged from the bushes and went back to the camp, passing the artillery wagons, where some soldiers called out to her with lewd comments. She felt lonely and unsafe. There was no sign of Mistress Erlam; and in any case she felt she could not trail in the older woman's wake for ever. There were women here nearer her age, but they all seemed to have their own groups and friendships. Some of them talked in foreign languages or strange accents, making her feel even more shut out. As the train began to move off, she walked by herself, on the fringe of one of the groups.

It was not long before a soldier started to bother her, one of those who guarded the train.

"All alone, are you? Want some company?"

He was a lanky fellow with a cocksure, pimply

face. She did not like his looks or his conversation, and quickened her pace, trying to shake him off.

He took offence, strode after her, seized her arm. "Think you're better than me, do you? You puffed-up whore!"

"Let me go!" Alice struggled to free herself. His companions laughed. Any moment now and they would join in. Her heart beat fast. She looked around for help – and saw two young women striding towards her.

"Leave her! She's with us!" shouted the shorter one, and Alice recognized the girl whose pail she had given back at the well; and she saw that the girl remembered her. Her two rescuers took hold of her, one on either side, and the soldier walked off, muttering about "bitches" and "drabs".

The woman had spoken in English, but now they both laughed and exchanged a joke in their own language. And then the shorter one squeezed Alice's arm and said, "Walk with us – if you wish? You'll be safer."

"Oh, yes! Thank you," said Alice.

The two of them – the little sturdy brown-haired girl and the taller one with red-gold curls – regarded her with undisguised curiosity. She, in turn, looked at them and saw two dirty, unkempt women, their gowns stained, their skins grimy and weathered from weeks or months on the road. Even as she noticed their appearance, she felt ashamed of herself for doing so. They were both smiling.

The brown-haired girl said, "I am Nia, and this is Rhian."

Strange names. She replied, "I'm Alice."

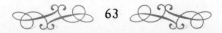

"Alice. You must have joined us at the camp? The village on the moor?"

Alice nodded. "I lived on a farm there. But I've left – for good."

"You came with a soldier, didn't you?" Nia persisted. "That dark, handsome man?"

"Yes." She knew she would end by telling them everything, and she saw that they knew it too, and would wait.

"Come and meet Bronwen," said Nia.

There was another girl looking back at them. They ran to catch her up, calling out in their own language.

"Are you Welsh?" Alice asked.

"Yes! Our husbands are soldiers. Come!"

Bronwen was older than the other two, quiet-spoken, more restrained in her manner than Nia. "So they have brought you with them," she said. "That's good. You should not walk alone."

"You three are lucky to be together," said Alice.

"We are all from one village, near Y Trallwng – Pool, the English call it. Rhian and I are sisters, and Nia is married to our brother Bryn."

"Who I love and adore and would not be parted from!" said Nia. "Oh! How I cried when he said he'd joined up and was going to war. We'd not been married a month!"

"Then why…?" asked Alice.

"We are poor. Everyone in the village is poor. The men are farm labourers. We all work for Sir John Leal, on his land, and live in his cottages. Sir John's men came

recruiting. Free uniforms: good strong shoes, two shirts, a coat and breeches. And the pay is good too – when they get it."

"But ... why would he recruit his own workers and send them away?"

"To find favour with the king! These gentlemen, they promise the king men, foot soldiers, a regiment. Their honour requires that they keep their promises."

"And they hope to be rewarded when the rebellion is over," said Bronwen more cynically. "The young men all joined up together. Truth is, they had little choice, our landlord being loyal to the king, and it being his wish."

"But – oh, we three did cry and complain!" exclaimed Nia.

"We did," said Bronwen. "And then we agreed between us that we'd go too, and look after our men and each other."

"Rhian and Gethin were not even married then," Nia said, with a teasing glance at the golden-haired girl. "Gethin is always slow to make a move; needs a push, he does." Rhian blushed. "Well, we pushed them into it, got them wed, and here we are."

Alice felt her loneliness melt away as their chatter surrounded her. If I'd had such a group of friends, she thought, or a sister, I might have been happy, even at Tor Farm. But what would these girls think of her? Nobody had pushed *her*, got *her* wed, before she ran away with Robin. Would they call her a slut? Would they still want her to walk with them?

The miles seemed less tiring that day, and the time

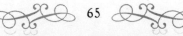

passed more quickly. A large part of the king's army was Welsh, and there were many of their women on the march. Although they did not all know each other, or come from the same places, they formed a distinct community. It was strange to be in a crowd of people all talking in a foreign language, but Nia made sure to translate if anything interesting was said.

"You speak English well," Alice said in some surprise, for surely these girls had had no schooling?

"Oh, that's because we are from near the border," said Nia. "Y Trallwng is just inside Wales, and the traders come and go from Shrewsbury. But some of the Welsh-women here speak no English at all."

Alice had never heard of Y Trallwng or Shrewsbury. I would like to see this kingdom, she thought, all laid out on a map. I would like to know where I am, and where Wales is, and Ireland. And Oxford. Yes, especially Oxford, because Robin's home is near there.

In mid-afternoon they paused near Crediton, and the camp followers took advantage of the brief stop to sit down and eat. Alice had water – she and Robin had refilled their leather bottles from a spring that morning – but she had only a bit of hard cheese and stale bread to eat; and nothing for the next day. Many of the others, she saw, fared little better. She looked out for Robin, but he did not appear, and neither did any of the Welsh girls' husbands. They were probably far away. The army, like a great untidy snake, straggled for miles along the country roads. Word came back to them that the king and his generals and Lifeguards were riding into Crediton

and would dine there, and then the king would travel in state to Exeter that night.

"We are to move on, to the far side of Exeter." It was a soldier – one of their guards – who passed on the news. "So it's wine and soft beds for the officers and a cold field for the rest of us, I reckon."

He was right. Their destination was a small village, unable to provide lodging for an army. By the time the women arrived they found the camp established over several fields, fires lit, huts being built.

It had been a mild day, but now, as the light started to fade, the September evening air struck cold. People went into the patches of woodland all around and began cutting branches. Some soldiers from the ammunition train appeared carrying a broken gate and several posts. Her friends got out knives and headed for the woods.

Alice stood still, uncertain what to do. Should she wait for Robin? She could see a lot of activity some way off, soldiers moving about, and hear orders being shouted.

Nia ran back to her. "Come with us, Alice. The men will be building huts and putting up the officers' tents. We make our own shelters. Come and help. Do you have a knife?"

Alice did, though it was a meat knife, not as robust as the ones the women were using. She was surprised at the speed with which they built simple lean-to huts. When the frames were made they stretched pieces of hide over them, tied them in place and pegged them down.

"We've done this often before," said Bronwen.

And, indeed, all the women were establishing their own shelters, whether huts, rough tents or covered carts. Some way off were a few carriages: officers' whores, Nia said.

"We'll help you make a hut, if you like?" offered Bronwen.

"I don't know…" Would Robin expect it?

Some of the other women had got fires lit. There was a warm savoury smell on the air, and she became aware of how hungry she was. She realized that the women were cooking together for their men. Several large communal pots were in use. Her friends began talking in Welsh to the women around one of the fires.

Then Nia exclaimed, "Bryn!"

Three soldiers were walking towards them. Nia ran to a young man, dark like his sister Bronwen, and with an open, amiable face. He looks kind, Alice thought; a good man.

"This is Bryn," Nia told Alice, smiling from one to the other, "and there is Bronwen's husband, Edryd. And here's Gethin."

The men were dressed in worn, patched uniforms. All were dark, small but strong-looking; all – at first sight – rather alike. Alice felt shy as they acknowledged her with nods.

"Will you eat with us, Alice?" asked Bronwen.

But Alice had seen Robin. She shook her head, stammered thanks and apologies, and ran to Robin's embrace.

"We've been hut-building," he said. "Are you

hungry? The cooking fires are lit now."

He tried to lead her in that direction, but it seemed rude to walk off so abruptly, and Alice said, "I've made some friends! Come and meet them."

The Welsh group were now clustered around their fire, talking together in their own language. Robin threw a glance in their direction and said, "Those Welsh? Don't trouble with *them*, sweetheart. They're clods, the Welsh. Can't tell one end of a musket from the other."

"But the women have been kind to me!" Alice insisted. "Come…"

She felt hurt on their behalf. But already he was leaving, drawing her towards his own group. She glanced back and waved an apology, but in the gathering dusk she could not see whether her new friends had noticed.

At Robin's fire there was meat. Someone had shot a rabbit, and others had requisitioned bread and turnips from one of the nearby farms. She ate gratefully, sharing Robin's bowl, since she did not have one of her own. I must get a bowl, she thought, and a spoon; and I must learn to forage and make myself useful. She kept quiet in the presence of Robin's companions. Will and Jacob, they were called; she remembered them from Tor Farm. She was aware of their eyes on her, and suspected that they were thinking about her and Robin together; and it made her feel ashamed and uneasy. Across the field, in the darkness, she saw the lights of other fires and sparks flying up. From where her Welsh friends were sitting she heard snatches of song; and, despite being with Robin, she felt almost regretful that she had left them.

When they had eaten, Robin got up and drew her away from the fire, his arm round her waist. "We won't sleep in the huts," he said. "There's a barn in the next field – I got a lad to hold us a place." He gave her a squeeze. "We'll be warm enough there."

She looked up at his face. "My courses have come today."

"Ah." She heard the disappointment in his voice. Then he laughed, and hugged her again. "Well, that's good news! You don't want a child yet, do you?"

"I would like to be married first," she said.

"Of course." But he said no more on that. "The word is," he told her, "that we'll stay here a few days. So you can rest awhile."

When they reached the barn, there were women loitering by the entrance, looking for business. They ignored Alice and Robin. The place Robin had found was set back, softened by hay. But there were other men all around, and more coming in all the time, some with the whores. Alice felt glad she had the excuse of her courses and could simply lie wrapped in Robin's arms.

Perhaps we'll go into Exeter tomorrow, she thought.

Six

"*Exeter?*" said Nia. "You'd be lucky! The officers might go into the city, but not the men. We are always stuck in places like this: wet, muddy and surrounded by sheep." She laughed. "I don't know why I left Wales!"

"You *do*," said Alice.

Nia had told her something of their life in Wales: a life of unrelenting labour on the land, morning till night; of damp cottages with only one room; of little pay, few rights, and no chance of improvement. Life in the camps did not seem hard or difficult by contrast; and they enjoyed the freedom of the open road and the companionship of a larger group of people. Alice could understand how they felt. For herself, it was not so easy to adapt. Her feet ached from walking and she missed the comforts of Tor Farm – the good food and clean beds. But I am free now, she told herself. Free, and with Robin, as I wanted.

In fact she saw far less of Robin than she had hoped; his time was taken up with drill and weapons training. Alice saw him only in the evenings – when they ate around a campfire with his companions – or at night, in the barn, where there was little privacy. She wanted to cook for him, to feel that they belonged together, but the army rations were mostly prepared by soldiers in a field kitchen. Some groups of English soldiers' women cooked together, but she was too shy to approach them. Instead she stayed with the Welshwomen, those who had first been kind to her. She was glad of their friendship – especially Nia's – in this rough, unfamiliar world. Nia became her constant companion, taking her around, introducing her to people and translating what they said.

The army had now been encamped near Exeter for three days and looked set to stay longer. Alice had been surprised that there was no fighting, no sign of the enemy, but Nia said, "Oh, it's usually like this! We go weeks without so much as a skirmish. They spend all their time looking for each other, sending out scouts, waiting."

This morning the sun was bright, and Alice and Nia had joined a large group of women washing clothes in the stream at the bottom of the field. They beat the linen on flat stones and rinsed it in the water that ran rippling over the pebbles. It felt good to see the sun for once and to enjoy its warmth. A woman along the line began to sing, and the song was taken up and set the rhythm for the pounding of the linen. Alice soon learned the tune and hummed along, but the Welsh words were impossible to catch.

"Did you sing at home, Lisi?" asked Nia.

She had taken to calling Alice "Lisi", which she said was short for Alice in Wales. Alice liked the name; it made her feel as if she belonged.

"At home in Bideford we sang," she said. "But at my uncle's it was only when we went to church. I've missed it."

The song changed, to something with a more romantic melody. Nia, Bronwen and Rhian all joined in, rinsing and wringing out the linen with strong turns of their wrists.

Later they strung lines between the shelters and hung the clothes to dry. Alice had washed Robin's shirt along with her own shift. She was glad to do it; glad to hang the two garments side by side to dry. It made her feel as if Robin were already her husband.

Nia teased her. "You're like the girl in the song."

"That last one?" Alice tried to remember the tune, but it had gone. "Tell me the words."

Nia began teaching her the song. It was about a girl who was at the riverside, washing her lover's shirt, when a knight came by and asked if she would sell it.

"But of course she won't sell," said Nia. "'Not for a hundred pounds,' she says, 'not for two hillsides full of sheep, not for two fields of oxen under yoke, not for all the herbs of Llandewi, trodden and pressed, not for anything would I sell the shirt of the boy I love.' You've got Robin's shirt there, Lisi. Wouldn't you say the same?"

"Yes," said Alice, laughing. "I would!"

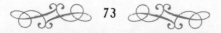

When all the linen was blowing on the lines, they rested, sharing beer and some oatcakes that Bronwen had bought from one of the traders. Bronwen, Alice realized, saw herself as the one responsible for the three – now grown to four with the addition of Alice. She was a strong, quiet woman, protective of her younger sister Rhian, who seemed shy and childlike – "A bit of a daydreamer," Nia said fondly. Rhian was playing now with her kitten, a little bold black thing with startled eyes. It crawled around her shoulders, tangling in her hair, then sprang down into her lap, breaking the oatcake she was holding into flying fragments.

"Oh, Rhian!" Bronwen sounded exasperated.

Rhian had been given the kitten on one of their expeditions around the village and farms when they knocked on doors, seeking food. She had bought a jugful of milk too but, as Bronwen pointed out, some of their milk now went to the animal.

"There were five of them, all to be drowned," Rhian had said. "I only took one."

"We should go around the farms again before we move on," said Nia, "though I doubt they'll have much to sell."

Alice knew the farmers must be preparing for a hungry winter. The harvest was ruined; and the army had already swept through these villages in July on its way west, eating everything, "like the plague of locusts in the Bible", one woman had said, "and now here you are again". Robin had told Alice that these same people, or others near by, had beaten and robbed the captured rebel

foot soldiers as the king's men forced them to march east from Lostwithiel. There was no love here for soldiers of any army, and still less for the women they called "Welsh whores" or, as often as not, "Irish whores". They could not tell the difference but particularly hated the Irish, remembering the stories they had heard of how Irish Catholics had attacked and butchered English Protestants only three years before.

Alice fared better on these forays. She was young and not yet as dirty and ragged-looking as the others, and she spoke the local dialect. She often came back with some bacon or cheese when others had been refused.

On one occasion she and Nia came to a house where a woman was in pain with a toothache. Alice felt sorry for her, and struggled to recall one of her father's remedies. "Daisy roots," she said, "and salt. Pounded together, strained, and mixed with the leaves of sweet flag. I think that was all. It makes a juice."

She helped the woman dig up roots and pound the fibrous mass in a mortar while Nia went to gather flag leaves. "You breathe it in," she said. "The scent eases the pain."

The woman was grateful, and gave Alice a pudding in a bag, in addition to the milk she and Nia had come to buy.

"You could be useful in the women's camp," Nia said afterwards.

"But I don't know much! And I've no supplies. Besides, there must be apothecaries with the army – and

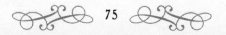

other women who have some knowledge."

"Oh, there are. Sian, she'll pull teeth and give you powders to bring on your courses or tisanes for the rheum; and Anwen can see your future in the stars. But I'd trust you more than most, Lisi. You have a gentle way about you."

Maybe, thought Alice. But she was wary of putting herself forward, and perhaps antagonizing the likes of Sian and Anwen. She was young, a newcomer here, and a foreigner in the Welsh camp. She'd respond quietly, she decided, if and when the need arose.

The next day, the girls planned to go afield, foraging for autumn berries and nuts.

Mistress Erlam tossed Alice a bundle. "Try these on. You don't want to attract the attention of men while you're away from the camp." There was a pair of breeches, well worn and patched, and a felted cap of dark red wool.

Alice climbed into the covered wagon and took off her skirt. She bunched up the length of her shift and stepped into the legs of the loose knee-length breeches. She removed her woman's cap of linen and put on the felted one, tucking her hair inside it. The breeches felt strange, and she was embarrassed by the sight of her stockinged calves, exposed like a man's.

She emerged shyly, and Mistress Erlam clapped her hands in delight. "You look like a boy player on the stage! You could leave off your stays and put a few more pins in your hair. But you'll do, from a distance."

Alice found her Welsh friends clothed in the same way. She felt afraid at first; she knew the king had forbidden women to dress like this. But as the day wore on she found she could climb trees, clamber over gates, stride across small streams, all without the need to pick up her skirts. She experienced a great sense of freedom.

The group of women had split into pairs. Alice was with Nia. In a woodland clearing they found mushrooms. They ate some raw, brushing the dirt off them and savouring the pungent, earthy flavour, then laid the remainder in a flat basket, taking care not to break or bruise them. They picked cobnuts and crab apples at the edge of the woods. Then Nia exclaimed, *"Mwyar!"* and led Alice across a rough field to a hedge where ripe fruit hung in glossy clusters: blackberries.

"No one has been here!" she said in amazement.

Most of the blackberry bushes around the camp had been picked clean by locals. Here the fruit was so ripe it burst and stained their fingers purple. Nia lined her basket with soft leaves and they dropped the berries in gently.

"They are too ripe to save," said Alice, and Nia agreed.

The two of them went to sit on a grassy bank. They could hear Bronwen and Rhian talking a little way off, and other women's voices around.

They shared half a loaf of hard bread, along with some of the freshly picked berries. Nia spilled purple juice on her breeches and rubbed at the cloth, spreading the stain and laughing. "Bryn says I look like a bugbear

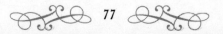

dressed this way!" she said cheerfully.

Alice thought that certainly Nia's small rounded shape showed to better advantage in women's clothes. She wondered about herself. "I don't know what Robin will say," she admitted. Would he be amused, or shocked? She could not guess.

"How long have you known him?" asked Nia.

Alice felt herself blushing. "Not long." She looked up defiantly. "He came to the farm when the army was camped in the village."

It was time to tell her story, and she did. Nia listened, little sighs and head-shakings escaping her now and then. Alice knew she would be telling the other two later that day.

"I love him," she insisted. "And he loves me. He said so."

"But will he marry you, Lisi?"

"Why not? I'm sure he will. If we'd had the chance to go into Exeter, I believe we'd have been married by now."

"Has he spoken of marriage?"

"Yes…" Alice struggled to recall exactly what Robin *had* said. "He spoke of it in a general way, as a thing that happens."

Nia was silent for a moment. Then she said, "It will be a long way home to your aunt and uncle if he does not marry you … if you should find yourself abandoned, and with child."

At this picture of herself alone, all Alice's unacknowledged fear rose to the surface. Robin loved

her! He would marry her – surely he would!

"Tor Farm is not my home," she said. "I can never go back there." Her eyes brimmed with tears.

Nia put her arms around her. "Oh, Lisi, I'm sorry! I didn't mean to make you cry. It's only that I'm concerned about you, you being so young. How old *are* you?"

"Sixteen. Seventeen, almost," Alice said, wiping her eyes.

"Too young for this. To be on the run with a young man you hardly know. And with such disreputable women as us! Welsh riff-raff who go about in men's breeches!"

They giggled together.

"I suppose," Alice said, sniffing back tears and laughter, "you've known Bryn a long time?"

"All my life," said Nia. "Our two families lived almost next door, and we used to play together when we were tiny, and then work together in the fields as soon as we were old enough to labour. I always loved Bryn, even when I was a little girl. He's two years older than I am and he used to look after me – champion me. I remember once, when we were harvesting peas, I couldn't help eating some of them. We were always hungry and they were so sweet and tender. The man in charge hit me and shouted at me to get back to work, but Bryn stood up to him – got between us and said he'd fight him if he hit me again. I walked home with Bryn that evening, and made up my mind right then that I'd marry him one day."

"Do you have brothers and sisters at home?" Alice

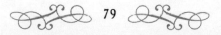

asked. She felt envious of Nia, despite the obvious poverty.

"Three sisters and five brothers. I'm somewhere in the middle. We joke that my mam probably hasn't missed me yet! But our cottage was so crowded, Lisi, and my father drank, and he beat my mother. I always wanted to be at Bryn's. They had just Bronwen, Bryn and Rhian – Rhian's the youngest, only a year older than you. And their father played music, and they all sang. It was a lovely house – the spirit in it, I mean; they were very poor. And then Bronwen got married, and later I married Bryn, and Gethin was courting Rhian; and all the talk among the young men was of going to the wars…"

"Bronwen has no children, then?"

"No. Bronwen is barren. It's a great sorrow to her, but it left her free to travel with Edryd."

"But you – you and Bryn… How do you…?" Alice stumbled, embarrassed.

"We are careful. And we trust to luck."

But Nia looked as if the question had troubled her. Alice briefly wondered why, before Nia began talking of other things.

It was their last day at the camp. Tomorrow they were bound for Chard, in Somerset, and it would be a long day's march. The Welshwomen lit their evening campfire early and began cooking: a stew with turnips, mushrooms and cabbage. No meat. They'd had rabbit two nights out of the six, and there was cheese packed for the march, but supplies were low.

 80

Alice helped with the cooking, and carried a jug of stew across the field for herself and Robin, along with new bread, and some blackberries in a fold of linen. He was pleased with her efforts, and amused at the thought of her foraging, dressed as a boy. Later, as they walked to the barn together, his arm round her, tight against the chill of evening, she thought, he *does* love me, and he's glad to have me with him. And the doubts that Nia's questions had raised in her mind faded away.

Seven

"*Prince* Rupert is coming," Robin said.

They had stayed a week near Chard, and during that time the camp had buzzed with an alarm that the enemy – General Waller's men – had been sighted near the coast at Bridport, raising troops. And now Prince Rupert, the king's nephew, was come from Bristol with his army. There was a great rendezvous on the Downs. The women, left behind with the wagons, heard the drums and fifes and saw soldiers in the lanes and on the hills all around. When at last the army took to the road its numbers were hugely increased.

Mistress Erlam told Alice that the shire they were now passing through was Dorset. It was a land of high ridges and deep green combes: a beautiful place, though the weather was wet and the people unwelcoming. Everywhere the harvest had been bad, and there was little food for hungry soldiers. Another long day's march

brought them to a place called Sherborne, where they remained almost a week, and where the alarms subsided and no one knew what was happening or why they were waiting there.

The gentry and officers stayed in a great house, the army in cottages, barns and farms all around. Alice was separated from the Welsh girls.

"I've got us a billet at a farm," Robin told her.

He was smiling, and she soon saw why. They had a tiny room to themselves – the first time they had been truly alone together since they left Dartmoor – and there was an outhouse, chilly and stone-floored, but with a tub and water for washing. They both stripped and cleaned away more than two weeks of filth.

"We could wash together," he'd suggested.

"No! I want to undress."

"So do I!"

"Go away!" She laughed and shut the door on him.

She washed quickly, dried herself with the shift she'd been wearing, and put on a fresher one. Then she darted barefoot up the steps to their room.

Later she let him persuade her to take off the shift and sit beside him on the bed, her hair damp and long over her bare shoulders. It was the first time they had seen each other naked.

"You're beautiful," he said.

And she looked shyly at him, and thought how perfect he was, and how much she loved him. They kissed, and drew together slowly, spinning out this new delight of being naked, of the touch and warmth

 83

of each other's bodies. The little room, with its broken floorboards and straw-filled mattress, was theirs alone. That night, and every night that week, they were able to lie and talk and make love without being overheard. Alice felt an intense happiness and desire for Robin. She did not care about the risks she took. Nothing, she thought, could make her happier than to have Robin's child. In the passion of the moment even the fear of childbirth could not frighten her.

She did not see Nia again until the day they left Sherborne, but that morning she went to join the other camp followers, and found her friends.

Nia hugged her. "We've missed you, Lisi."

And Alice felt guilty because she had not missed them at all and had thought only of Robin.

Now she noticed that Nia looked pink around the eyes, as if she had been crying. "Something's wrong, isn't it?" she asked. "Tell me, Nia. What's the matter?"

Nia bit her lip. "My courses have not come. Not last month either."

"You are with child...?"

Alice thought, then, of her own lovemaking, all the last week; this could happen to her too. And she realized, seeing Nia's face, that it would be momentous, terrifying; not at all to be wished for.

"Are you sure?" she asked. "Do you keep count of the days?"

"No. I've always looked at the moon. That's how I remember. I think it's two and a half months since

I last had any bleeding." She gave a little gasping sob. "I ought to be happy. I love Bryn. And I want a child. But I'm so afraid of giving birth – and on campaign! I'd always thought I'd be at home for that." Her voice broke. "We've tried to be careful, but – oh, Lisi, I wish this wasn't happening now!"

Alice said, tentatively, "There are herbs you might try. Parsley…"

"I've tried it. And jumping off a wall." She managed a smile. "This one means to be born. I won't try anything else; I see now that it is God's will. But Bryn is anxious for me. He says when we reach our winter quarters he'll find me somewhere safe, among women, where I can stay on after the army leaves in the spring."

"That might be wise," said Alice, knowing what her friend would say, because it was what she herself would have said.

"I won't be left behind," said Nia. "I won't let him go on without me."

Eight

Alice and Nia scurried along a cobbled street in Salisbury, heads down against the driving rain. They were looking for a cobbler's shop they had been told was near. Nia spotted it first – its sign, with a shoe painted on it, swinging in the wind. Because of the wild weather the shop counter had been pulled up, but the door was opened to their knock.

"I've nothing for the likes of you!"

The shoemaker was hostile, and Alice realized he had taken them for vagrants, they were so patched and bedraggled. But when they produced money and he'd bitten and tested it, he was glad enough of two new customers. Alice's feet were sore from the sharp stones of the road. It was mid-October. She had been following the army now for over a month and the soles of her shoes were worn through. Nia wore sturdier boots, but even these were in need of repair. She showed the man how

86

the upper of one of her boots had split from the sole.

He set to work while the two girls sat on a bench and waited, since they had no other shoes. Alice tucked her feet under her skirts, ashamed of the holes in her stockings. She was made aware, here in town, of how dirty she had become. It was an effort to wash, in public view, in the cold wet fields. There was dirt under her fingernails and ingrained in the skin of her hands. The hem of her gown was muddy, and the skirt was stained with grass and grime and had a long tear that she had mended with thread of a darker brown. On the march she was no dirtier than anyone else, but here respectable people stepped away from her.

"Parliament troops have been around," the cobbler remarked. "Manoeuvres. Reckon a battle's coming?"

"We don't know," said Nia. "We follow our men, that's all."

The man's wife watched them from an inner room. She was hanging children's linen around the fire to dry. Two little boys played with wooden blocks, and a baby lay whimpering in a cradle. Now and again the woman rocked the cradle with her foot, and the baby's cries briefly subsided.

Alice saw that Nia was looking at the baby. Nia was sure now that she was with child and, despite her fears, was happy enough about it. Alice had bought dried camomile flowers and a tiny piece of ginger root from one of the army apothecaries; with these she was able to make Nia a tisane to relieve the sickness she had begun to feel in the mornings.

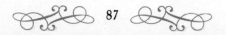

"Take it every day," she said. "And later, when your time is near, I'll make you raspberry leaf tea. It will ease the birth."

"I'm glad you'll be with me, Lisi."

"I'm no midwife."

"No. But I trust you."

Nia had been greatly impressed by Alice's book, the one her father had left her, and which Alice had consulted on the properties of camomile and raspberry. Nia, who could not read, even in her own language, had turned the pages reverently, exclaiming when she saw a drawing of a plant she recognized, such as dandelion or fennel. Alice realized that for Nia the book was almost a magical object.

"These herbs and their uses are all God's work," she assured her. "My father taught me how God has given us signs to show us which plants to use."

Nia understood. "Like woundwort? With its flowers like drops of blood?"

"Yes! And lungwort. And aspen leaves, which help those with the shaking palsy."

Alice knew how important it was for Nia to have faith in her, to believe she could achieve what both of them wanted. Once, as a child, she had asked her father about the dried turtle that hung from the ceiling of his dispensing room.

"What is it for?"

"What do you think it might be for?"

She regarded the strange creature from foreign seas. "Some remedy. Something very powerful – rare and costly."

He smiled. "It has no medical use whatsoever."

She looked at him shrewdly, to see if he was teasing her; but he was not. "Then why...?"

"It gives my customers belief in me. They see it hanging there and, like you, they think it must be some rare medicine, or perhaps a charm."

"Isn't that cheating?"

"Not at all. If they don't believe in me they may not get better. It helps their recovery."

"Then it *is* a medicine!"

He had laughed then. "You are sharp, Alice. Yes, perhaps it is."

Thinking now about Nia and her unborn child, Alice became aware of a familiar ache in her own back and thighs, and thought, My courses will come soon. It was a burden lifted; and yet, after her week of love with Robin at Sherborne she had half hoped to find herself with child, so that he might make haste to marry her. Here, in Salisbury, would surely have been an opportunity, but Robin had said nothing. Of course he's busy, she thought. The army may move on to battle at any time. His mind is on manoeuvres and drill. He'll marry me in the winter, for sure, when the campaigning season is over. She wished, though, that she felt closer to Robin: close enough to argue, quarrel, kiss and make up, as the Welshwomen did all the time with their men. Instead she took delight in his affection when it came her way but never really knew what was in his mind.

The cobbler had finished. He gave them their shoes,

and they went out again into the rain and scampered back to the outbuildings where they were lodged.

Later that day Alice saw a few of the soldiers standing in groups holding letters, some helping others to read them. There was great excitement. It seemed that a carrier with letters for Salisbury had brought mail to the army – most of it for officers and much of it months late.

None of Alice's friends could read, and she was not surprised that they had no news from home. But a young woman came to her, holding a letter. She had the hard, blank face of a whore, but she spoke diffidently to Alice. "They say you can read. Would you read this to me? I'd be much obliged."

Alice took the letter, embarrassed, and fearful too, wondering what news she might be required to pass on.

The handwriting was difficult, and she stumbled often as she read aloud:

> *"To Margaret Evans, travelling with the king's army, from her sister Elizabeth Evans of Newell near Buckingham, the eighteenth of September, 1644.*
>
> *Dear Sister, Master Holdom at the parsonage writes this for me, it being necessary to tell you in all sorrow that our mother has departed this life but is gone into that greater life of the spirit which is the reward of true believers."*

Alice looked up to see tears in the girl's eyes. "I am sorry," she said.

"Read on," the girl replied.

> *"She fell sick of a fever and died this Saturday last, and was buried at St Martin's beside our brother Richard. She spoke of you at the end, and forgave you, and wished that you had never left home, as I do wish also, dear Meg..."*

The girl dashed a hand across her face. "Would you write me an answer? If I can find paper for it? I'll pay you."

"Yes. Of course," said Alice.

That evening she told Robin about the girl and her letter, and how she'd felt pity for her. He was with his friends, and joked, "You could make a living there, sweet – writing letters home for drabs."

His friends laughed, but Alice felt hurt on behalf of the bereaved girl.

Next day they moved off and marched towards Andover. The women, camped in fields a few miles outside the town, saw nothing of the fighting, but they heard distant sounds of gunfire and saw smoke rising on the horizon. By nightfall the town was in Royalist hands and the enemy in flight. From the lanes all around came shouts and the clash of weapons as the defenders were pursued and taken prisoner.

Alice stayed with her Welsh friends while she waited for Robin.

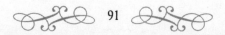

"There will be more fighting tomorrow," Bryn predicted. "We'll go after the rebels."

But for now they celebrated, singing, joking and playing music; a group of the men lined up and linked arms and, despite their long march, danced while the onlookers clapped and sang.

Over the next week there were skirmishes and movements of troops all around. Alice heard names: Newbury, Basing House, Donnington Castle.

"What's happening?" she asked Robin. "We go round about the same places, day after day. Nothing makes sense."

"We don't try to make sense of it," Robin said. "We obey orders, go where they send us."

"But will there be a battle?"

"How should *I* know?"

He stared moodily at the ground. He'd been distant with her lately, as if there was something on his mind. She supposed it was all the extra drills and alarms, the prospect of fighting to come. It made her feel very alone.

"I'm afraid for you," she said, and put out a hand to him.

He shook it off. "Then you should not have come with me!" Her obvious hurt seemed to provoke rather than soften him, and he said roughly, "This is war, Alice; not some game."

"I know." She spoke in a small voice and turned away, afraid she might cry and so anger him more.

* * *

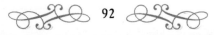

They were woken next morning by the drumbeat that she now knew was to summon the men to their quarters. Word flew about that the enemy had been sighted, drawn up on the hills to the east of Newbury. There was a ferment of activity in the camp, but it was nightfall before the fighting began. Alice huddled with the Welsh girls, all four of them crowded into Bronwen's shelter, listening to the guns: the distant sound of the rebels' cannon, and the deafening roar and flash of their own. When all was quiet for a while they fell asleep, lolling against each other, only to wake again towards dawn to the sound of more cannon fire. The air was full of smoke.

The sounds of battle continued on and off all day. Mistress Erlam called on Alice to help make ready with linen strips and salves. The surgeon would deal with the officers and those who were badly wounded, she explained, but those with lesser injuries would be sent to the women's camp. Alice was glad of the work. It took her mind off her fear for Robin. His harshness of the evening before had only made it more important to her that he should be safe, that they should not lose each other.

In the afternoon a cry went up: "They are bringing the wounded!" and she became too busy to think of anything else for a while.

A woman's voice rose, keening. The sound went on and on.

"It's that girl from Bristol," someone said. "Poor soul, to lose her man."

"What will become of her?" Alice asked her friends later.

Nia shrugged. "She'll get work, maybe, on the baggage train; find another man, if she's lucky."

"Or, more likely, become a whore," said Bronwen. "That's often the only way to survive."

For the first time, Alice realized that this could happen to her; that she herself might end up like the whores she had so much despised. It would be all too easy if she was left alone, without Robin, without a home or family. Whatever would my father have thought? she wondered; and she imagined his shock and distress at seeing her as she was now. Her eyes filled with tears, and Bronwen, misunderstanding the reason, took her hand in her own rough, grimy hand, and said, "Don't cry, Lisi. He has a lucky face, your Robin. He'll survive. And you'll live to be wed."

Alice turned to her gratefully. "You think so?"

"I do."

The next night was quiet, but the men did not return to the shelters, and the women sat together, talking, singing and mending clothes. Alice was beginning to learn the words of some of the Welsh songs, which were mostly romantic: the shirt song; the ballad called "The Slender Lad", about a girl who refused to marry unless she could have the boy she loved; the song about the garden of love:

> *I left the lily, the lavender and rose,*
> *Instead the nettle's sting I chose.*

Later she slept in Nia's shelter, the two of them close together under a rough blanket and their woollen cloaks. At dawn they woke to the sound of cannon fire. The guns thundered most of the day, and once again Alice tended the wounded. Towards evening her fears became real when Robin appeared in the camp, white-faced and bleeding from a shoulder wound.

"Robin!" She tried to still the trembling that gripped her: ran to help him, made him sit down, gently removed his jacket to reveal the shirt saturated with blood.

"Have you been to the surgeon's tent?"

"No. He only sees officers. This is nothing..." – though he was shaking and his teeth were clenched so that he struggled to speak. "A sword cut. They always bleed a lot."

Alice peeled the cloth away from the wound, swabbed it with warm water and saw that he was right: the flesh had been sliced open and the wound was bleeding heavily, but it did not look serious. Now that she was sure he was in less danger, she felt almost pleased that he had been injured. It gave her a chance to care for him and perhaps regain the love she had feared might be slipping away from her.

He *was* grateful. He praised her skill in binding the wound and seemed glad of her company.

"How goes the fight?" she asked.

He shrugged. "I don't know. I've been stuck beside a hedge all day, with a row of others, firing at any rebels that come past – when we can see them through the smoke."

He struggled to put his arm back into the bloodstained sleeve. She helped him.

"You're not going back there?"

"No." He grinned. "It's my firing side, so I'm spared that." He put his left arm, the good one, round her and pulled her close and kissed her. "I'll stay with you tonight."

And Alice felt happy, secure again in his affection, even though the smoke of battle was blowing across the campsite, and they could hear gunfire, and no one seemed to know which side, if either, had the upper hand.

"Fetch my snapsack, sweet, will you?" he asked. "I need a smoke."

He opened the bag and rummaged awkwardly, left-handed, for his pipe. Something else fell out – something that showed white in the fading light: a letter, its seal of red wax broken.

"Oh!" she exclaimed. "You had a letter! Did that come at Salisbury?"

"Yes."

She was surprised he had not told her, since they had talked about the arrival of the mail and the letter she had read aloud for the girl. He must have received his own letter that day, and yet had said nothing of it.

"Is it from home?" she asked.

He nodded. "Family." And he thrust the letter to the bottom of the bag, pulling out his clay pipe and tobacco pouch.

She waited for him to say more, if only that his parents

were well. She longed to be drawn into his family, to feel part of his life. But he simply lit his pipe and puffed on it, his mood distant now. She wondered if the letter had contained bad news; perhaps that was the reason for his changed manner towards her. But if he would not tell her, how could she comfort him?

He did stay with her that night, as he had promised; and they made love, despite his painful shoulder. But she still felt shut out from his heart and his concerns.

It was later that night, as she lay listening to the guns, that she remembered, in Salisbury – about ten days ago, was it? – feeling that her courses were about to begin. She had not thought about them since. But they had not come; and the heavy feeling in her back and thighs had gone. She was very late. And yet she'd been quite certain of that feeling. Surely it meant all must be as usual? Beside her, in the darkness, Robin breathed steadily, asleep and apart. She felt lonely and frightened, uncertain even of what she wanted. What would he say if she told him she might be with child? I don't know him, she thought; he's a stranger to me.

Two weeks passed, and still nothing.

There was no parsley growing now, to make into a tea that might bring on her courses.

"Ask Sian," said Nia. "She'll give you a remedy."

"Maybe. But I'm not sure yet..."

She could go to Sian, or she could buy rue from the apothecary. But her father had taught her to be cautious of powerful ingredients; and besides, in spite of

everything, she was reluctant to lose this child, if indeed one was there. If she had a child, she thought, it might bind Robin closer to her.

The weather was cold now, the days short.

"We'll move to quarters near Oxford soon," Robin told her, "and stay there for the winter."

He did not seem happy at the thought. His mood was strange these days, and Alice lacked the courage to ask him whether they might be married in Oxford.

Nine

"*You* women – out! Come on! Get down! We're stuck!"

The carter, grim-faced, the shoulders of his coat soaked dark with rain, shouted up at the four of them. He hauled on the wagon while the younger carter – the one who had allowed the girls on board – whipped the horses. The horses laboured. The carters swore. The wheels slipped and stuck in the marshy ground.

Alice had been barefoot since morning, her skirts hitched up to her knees. Now, as she climbed down, she sank into mud above her ankles. The mud was cold and full of sharp stones, and the rain drove against her, soaking her in minutes. She could hear Rhian complaining with little squeals of shock. Bronwen and Nia were clinging to each other as they staggered in the mud.

"Get behind the wheel and push!" said the carter.

Alice obeyed, but her weight was nothing. They

all – carters and women – pushed and felt no response. Two men from the wagon in front ran to help. Behind stretched a long line of stalled carts and wagons, waiting. Shouts of advice reached them, followed by men with ropes.

They had come down from the Ridgeway that morning onto a flooded plain crossed by swollen streams. The heavy ammunition wagons pulled by oxen had passed through ahead of the baggage train, turning the track they were following into a morass.

"Heave! Heave!" yelled the carters.

With men and ropes all around it, the wagon at last began to move.

"Heave!"

The women stood well back, shivering, arms crossed against the cold. Above them the view of the Downs was blotted out by rain. The horses struggled; the men strained against the ropes. Slowly, slowly, the wagon came free, the wheels turned; it was out, and moving. They clambered back on board – Rhian, going up ahead of Alice, showing a flash of white, mud-spattered thigh that caught the younger carter's attention.

"Give us a bit more!" he shouted.

The older one uttered a stream of curses as he whipped up the horses. "I should have gone with those men that ran off," he said. "Couldn't be worse than this."

The other man disagreed. "They'll freeze to death tonight – if they're not caught and hanged first."

A large group of Welsh soldiers had deserted and were being sought, and everyone was wondering how

they would fare in this cold and rain. In the few villages the army had passed through, the inhabitants had been hostile. Alice could not imagine those people giving food or help to deserters – especially foreigners.

Everyone on the march was hungry. The bad harvest had left farmers with nothing to spare, and the wild crop of berries and mushrooms was over. People thought about food, and how to get it, all the time, and would dart into hedgerows to gather a few mouldy hazelnuts, pick up long-rotted summer fruit, or steal from cottage kitchens, the soldiers threatening householders with their swords. Alice's skirt felt loose on her. I can't be with child, she thought, not if I'm so thin. Perhaps it's hunger that has stopped my courses.

It was not far to the king's destination – a great house in Marlborough. The troops pressed on for another two miles to a village built all of grey stone: Fyfield. The same grey stone lay underfoot and bruised their feet as they walked across it in their soaked shoes and boots. The inhabitants' manner was as stony as their dwellings, and the soldiers found themselves lodged for the most part in dank, miserable quarters.

Alice was glad she was with Robin, who always made sure those in his charge were fed. They ate pottage, hot, with a few pieces of bacon in it, and a hunk of bread. Alice was never more glad of food as she sat shivering, warming her hands on the bowl. Her gown was drenched and mud-soaked, but she had nothing dry to wear. The day before she had worn her boys' breeches, but those were now wet through. Even her spare linen was wet.

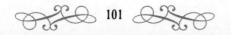

They stayed two days at Fyfield. Alice's friends did not know any of the deserters, but they were thinking about them; they were, after all, Welsh – their countrymen. On that first long evening the men sang sad songs of home, their voices mingling and harmonizing. They were easily moved, and the songs carried a charge of emotion that had some of them in tears. Later they fell to telling ghost stories, while the wind howled outside and the unfriendly dark closed in. Alice could not understand the language, but she was caught up in the drama of the stories all the same: the way the tellers used their voices, the sudden dramatic pauses, the listeners' intakes of breath.

"They're frightening themselves half to death," said Bronwen, and Alice looked at the men's faces and saw that she was right.

It was dusk of the following day when word began to spread around the billets that most of the deserters had been caught and brought back. They were imprisoned in the village lock-up. Alice looked out and saw the guards standing outside, puffing on their clay pipes and stamping their feet to keep warm. She thought of the men lying shackled within – wet through, beaten, vanquished – and pitied them. Robin told her that in the morning two of them would be chosen to hang, the rest returned to the ranks.

Alice was shocked. "To hang?" she exclaimed. "Why those two?"

"No reason."

"But that's unjust!"

"It's what happens, sweet. The army must set an example."

Everyone was in subdued mood that night. Next morning the soldiers were all summoned to witness the executions. Alice heard a drum roll and knew the two men were being led to the scaffold. The insistent drumming continued, and when it stopped, suddenly, the silence seemed loud. She saw, in her imagination, a young man throttled and kicking at the end of a rope, and felt distressed at the cruel unfairness of the punishment. Later the entire army marched past the place where the bodies hung. Already, it seemed to Alice, they looked like bundles of rags, as if they had never lived.

"Oh! That any man should have come to this!" exclaimed Nia.

And Alice, shaken and afraid, wondered what would become of them all, what *she* would come to; where this cold, wet march was leading them.

On a dark day in late November they turned north-west, towards Faringdon.

"We've finished now, for the season," Mistress Erlam told Alice. "We'll be sent to our winter quarters."

"In Faringdon?"

"Some in the town, some in the countryside around. The king will go on to Oxford."

"Is Faringdon close to Oxford?"

"Twelve miles or so."

Alice thought of Robin, of his home near Oxford, their chance to marry now that the campaign was over.

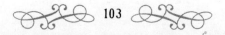

Would it happen? She wished she could be certain; wished he would turn to her and say, in that easy way of his, "Let's be married, sweet." But he said nothing; and although he was still casually affectionate, and still made love to her, the passion they had shared at Sherborne scarcely two months ago seemed to have waned.

And now she would have to part from Nia and her other friends. On that last day they embraced one another and said the goodbyes that they would not have time for later. By afternoon they would go to whatever quarters their men were assigned to, and it might be spring before they met again. Alice felt sad, and apprehensive about the months to come without Nia.

"I think this baby will be born in May," said Nia. "We should be together again by then. If only we didn't have to separate now!"

"But you'll be with Bronwen and Rhian through the winter," said Alice. "You three are sure to be quartered together. *I'll* be with strangers."

"You'll have Robin."

"Yes." But it had been good, Alice realized, having a friend, another girl, to talk to. Nia had become a steady, reliable source of comfort and gossip and giggles in a way that Robin never could. "It's not the same," she said.

Nia understood. "No, it's not. Oh, but we'll meet up again in the spring, won't we? And you'll look in your father's book, and help me when my time comes? I'm so afraid of the birth."

"Don't be afraid! I'll be there. I promise."

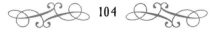

"I'll feel safer if you are with me." Nia glanced at Alice's flat stomach. "You were mistaken, weren't you? That's lucky."

Alice bit her lip. This was another reason why she wanted her friends around her. It was a long time since she had taken off her shift, but that morning her breasts had felt full and tender, and when she was alone for a moment she had untied the gathered neckline and looked down at them. She had seen enlarged nipples and a network of blue veins showing on the white skin.

"I think perhaps I *am* with child," she said.

Nia's gaze was startled, full of concern. "Are you sure? Last week you thought—"

Alice explained. She hoped Nia would say, "Oh, that's nothing! It doesn't happen like that." But Nia didn't. She looked into Alice's eyes and said, "Tell Robin, Lisi. *Tell* him. You must be married." She tried to make a joke of it. "You know what we said about Rhian and Gethin – you have to give these men a push!" She hugged Alice tightly. "All will be well. We are in God's hands."

Alice felt heavy-hearted, but she told herself that she would be with Robin for the winter, and that was what she wanted above all else. And with the end of the campaigning season, surely he would have more time. Her fears were unnecessary. She would tell him she was with child; they would marry; and he would take her to his home.

Robin came to fetch her later, and she joined the draggle of women following his company of foot soldiers

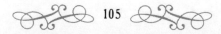

along a muddy, rutted road between dripping hedges. A slippery mush of fallen leaves lay underfoot. The day had closed in early, and Alice shook with cold.

"I'd kill for a bite to eat," one of the women said.

Alice felt hunger pains too. She was always hungry these days.

The road led on into the countryside east of Faringdon – for mile after mile, it seemed to Alice. She wondered which way the Welsh troops had gone; whether her friends would be anywhere near. At last, as evening fell early, they turned off the road and marched along a lane that wound downhill into a darkness of wintry trees wreathed in fog. A lantern appeared ahead, bobbing and flickering in the mist, and she heard dogs barking and saw, a little way off, the glow of candlelight in windows.

It was an inn – a substantial place, surrounded by stables and sheds. Not far away were several cottages. They tramped through squelching mud into the yard. Two dogs barked over a hubbub of raised voices, confusion, shouted orders, groups of men milling about. It was dark now, and difficult to see what was happening. Alice felt faint with hunger.

Robin appeared and said, "Alice! Come – there's food!" and led her into the inn's parlour, which was full of a great stinking press of men in sodden clothing. They squeezed between bodies until they came near the fire. It was piled with logs that blazed and spat sparks and drew out the smell of wet wool. There was nowhere to sit, so they stood close together, scorched on one side

by the fire, and chilled on the other whenever the door opened and more people came in. The innkeeper and several servants were handing out beer.

Robin passed Alice a tankard. "Here, drink some of this. It'll warm you."

She obeyed, but almost at once began to feel light-headed. She was relieved when the food arrived: army rations of bread and cheese – and some meat too, for those who were quick. Robin was quick. He managed to grab a leg of mutton, hot and fatty, and they shared it between them. They ate ravenously, stuffing food into their mouths, hardly bothering to chew.

When her hunger was eased, Alice asked, "What's happening? What were they shouting about out there?"

"Too many of us for the billets," said Robin. "Some of us – and all the officers – were to go up the road to Weston Hall, but it seems there's sickness there; so they've split the company, moved some on to another place." He wiped his greasy mouth with the back of his hand. "Quartermaster doesn't like it. Small groups are more at risk from the enemy. But there's naught to be done. And you're lucky: I got us a space here, at the inn, in the attics."

But he didn't seem eager to go up, as he usually would be. He lit his pipe, and they stayed in the parlour, surrounded by damp, steaming clothes, slopped beer and loud drunken voices until Alice was so weary she could no longer stand, but sagged against him. Even then he merely searched out a stool for her, and continued to stand and puff at his pipe and occasionally frown or stare

into the distance. Alice felt unable to reach him.

At last the parlour began to empty. Most of the men were billeted in surrounding cottages and farms, and went out.

"I need to rest – to sleep," Alice pleaded.

Robin nodded then, knocked out his pipe on the fireplace and – almost reluctantly, she felt – led her up two flights of narrow stairs to the attics. There were others sleeping there, but Robin had found them a space in a little side room where they could be alone. It was warm from the rising heat of the fire downstairs, and with their layered blankets and outer clothes over them they were cosy enough.

"This is good," she said, snuggling close to him. "You always find good places for us."

She knew it was because of his way with women – even busy innkeepers' wives, or frosty women like her aunt.

He kissed her forehead. "Yes. You'll be safe here."

"I'll be *safe*?" She searched his eyes in the darkness, suddenly afraid, as she'd been at Tor Farm when he said the army was moving on.

He rolled away from her and lay on his back. "I'm going home, Alice. I've been given leave—"

"Home?" Her breath came short. "When?"

"Tomorrow. I meant to tell—"

"But – when will you be back?"

There was a silence – and she knew. She knew he would be there for the entire winter and would not return until the army was on the move again. But he

said, awkwardly, "Weeks. Several weeks," and added, "it's an advantage for the army if men go home. No billets or provisions needed. And my family – I haven't seen them this long time…"

"Can't I come with you?" she asked in a small voice. "Robin? Can't I meet them? You said—" Her voice broke. "You said you loved me. I thought…"

He turned towards her and held her close. "I'll come and visit you, I promise. There are army carriers going to and from Oxford all the time, delivering supplies. It's no distance, sweet. I'll come and see you."

"But I don't know anyone here!"

Her voice was a wail, and he shushed her as someone snarled a curse from the adjoining room.

"You'll do well enough. Make yourself useful to the goodwife. She'll look out for you, keep you safe. I spoke to her earlier."

It's all planned, she thought. He's been planning this awhile, and never told me. Why won't he take me to his home? And where *is* his home? He had never told her the name of the place where he lived, only that it was near Oxford.

She said, "Robin, you can't leave me. I'm with child by you."

She felt him stiffen. "Are you sure? You don't look… You must be mistaken?"

"No. I'm sure." Why should he think it so unlikely, she thought bitterly, given what they'd been doing? "We should go to Oxford *together*," she said. "We ought to be married."

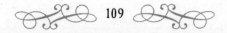

"Oxford's no place for you, sweet. They've got plague there. Had it since the summer."

"Well, *here*, then. We could be married here."

"Ah," he said. "I must go home first—"

"Why can't we be married first? Why can't I come with you?" Her voice rose, and he hushed her again.

"I'll see what can be done. But don't fear, love. I'll come back soon, soon as I can."

"It won't be long? Promise me?"

"Of course."

She wanted to believe him. And when he began to kiss and cuddle her, his touch was so gentle, and the smell and feel of him so familiar, that she thought he must love her; it must be true. And yet she lay awake for hours afterwards, thinking, and worrying, and wishing she had Nia to turn to for advice. She suspected that Robin was also awake, but he gave no sign. Tomorrow, she thought, I'll insist he gives me an address to send to if I should need him. I'll make him write it in my father's book. The decision comforted her, and at last she fell asleep.

When she woke, he was gone.

For a moment, she thought he had simply stepped outside, to the privy. Then she saw a small leather bag lying on the blanket beside her, and a folded piece of paper.

"Robin!"

She sprang up and opened the door, but the main attic room was full of huddled, snoring bodies. She picked her way between them and peered out of the

grimy window. It was early morning, still dark. A stable boy was walking across the yard with a lantern, and a maid leaned on her broom and chatted with him. There was no sign of Robin.

She returned to her bed. She knew what the bag would contain. She unfolded the note. His handwriting was like a child's, unpractised; but the words were clear enough.

> Sweetheart, don't be sad. I'll come when I can.
> The money is for your needs.
> Your loving Robin Hillier

No mention of marriage. No address, not even the name of his village. Only *I'll come when I can*. She picked up the bag and tipped its contents onto the bed, surprised at how much was there: several months' pay, she reckoned, and perhaps coin looted from the rebels at Lostwithiel.

She began to cry, stifling the sound of her tears in the blanket. The money should have given her some comfort, but it didn't. It made her feel like a whore.

Ten

"*Got* you in pod, has he? Moved on?"

Alice winced at the maidservant's accuracy. How could the girl know? She didn't, of course; she was guessing. Alice held her head high and ignored the questions.

The two maidservants goaded her every hour, every day. Sib and Nell, they were called: Sib a stringy-haired blonde with a weasel face; Nell heavy and spiteful, given to lying in wait to trip or pinch her victim. Alice had to share the tiny attic room with them: the same room she had shared with Robin that first night here at the King's Arms in Copsey. They had resented her from the start, it seemed; or perhaps they simply enjoyed having a friendless newcomer to torment. Alice, in exchange for work, had been granted free board and lodging and a payment to be made when the army left. The arrangement suited the innkeeper and his wife, the place

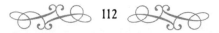

112

being so much busier with the army quartered in the village.

"He's moved on," Sib repeated, taunting her. "Got another girl."

Nell sniggered. "He can move on top of me any time he likes."

"Fight you for him!"

They laughed and jostled each other.

Oh, Robin! Alice thought. Why don't you come? Why have you left me here?

It was more than three weeks now. Every day she watched for the army carrier. A constant flow of traffic came through the village: the mail, the brewers, pedlars, carriers, coaches. The Oxford army supplied bread to all its regiments billeted around Faringdon, Wallingford and Kidlington. Other army suppliers also came from Oxford; and often she saw soldiers alighting or catching a ride into the city. Copsey was five miles out of Faringdon, off the Oxford road. It would not be a long or difficult journey, even if he lived on the far side of Oxford. Why didn't he come?

She thought of many reasons, most of them alarming. He was dead – but no, she dreaded even to think that, for fear of making it true. He was injured, ill. His mother was ill, or some other of his family. He'd been attacked and robbed. He'd found another girl.

Another girl. Sib or Nell would have had him, given a chance. Anyone would. And yet… He wouldn't even glance at the likes of Sib or Nell. And he'd given her money; he'd settled her here; he knew she was with

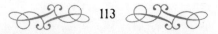

113

child and had promised to come back. He was always so loving and careful towards her. He could not be tired of her. She would not believe it.

The army provisions carrier was here now, the wagon wheels clattering over the cobbles of the inn yard. She flung a shawl around her shoulders and ran outside, hearing behind her the maidservants' mocking laughter.

A party of dragoons guarded the wagon. One of them gave her the eye as he dismounted, and she looked quickly away. She hated being so unprotected in this male wartime world. Without Robin she was prey to any man.

She stepped cautiously across the icy cobbles and approached the driver, an older man with a slouch hat, a pipe between his teeth and flamboyant side whiskers.

"Do you know Robin Hillier? A corporal of foot? He's staying with his parents near Oxford."

But the man could tell her nothing. In desperation she asked, "Do you deliver all around Faringdon?"

"I do."

"I want to find my friend, a Welsh girl, a soldier's wife. Do you know where the Welsh foot are billeted?"

He shrugged. "There are Welsh in all the quarters around here. Could be any of them." He reeled off a list of place names that meant nothing to her. None, it seemed, were less than five or six miles away, across marshy country, in winter.

"Thank you."

She retreated indoors, away from the cold wind.

There was always plenty of work to do. The

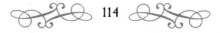

innkeeper's wife, Mistress Tyrrell, set her to sweeping the upper chambers. The other two were scouring pots, cackling together in the scullery. Alice was glad to get away from them, and went upstairs and swept her way down from the attics, sneezing as the dust flew. At the top of the stairs above the parlour she sneezed harder than before and felt a sudden wetness between her legs.

She stood still, aware of her breath, her heartbeat. Could this be...? There was no one about. She caught up her skirts, put a hand there and drew it away. Blood. Bright red.

So she was not with child. That was her first thought, and with it came a wash of relief and then, perversely, disappointment. And yet ... it had been so long. It was October when they were in Salisbury and she had first thought her courses were about to come. How many weeks ago was that? Eight? Nine? Ten? Today was the eighteenth of December. She knew because Master Tyrrell had an almanac downstairs, like the one they'd used at Tor Farm.

I *must* be with child, she thought. I must be nearly three months gone. And now I'm bleeding. She began to tremble with fright. She propped the broom against the wall and ran up to the attics and rummaged in her pack for rags. Robin's heavy purse, in a pocket under her gown, bumped against her hip. She wished she could hide the money somewhere else, but feared Sib and Nell would find it. She had padded the coins with cloth to prevent them from jingling. Her father's book was hidden too, pushed down inside the front of her

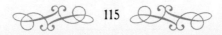

stays. She'd made the mistake, once, of picking up the latest newsbook that lay on a table in the parlour. One of the regular customers would occasionally read aloud from these to the assembled company. But that day Alice had read alone, in silence, following the words with a finger.

Sib had jeered, "Look at *her*! We have a scholar among us!"

And Alice knew she had distanced herself even further from those two. They would have no mercy on her book if they found it. "Bum fodder!" they'd crow, and rip out the pages to use in the privy.

They would have no mercy on her, either, if they knew she might be about to miscarry. As she tied the rags in place she noticed several dried blood spots on her shift; and she became aware, now, of a low backache that she realized had been with her for most of the day.

I should rest, she thought. But that would mean admitting she was with child, and she had been pushing that revelation away into the future, thinking – hoping – that Robin would come and remove her from this place before she needed to tell.

Should she tell Mistress Tyrrell now? The woman was not unkind, but she was brusque, busy, unapproachable. A girl who needed to rest was no good to her. And if she did tell Mistress Tyrrell, it wouldn't be long before Sib and Nell knew.

She'd do better to keep quiet, keep her shift on, not be seen washing it, hope … what?

"He's moved on." Perhaps it would better if she

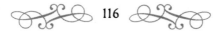

miscarried. No, she thought. No. She clung to her dream of a baby, a husband, a new life as Robin's wife.

"Alice! Have you gone to ground, wench?" Mistress Tyrrell's voice rose up from the foot of the stairs.

Alice hurried down, seized the broom and began banging it busily around the skirting boards.

Next morning, on waking, she felt a dragging ache in her hips and back. She got up and dressed quickly, hiding her stained shift under her skirt while the other two maids were still half asleep. She went about her work, cleaning, scouring pots, fetching and carrying. She bled again, and the ache was worse. Once, in the afternoon, she felt a cramp that took her breath away. She had to put down her kitchen knife and press with both hands on the table till it passed. Fortunately no one noticed, and when nothing more happened she relaxed a little, and continued her work. Later, she took out a pail of warm mash to the hens, flinching at the shock of cold air as she opened the kitchen door. The wind was from the north and had flecks of snow in it. She saw that the water in the horse trough was covered in a film of ice.

"You can take a walk to the glover's for me before it gets dark," Mistress Tyrrell said. She showed Alice a pair of well-worn leather gloves, split at the seams, the thumb coming away on the right-hand glove. "See what can be done. And call in at the butcher's − Crockford's, not Loosley's − and tell Master Crockford I'd like a dozen more of those pies he sent last week, to be delivered on Saturday."

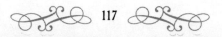

Alice took the gloves, put on her red cloak and a hood, and went out. The King's Arms was at the edge of the village, the glover's and butcher's a five-minute walk away along a road lined with cottages and shops. The cold wind stung her eyes as she set off.

She had not gone more than a few yards when a cramp made her double over. She looked around. People scurried by, heads down against the wind, unaware of her. She walked on, but almost at once the pain came again, and she felt a gush of blood.

Not here, she thought in panic. It can't happen here, in the street. The shops ahead were busy with customers going in and out. She imagined collapsing there, on someone's doorstep; the shame of it; the news reaching the inn.

She had to find somewhere private. A road went off to her left – a deserted road that led past a paddock into woodland. Those woods, she knew, belonged to Weston Hall, the place where the officers had expected to stay. Between the trees, which were now almost leafless, she could see its tall, decorated chimneys.

The house was some way off, and already dusk was gathering in the shady places under the trees. She turned aside onto the road and hurried, hunched over, afraid that at any moment events would overwhelm her.

When she reached the woods, she plunged in among the trees and bushes without waiting to look for a path. The cramps were coming regularly now, and the urge to hide was powerful.

Even here the wind bit like a blade. She dropped to

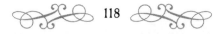

her knees beside a tree in the shelter of a holly bush. A pain came like a band of iron tightening around her back and belly, and she cried out and squatted, bundling her clothes out of the way.

The pain gripped her again, and now she pushed and felt something pass, something substantial; and she knew this was the child, hers and Robin's, and she had lost it. Warm blood flowed. Another pain came, followed by more loss. And then her body relaxed. It was over. She waited a few moments, then tried to stand, but at once black specks gathered in front of her eyes, and she sank down again. She felt weak and nauseous, and extraordinarily tired. I'll rest a bit, she decided. When she tried to move away, to a cleaner place, the faintness came again, so she simply leaned back against the tree and closed her eyes.

Eleven

Sounds roused her: barking, and then snuffling, breathing; wet muzzles pushing against her legs and face. Dogs! Three or four of them. They were all around her. Alice yelped in fright; and at the same moment, a female voice called out, "Keeper! Jewel! Here, here!" And she looked up and saw the dogs running towards a woman who had emerged on horseback from a woodland path, accompanied by a young groom.

"Thank the Lord!" said the woman. "I feared you were a corpse!"

Alice remained crouching and lowered her gaze, overcome with shame at being found in such a condition. She heard the woman draw nearer, and saw, on the snowy ground in front of her, a pair of feet in high-sided brown leather shoes and the hem of a dark skirt brushing them. The shoes and skirt – polished leather and soft heavy wool – told her that this was no servant,

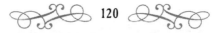

but a woman of quality, perhaps one of the gentry who owned the house. Was she trespassing, she wondered? Trembling, she raised her eyes.

The woman's voice had sounded younger than she now appeared. This was an old woman of fifty, perhaps even sixty: tall and strongly built. She wore a black velvet hood that draped softly around her face. A wing of white hair showed beneath the hood, and her eyes were dark.

She looked at Alice, and frowned in concern. "You are not one of my people, I think? How came you here? Have you been ill-used by soldiers?"

Alice knew the woman must have seen the blood on her stockings as she scrambled away from the dogs. She flicked her skirt to cover them, and struggled to rise, holding on to the tree, and shaking her head at the question.

"No. No man has hurt me," she whispered.

"Then what … ah, I see how it is…"

She turned to the boy, who stood some way off. "Tom, this is no sight for you. Go back to the house. Send two wenches with a pallet – and a spade."

"No!" said Alice. "No, I can't. I work at the King's Arms. I must go back…"

"On foot? Child, if you could see yourself! You are as white as bone. You should thank God we found you in time. Much longer, and you might have frozen to death."

"I do thank God," said Alice. "And you, my lady. But I can walk." She let go of the tree and took a few steps forward, determined to prove it. She could not

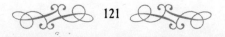

bring herself to look at what had come out of her body.

But the woman looked. She said, "You have miscarried of a child. Three months, I'd say?"

Alice felt tears sliding down her cheeks. She nodded. The dark eyes appraised her, head to foot, and Alice knew she was thinking: this girl is young, and no doubt unwed.

"Not a village girl, are you? Is that a West Country accent?"

"Yes. It is. I … came with the army."

"Ah. I see."

Alice knew from the woman's tone that she thought her a whore. She insisted, "I'm to be married soon! He's gone home, my soldier, but he will come back. He promised me."

The look she got in response was one of mingled pity and exasperation. "You girls! You always believe that! Well" – she turned away – "here are Joan and Bess. They will take you to the house, where you can rest awhile."

Alice shrank from enduring more scrutiny, but the two servant girls were friendly, as different from Sib and Nell as could be imagined. They quickly took in the situation and helped her onto the pallet. They found Mistress Tyrrell's gloves, which Alice had dropped, and reassured her that they could carry her easily between them. Before they left, Bess, the sturdier of the two, dug into the hard soil with the spade and spread a covering of earth and twigs over the dead child.

The lady had ridden ahead of them back to the house, and by the time they arrived she had disappeared,

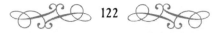

and the dogs with her. The maids set the pallet down in a courtyard where there was a well, a trough for horses, and a mounting block. There were several barns and outbuildings near by, and seeing them made Alice think of army quarters, and how she had heard that the army had avoided this place because of disease. It was clear that there were still no soldiers about.

"I heard there was sickness here," she said to the girls.

"Oh, you've nothing to fear," said Joan. "Lady Weston's grandchildren came with their mother and a maid from Oxford. The maid was ill, and then the eldest boy sickened, and at first they feared it was plague. You know there was plague in Oxford all summer?"

"Dirty, overcrowded place," said Bess, shaking her head.

"Oh, Bessy! Proper country girl, you are! I love to see the town. Well, it wasn't the plague, thank the Lord, but it kept us free of the army. They went to Haden Hall instead, and it seems they'll stay there."

She went inside, while Bess supported Alice with an arm about her shoulders. "Come into the kitchen and sit on the settle by the fire. I'll warm some ale for you. Joan's gone to fetch water so that you can wash."

There were other people in the kitchen, a cook working at the big table, helped by a little maid of no more than twelve years. The cook nodded to Alice as she sat down. No one asked questions, but Alice knew they must be curious. She saw Bess, on her way to fetch the ale, encounter Joan in the doorway; the two of them

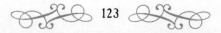

exchanged looks and whispers, and Alice heard "…one of the soldiers' drabs, I suppose…"

I'm not a drab, she thought, tears of anger pricking her eyes. And yet the girls were kind, whatever they assumed she was.

It felt odd to be sitting idle while others worked, but she felt too weak to do otherwise. She glanced around the kitchen: at rows of great pans hanging on the walls; ladles, sieves and serving dishes; a shelf of jugs and another of painted china plates; strings of onions and herbs dangling from the ceiling. The cook, a strong-looking woman with huge arms, was making pastry, while the young girl chopped onions, with much sniffing.

Bess came back with a little pan of spiced ale that she warmed over the fire before pouring it into a tankard. "Here, this'll bring you back to yourself." She shook her head. "You do look wan!"

Alice sipped the ale and felt it warm her from within. The fire was hot, sleepy-making. She felt very tired. Two cats, one tabby, one black, lay on the hearthstones, asleep and purring. As she watched the gentle rise and fall of their bodies, her trembling gradually ceased.

She looked up when Joan approached, accompanied by a young gentlewoman.

"Here's Mistress Christian to see you," the girl said.

Alice made to rise, but the woman gestured to her to remain seated, and sat down beside her. From her dress Alice thought she must be an upper servant of some kind, or even a member of the family. She was perhaps in her late twenties, slender in a gown of green wool

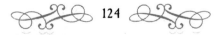

with a wide white collar edged with lace and a white linen apron, and with tawny-coloured hair drawn back under a neat cap. Her eyes were hazel brown, flecked with green. They studied Alice with concern.

"Lady Weston sent me to see you," she said. "I'm no apothecary, but I have some knowledge of medicine."

Alice drew in her legs and elbows defensively. "I'm not hurt."

"But do you still have any pain?" The woman's voice was gentle but authoritative. "If it did not all come away…"

"I believe it did," said Alice.

"That's good. But if you have more pain or loss you must tell someone. Don't hide away again, if you value your life." She smiled. "My name is Christian Aubrey. I am a kinswoman of Lady Weston's. And your name?"

"Alice Newcombe."

"There is water for you to wash, Alice, in the scullery. And you must stay here at Weston Hall until you are warm and rested."

"I can't stay! I have to go back. Mistress Tyrrell expects me—"

Christian Aubrey shook her head. "My lady's orders. She won't be gainsaid. She believes you were sent to her by God in this time of Advent, and she has instructed us to take care of you. Come. The water is warm."

She led Alice to the scullery, where Joan had left a bowl of water, a jug to top it up, a wash-ball and clean cloths.

"I'll leave you," she said. "No one will come in."

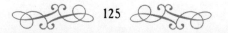

And she closed the door.

Alone at last, Alice found a stool and sat down. She felt weak, overwhelmed with shock. She had lost her child – Robin's child. All connection to him was now severed. If he did not come back for her, she would be quite alone in a world that seemed suddenly huge and threatening.

She moved, and felt her thighs sticky with blood. I must wash, she thought. Warm water and scented soap awaited her – a comfort she had not known for many weeks. She stood up, and took advantage of this rare moment of privacy to take off not only her skirt and stockings but also her bodice, stays and shift. The shift would need to be soaked in cold water to release the bloodstains. For now, she bundled it up and hid it under her other clothes.

She stood naked and took a cloth and washed down from neck to feet, sluicing away all trace of her ordeal. The wash-ball was scented with rosemary, a cleansing smell that Alice liked. Unable to lift the jug in her weakened condition, she tilted it to add fresh water to the bowl, rinsed away the soap, and picked up a soft drying cloth. Underneath it she saw that Joan had left a linen shift – old and patched, but clean – and a pair of brown woollen stockings. Such kindness, she thought; these are truly good people. She dried herself, and put on the stockings and shift.

Someone tapped at the door. "Are you seemly?"

It was Christian.

"You are kind, mistress," Alice said, glancing down

at the shift as the woman came in.

"Oh! We have plenty of linen stored." She approached the bowl of water to remove it.

"It's full of filth," Alice said, ashamed.

"I've seen worse."

She lifted it, and tipped the water into a funnel that led outside, then washed out the bowl with clean water. It was maids' work, and Alice knew this woman should not be doing it; she was shielding Alice, as far as she could, from kitchen gossip.

Alice put on her stays over the shift.

"What's this?" asked Christian, her voice sharp with surprise. She had found Alice's book lying on the table.

"It was my father's," said Alice. "He was an apothecary."

The woman turned to her with new interest. "May I look at it?"

"Yes, indeed. It is all remedies and observations and the properties of herbs."

"So I see. It is most full, and detailed. Can you read this, Alice?"

"Yes. And write."

"And did you work with your father? He taught you his skills?"

"Yes. I learned a little from him. But I was only a child. He died when I was eleven."

Christian studied the book a few moments longer, then closed it and handed it back; and Alice, who was now dressed, took it and, without thinking, pushed it down between her bodice and stays.

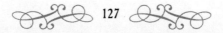

Christian laughed. "Why do you do that?"

Alice felt herself blushing. "To keep it safe. It's all I have of my father – and the maids at the inn would take it from me if they knew."

"*Would* they?" Christian frowned. "Come back to the kitchen. You must be hungry. I'll send for some bread and pottage."

"Mistress Aubrey, I have to go back."

"But eat first, to give you strength. It's dark already. We've sent a boy to return the gloves and tell the innkeeper's wife where you are. Don't fear."

But Alice was alarmed. "What will he say about me? About what happened?"

"Only that you were taken ill and fainted, and that Lady Weston chooses to keep you here till you recover."

She called Bess, and asked for food for Alice; and when it was brought she sat with her on the settle while she ate. In that large kitchen they were some distance from the others and not likely to be overheard. After a while Christian said, "You are not quite what I first thought, Alice Newcombe."

"Not a baggage train whore?" Alice retorted, with a burst of spirit. She knew that was what they must all have believed her to be.

"Not an ignorant girl, fit only for rough tasks. What work have you done since your father died?"

"Farm work, on my uncle's farm. Dairying, and suchlike."

"Did you like the dairy work?"

Alice paused. "Yes," she said, surprised to admit she had liked anything at Tor Farm. "Yes, I did. It was clean work, and suited me."

"And yet you left?"

Alice explained: told the woman briefly about her life at Tor Farm, about Robin, and the baggage train, and the King's Arms.

"So you are not happy at the inn?"

"No. I'm only waiting there. Waiting for Robin..." Her voice had turned husky.

"Oh, you poor child! Did he know?"

"Yes. I told him."

"And still he left you? But if he is with his parents it may perhaps be difficult. Can you write to him? Tell him what has happened to you?"

Alice looked down. "He never gave me his address."

They fell silent, and Alice knew that Christian was thinking, as Lady Weston had, that Robin had abandoned her. She thought it herself, often, but always pushed the thought away. "Thank you, mistress," she said, and put down her bowl on the hearth. "That was good."

Christian smiled. "You look a better colour now." She stood up. "Wait here. I must speak to Lady Weston before we send you back to the inn."

Alice sat quietly when Christian left, trying not to attract attention to herself. The kitchen women talked together as they prepared supper for the household. A door opened, and a lad came in shivering and hugging his arms. It was the boy Christian had spoken of, Alice realized, back from his errand to Mistress Tyrrell.

"You look perished, Walt," said the cook.

"I am. Gone bitter cold, it has. Roads'll freeze tonight."

Christian returned soon after. She looked purposeful. "It's dark, Alice, and slippery underfoot, and you are not yet fit to walk. You must stay the night here and we will see about getting you back in the morning."

Alice felt too exhausted to argue. She had no desire to arrive late at the inn and face the curiosity and questions of Mistress Tyrrell, still less endure Sib and Nell's attentions. It was easier to do as she was told.

"Joan, come! We'll make up a bed in the room next to mine," said Christian.

A little later she reappeared with a candle and led Alice into a large dining hall, then upstairs and along a wood-panelled corridor to a pleasant room containing a curtained four-poster bed, a washstand, a chest, and a toilet table and stool. From this room a doorway led into a smaller room, little more than a closet, and cluttered with boxes and piles of cloth. There the women had made up a bed for her with clean sheets, and provided a chamber pot.

"Sleep now," said Christian. "You must be tired. But I have put you here, near me, so that you may call me in the night if you are in pain, or need help. In the morning I have something I want to show you."

Twelve

Alice woke early, after a deep sleep. For a moment, she could not think where she was, and reached out, expecting to encounter the warm solidity of Robin's body beside hers. But the bed was narrow and cold. She remembered then, and felt empty, hollow, both in body and mind. Her baby was gone. Robin was gone. There was no one in the world she belonged to. She looked at the shrouded bales and boxes stored around her and the pale winter daylight showing between the gaps in the shutters and felt tears leaking from her eyes.

After a while she got up to use the chamber pot. There was blood, but not too much, and she felt recovered, if weak. She went to the window and opened the shutters. The view was from the back of the house. She saw outbuildings, stables and a boy – Lady Weston's fair-haired young groom – coming down the stairs from the loft, yawning and pulling on his jerkin. Ice glittered

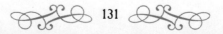

on the stones of the yard. Beyond the buildings were fields and trees, white with frost. The sky was barely light, pale as a pearl; but to her right, in what must be the east, a pink glow was spreading.

A new day. The sight gave her hope, and she chided herself for succumbing to self-pity. She was among kindly people and would be spared the taunting of Sib and Nell, at least for a time. And Christian Aubrey had said last night that she had something to show her. What could that be? She closed the curtains again, and put on her stays over the borrowed shift and began lacing them. From somewhere in the house she heard children's voices: perhaps the family who had come from Oxford?

When she was dressed and her hair combed – with her fingers, since her comb was at the King's Arms – she tapped on the connecting door between her room and Christian's. "Mistress Christian?"

No answer. She opened the door and looked in. She caught a flicker of movement, and thought at first that someone was there – then saw that it was her own reflection in a mirror. She felt drawn towards it. She had not seen herself for many months.

The mirror was a small one in a carved oval frame, standing on the table with a comb and several little glass and china pots beside it. Her aunt too had possessed a bedroom mirror, though not so fine as this one, and Alice had been in the habit of glancing into it when she swept the room or made the bed. Now she felt instinctively that she must look different. She had a lover and had been with child. Surely some subtle change must have

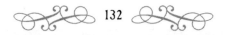

occurred in her appearance? But the face she saw, though somewhat dark-shadowed under the eyes, was the same as ever: young, pale, grey-eyed, and framed by mouse-brown hair that hung unfashionably straight and slack to below her shoulders. At Tor Farm she had coiled and pinned her hair out of sight under a cap; or curled it, for feast or fair days, with Jenefer's help, using tight twists of rag that were uncomfortable to sleep in. Her aunt, whose own hair curled becomingly from beneath her cap, had said Alice was without beauty – and yet Robin had made her feel beautiful. She bit her lower lip and pinched her cheeks to redden them, and instantly looked prettier. Perhaps that was how Robin saw her?

Christian Aubrey came in, and Alice jumped guiltily, even though she had not touched anything.

"You look better this morning," Christian said.

"I am. Thanks to you and the lady, Mistress Christian."

"Good. Then put your cap on and come downstairs with me."

"You wished to show me something?" Alice was intrigued, and a little anxious, wondering where they were going, and whether it would matter that she was so dishevelled. "My hair… I've lost its pins."

"Oh! You will do very well as you are."

They went downstairs and into the hall, which was now occupied by what seemed at first to be an army of little boys, all running about and squealing, pursued by a nursemaid holding coats and boots. It resolved itself

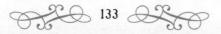

into two boys of five or six years – only one of them breeched; the other still in petticoats but wielding a toy sword – and a baby, just old enough to pull himself up to standing and try to join in with the others.

The eldest child grabbed at Christian's skirts. "Cousin Kit, we're going to the lake!"

"Then take care." Christian widened her eyes at the nursemaid, who rolled hers in return, before swooping to catch the second child and pinion him in his little fur-trimmed coat.

"Lady Weston's grandchildren," Christian told Alice. "She dotes on them."

She took a key from her belt and opened a door into a room that seemed immediately familiar to Alice – so much so that she gasped in surprise.

She noticed the smell first: a strong, sweet spicy mixture of cinnamon, cloves, anise, coriander, orange peel; and, underneath that, the more subtle fragrances of herbs – lavender, meadowsweet, thyme – and the bitterness of wormwood. There were flowers too: above all, a wondrous summery scent of roses. The room was in semi-darkness, but when Christian opened the shutters Alice saw, all around, shelves of phials and ceramic pots, carafes, mixing bowls, pestles and mortars, a set of scales, sieves, spoons and, at the far end of the room, two stills: a simple pewter one and a glass alembic.

She turned to Christian in amazement. "This is a preparation room! An apothecary's workroom!"

Christian smiled. "We call it the still room. All houses of the gentry have such a place where the ladies

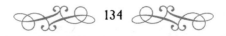

work. It is where we make remedies, cordials, sweet waters and the like; confections for feast days; wash-balls and lotions: everything the household needs. I have sole charge of this still room now. Lady Weston has never had much interest in it. Cis – her youngest daughter, Lady Cecily – and I used to work here together, but Cis was married in May, and is gone to Buckinghamshire. I like to gather the herbs myself, and dry them – we have a drying cupboard – and I make washing waters and keep a stock of remedies."

Alice was looking along the shelves. All the containers were neatly labelled: rhubarb, mugwort, aniseed, senna, cassia; several bottles of rose water and more of aqua vitae.

She approached the glass still. "What do you distil?"

"Rose petals, in great quantity, for rose water. Herbs, for their oils. And wine, for aqua vitae. Is it all familiar to you?"

"Yes. But my father's room was more cramped – crammed with medicines. And some different ingredients. Myrrh, gold, mercury, crushed bone. Poisons under lock and key."

"Less rose water, more purges?"

"Yes." They smiled together.

Alice said, "You are lucky to have such a workplace, mistress."

"I am. But, Alice, I need a still-room maid."

Alice's heart gave a jump. She guessed what was coming.

"With my cousin Cis gone, there is much to do, and

you have experience in this work. You will understand about the need for care and cleanliness, and you can read and write. I spoke to Lady Weston yesterday and she is willing to take you on—"

"Oh, but – I'm waiting for Robin!" Alice burst out. "When Robin comes I'll go with him. We'll be married."

Christian was silent, and Alice said desperately, "You don't believe he will come back, do you? Neither of you believes it. But you don't know him. He *will* come; I'm sure of it." It was less than a month since Robin had left. She would not give up hope yet.

"We understand that you are waiting," said Christian. "But until he does come, it seems you have nowhere to live but the King's Arms, with wenches you dislike. Would you not rather be here? Would you like to work with me?"

Alice looked around at the still room; inhaled its familiar smell. She hadn't objected to her work at the inn, but this would be a hundred times better. And she'd be away from Sib and Nell.

"I would, Mistress Christian. Nothing would please me more than to work in such a place. But Robin said the king's army will be on campaign again by May. I could not be bound as maidservant for a year."

"We would not bind you at all. You would be free to leave whenever you wished. If you left in the spring, we'd pay you then. You see, you have nothing to lose."

Alice agreed. Indeed, she felt, like Lady Weston, that God must have brought her to this place, at this time; for

it seemed that she was not only welcome but needed.

"I must tell Mistress Tyrrell," she said. "I hope she will not be offended."

"She will not dispute with Lady Weston," Christian assured her. "You'll have belongings to collect?"

"Yes – my pack. Oh!" A dreadful thought struck her. "If Robin comes he won't know where I am!"

"The people at the inn will tell him."

"Not Sib! If she gets to him first, she'll send him astray, for sure." It had been her one comfort, these last weeks, to know that when Robin came he would alight at the inn, that she would see him straight away.

"*Alice!*" said Christian. "We are but half a mile from the King's Arms. If this man loves you, he'll find you soon enough."

She knew it was true. And yet she wanted to *see* the carrier arrive, to see Robin the moment he appeared.

"You may walk down to the inn whenever you have free time," Christian told her. "But Christmastide is almost upon us. If he is at home with his parents he may not come now till after Twelfth Night."

"Christmas..." She had quite forgotten it.

"We'll be busy," Christian said. "It's Christmas Eve next Tuesday. Our cook has been making plum puddings and mince pies. And we shall need washing waters and cordials, sweet wine, sweetmeats for the children..."

Alice was surprised. "Then you'll celebrate Christmas openly, as a feast?"

"Of course."

"But we heard that this year it was to be a fast day,

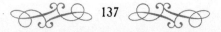

strictly observed, by order of Parliament."

"We heard that too. But Parliament is in London. And Lady Weston says that if the Members of Parliament wish to deny themselves they may do so, but here at Weston Hall we will celebrate Christmas as we have always done, with feasting and music, though our resources are much reduced because of the war. I hope you don't fear to join us?"

Alice laughed. "No! Even at Tor Farm we enjoyed Christmas. I can't believe most people will fast."

"In Oxford some will – the Puritan sort."

"Oxford? But the king is there! I thought Oxford was loyal."

"The university is loyal, but the town is for Parliament. Oxford has always been divided. Indeed, the whole country is divided. We have friends – neighbouring gentlemen and their families – who used to visit with us in the good times before the war. Sir Basil Thornton, Sir Antony Deere. Both declared for Parliament, and so we are become enemies and our families no longer meet. And Lady Weston's husband, Sir Richard, was captured in battle and is in prison in London. So you see, Alice, for us, celebrating Christmas is important: an act of defiance. "

Thirteen

The servants' sleeping quarters at Weston Hall were scattered all over the house and outbuildings, wherever there was space or need. The housekeeper and the cook each had her own small room; but the grooms slept over the stable, and the kitchen maids in the bakehouse. The ladies' maids had truckle beds in their mistresses' rooms, or slept in closets close by. As still-room maid, Alice had no obvious place, but the housekeeper, Mistress Denham, decided that at least while the house was full at Christmastide she should sleep with the maids in the bakehouse. Alice was glad to comply. She wanted to be accepted in this house, not only by Christian Aubrey and Lady Weston, but by the kitchen maids and cook – those who had the power to make life difficult for her.

She need not have feared. The kitchen people were gossips and teases, but no one seemed to be unkind. The cook, Mistress Florey, and the two maids were full of

curiosity about her. Mistress Florey told her she looked half starved and urged her to eat well. On that first day, when Alice came to the kitchen for dinner, she placed a bowl of fish broth in front of her and said, "Get some of that down you. You're too thin. When your soldier comes back he'll have nothing to get hold of."

Alice blushed. "We had to eat what we could find," she said. "It wasn't much. All the soldiers were hungry." She picked up her spoon.

"Meat's what you need," said Mistress Florey, herself a large woman with arms like hams. She set down bread, little pies and a dish of winter cabbage, shredded and mixed with dried fruit and spices. "But this being Advent, and Lady Weston sticking to the old ways, there's none to be had. You must wait till next week."

"Pease porridge and turnips till then!" joked Joan. She glanced curiously at Alice. "How long since you've seen him – your soldier?"

"Twenty-seven days," said Alice. She had kept a tally.

Bess tutted in sympathy.

Joan asked, "What's his name? What's he like?"

Alice answered briefly. She knew she was the centre of speculation and interest. The maids in particular found her story both shocking and romantic, and wanted to know all about her and Robin. It gave Alice the courage to do some delving of her own.

"Who is Christian Aubrey?" she asked. "I mean, *what* is she? Is she a lady?"

"No," said Mistress Florey. "Christian Aubrey is a

kinswoman of Lady Weston, but a distant one – a poor relation, you might say. Lady Weston took her in when both her parents died, twelve years ago. She's much of an age with the daughters of the house: Lady Grace – that's the one who's here with her children – and Lady Cecily."

"Lady Weston is seeking a husband for Mistress Christian," said Joan. "She's without a fortune, poor girl, and can't afford to be choosy."

"But she turned down Hugh Lyford," said Bess, grinning.

"Who wouldn't? A man who takes his horse to bed with him?"

"*Joan!* It *wasn't* his horse! You *know* it was his dogs!" Bess went off into a fit of the giggles.

"Now, you girls," said Mistress Florey. "Back to work."

There was plenty to be done: pies and puddings to bake for Christmas, as well as all the extra day-to-day meals with visitors in the house. Mistress Florey was indulgent towards the children. They ran in and out of the kitchen begging for treats, and were never disappointed.

Alice left the maids grating and sieving stale manchet bread to make gingerbread, and returned to the still room, where she and Christian were also preparing sweet things for Christmas. A block of refined sugar, saved from before the war, stood on the table. "It's twice as expensive as unrefined," said Christian, "but saves hours of work."

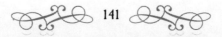

The sharp, tangy smell of oranges and lemons filled the room. Christian was peeling an orange, and beside her were two bowls, one of oranges and a smaller one of lemons. Alice had occasionally seen oranges and lemons being unloaded at the quay in Bideford, and sometimes her aunt might buy one in Tavistock market; but such luxury as this astonished her. What wouldn't we have given for these fruits on the march! she thought; and she exclaimed impulsively, "Oh, I wish my friends could see all this – could taste the orange juice and smell the spices! It would be such a wonder to them – like going through a door into Fairyland!"

Christian smiled. "You miss your friends?"

"Yes, especially Nia." She remembered sharing treats with Nia on the campaign: the excitement when they found the blackberries; the way they had eked out mushrooms and hazelnuts and tiny, worm-eaten crab apples. And she wondered how Nia was faring now, what sort of place she was staying in, whether *her* baby was still safe in the womb.

"I wish I knew where they were," she said.

"You'll find out in the spring, perhaps," said Christian.

She showed Alice how to peel the fruit. "Mistress Florey will use some of the juice," she said. "Nothing must be wasted. We will boil the peel several times until the bitterness goes. Then, when the pieces are dry, we'll make a sugar syrup and coat them with it. Tomorrow, if we have time, we can make some more comfits."

Alice had noticed the jar of comfits: little sugar balls with spice or fruit at their centres.

"You can buy them," said Christian, "but they are much better home-made."

She reached up and opened the jar and handed one to Alice. Alice put the tiny sugared ball in her mouth and sucked it. She loved the sweetness, and when she bit through the last brittle layer she released a fragrant spicy taste from the coriander seed at its centre.

"I like these," she said.

Christian looked pleased. "They are wholesome. Good for the digestion after a feast."

The two of them worked hard together all afternoon. Later, while they were laying out the crystallized peel to dry, Alice felt suddenly tired and asked if she might sit down.

"Of course," said Christian. She put a hand on Alice's shoulder as she drooped on the stool. "Rest while I make you a cordial."

Alice thanked her, then astonished herself by bursting into tears.

Christian was immediately concerned and dropped to her knees beside her. "Are you unwell?"

"No." Alice did not know why this sudden grief had come upon her, but she found herself sobbing helplessly, "My baby. My baby…"

Christian tried to comfort her. "Alice, until a child has quickened in the womb it has no life; it is not a living soul. You lost a child of three months or less. You never felt it move?"

"No."

"Then you must not grieve for it."

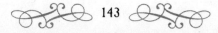

But Alice did. The thought that the child had never quickened into life saddened her even more.

"Lady Weston says you should go to church – to our chapel – and ask forgiveness for your sin. She says Advent is a time of joyful waiting but also of penitence. If you could confess your sin to God you might be healed of this grief."

Alice nodded, unable to speak. She knew she had committed the sin of fornication, and that she should do as Lady Weston said; but she felt that the only thing that would lessen her sorrow now would be the sight of Robin coming to claim her, and that if they were married her sin would be taken away.

"Lady Weston finds the chapel a place of solace," said Christian. "She goes there to pray for her husband's health in prison and for the souls of her dead children." And she added gently, "It is our family chapel, and gracious of Lady Weston to allow you to use it."

Alice went to the chapel the next day. It was close to the house, on the western side, and very small, with a High Church look that would be sure to offend the zealots in Parliament: Christ on the Cross hanging above the altar; the altar itself set back behind a rail; a painting of the Resurrection and another of the Madonna and Child; coloured windows full of saints and miracles; many candles and a smell of incense. Alice wondered whether Lady Weston might be secretly Catholic.

There was no one else in the chapel. Alice wanted to light a candle for her lost child, but hesitated because

Christian had said it had no soul. Instead she knelt and tried to feel penitent. The peace and silence of the place was calming, and she felt its beauty and the influence of Lady Weston and all those others who had worshipped here. But true repentance would not come. She knew that, given the chance, she would do the same again.

"Make way for the yule log!"

From outside, in the frosty morning, there was a beating on the door. Inside, the entire household was assembled: family, children, servants, dogs and cats, though the cats fled as Mistress Denham flung open the door and two old men – the gardener and the head groom – carried in the massive log between them. All the company broke into song. Alice soon picked up the words of the chorus and joined in. The song ended in clapping and cheers, and the children shrieked with excitement as the fire was kindled. Lucas Rowles, the gardener, lit a small piece of last year's log and used it to ignite the dry tinder surrounding the new one. When it was blazing, everyone filed past and made a wish. Bess had told Alice that as the yule log burned, it banished misfortune and healed old quarrels. Alice wondered what the others were wishing for. The end of this bitter war, perhaps, or the return of husbands and sons? Her own first thought was to wish for Robin to come to her. But she wished for that all the time; it was part of her being. Instead, when she reached the fire, she wished that Nia might stay well and strong and bear a healthy child in the spring.

On Christmas Eve, the night before, she had joined the servants gathered in the yard with lanterns, and walked to Copsey church for midnight mass, the holiest part of Christmas. In the morning the family had attended their chapel again while the servants made ready for the feast. With the bringing in of the yule log, Christmas had now truly begun. Earlier that day Alice had helped the women, ladies and servants together, to make the kissing bough, a ring of evergreens – ivy, holly and mistletoe – twisted and tied around a frame and entwined with ribbons of red and gold. Small gifts were tied with laces and hung from the bough. While the men put up greenery all around the hall and staircase, the women assembled the gifts. These were mostly sweetmeats: star-shaped biscuits, a bag of comfits, candied peel, sugar shapes, nuts, spices.

While they worked, the two little boys ran around, begging sweetmeats and crawling under the table to play with the dogs. Meanwhile the youngest, fastened into his wheeled walking frame, trundled around after them, shouting with laughter, then screaming when something he wanted was out of reach. The dogs too were indulged by Lady Weston, who tossed them treats which they caught and ate. The children wanted her to do the same for them. "Me! Me!" they cried – but missed and had to scamper in pursuit.

Mistress Florey laughed. "We'll have nothing left for the bough!"

Alice felt one of the hounds pushing at her hand; his pleading eyes looked up at her. She had learned the

dogs' names now: Keeper, Jewel, Holt and Bryce. This was Holt, her favourite because he always sought her out. She stroked his smooth soft head and slipped him a biscuit.

When the kissing bough was ready, the men hoisted it high to hang from the beam above the hall's entrance.

Now, with the greenery in place and the yule log lit, the day's feasting could begin: a leisurely dinner shared by all, seated along the length of a long table garlanded with ivy and coloured ribbons and illuminated by beeswax candles in gold holders. Everyone sang as Tobias Fairthorne carried in a roasted and garlanded goose. ("It would have been a boar's head before the war," Mistress Florey told Alice.) There was more meat – beef, duck and capon – and pies and rich sauces. After the meal the candies and comfits Alice and Christian had made were passed around in small bowls.

By the time the meal was over, the early dusk of winter was crowding against the windows. Lady Weston sent for candles. She lit them herself, handing them out to the maids to be set in sconces and windowsills and fill the hall with soft light and leaping shadows while they all sang another carol. Surely no edict from Parliament could ever suppress this, Alice thought.

The snow began in earnest before the end of December, and by Twelfth Night, Weston Hall was cut off from the village by deep drifts. The community turned inwards, relying even less than usual on the village and the world beyond. The livestock had been killed and there was

fresh meat in the larder, and Mistress Florey would soon be busy salting and preserving what could not be eaten. There were stocks of root vegetables, green beans layered with salt in earthenware crocks, summer fruits bottled or made into preserves. The wood stack in the yard was heaped with logs, and the baskets indoors with kindling; candles, both beeswax and tallow, were stored against the dark evenings and sunless days.

The servants had received presents on St Stephen's Day, mostly of clothing. Alice, so newly come to Weston and not a bound servant, was surprised and pleased to receive a gift of a pair of blue woollen stockings. During the days that followed there was plenty of merrymaking, and – until the snow set in – visitors coming and going. One of these was an elderly neighbour and widower, Sir Walter Clare, who, Alice noticed, paid particularly courteous attention to Christian.

Twelfth Night was the last great day of feasting. Christian told Alice that before the war they would have had a houseful of guests, the gentry from all around. Even so, it seemed grand to Alice. Lady Weston had hired musicians, and everyone danced and joined in the feasting. At dinner Mistress Florey carried in a Twelfth Night cake, baked with ginger, honey and cinnamon. Somewhere inside it was hidden a dried bean, and whoever found the bean would be king or queen of the revels. Mistress Florey cut the cake and made sure that everyone took a slice. Almost at once shy Bess found the bean and, in terror at the thought of being the centre of attention, put it back in and pushed her plate away,

 148

declaring that she wasn't hungry.

"Oh, Bessy!" exclaimed Joan. "Now everyone knows where it is!"

But it didn't matter. The young groom, Tom Pether, exchanged slices with Bess, brought out the bean with a flourish, and was crowned king with a wreath of ivy and a velvet cloak from the storeroom. Enthroned on a chair, he commanded, as if born to it, an evening of music, dancing and spiced wine, as well as a number of games of the kind that involved hiding and chasing.

Because this was a night when order was overthrown, Lady Weston danced with old Tobias Fairthorne, the head groom; and Lady Grace with Lucas Rowles. Alice was grabbed by Tom, who kissed her clumsily under the mistletoe. Nine-year-old Walter Nevell danced with young Anne Florey, the cook's niece, who helped out in the kitchen. Even the three little boys joined in. Alice found herself partnered by five-year-old Martin in his petticoats, and saw Mistress Florey holding the hands of baby John, who could not yet walk more than a few steps.

"None to dance with but boys and old 'uns!" said Joan. "The war has taken all the men away."

The evening ended late, with songs and kisses and wassails, and then they all retired to bed. The bakehouse was snug against the winter cold, and the girls lay close together, chatting and giggling.

"I reckon young Tom has a fancy for you, Alice," said Joan.

"What? He's only fourteen!"

"That don't stop 'em!"

They laughed, and Bess said, "You've taken his eye for sure. He's a well-enough-looking lad."

Joan lay flat, giggling from too much wine. "No. Little Master Martin. He's the one for me."

They subsided and drifted towards sleep, until Bess groaned, "Oh, that spiced pudding…" and stumbled out to the yard to be sick.

The next day order was restored. The ladies lay late in bed with headaches while the servants swept and cleaned and threw out the greenery or burned it on the fire. There was plenty of rich food left, but nobody fancied it.

"Lady Weston will send some down to the village, for the poor," said Mistress Florey, "if Rye can get through the drifts."

Rye was one of the six horses kept at the house. Lady Weston's own mount was Amor, a bay; Christian, when she needed to ride, rode Capel. There were more horses at the home farm, half a mile away.

Weston Hall, cut off now by the snow, was self-sufficient. Alice knew that there was no possibility of Robin coming to Copsey until the weather changed, and so, as January went by, she allowed herself to be happy. She grew to love the house, which always felt welcoming. It was built of warm golden stone, only two storeys high but with gabled attics; not a great house, but a comfortable home, built by Lady Weston's grandfather after he was knighted by Queen Elizabeth.

She worked steadily with Christian in the still room, making remedies for winter ills. Lucas Rowles had developed a cough that racked him at nights, and Tobias Fairthorne and Lady Weston both suffered with the aches and pains of old age. The children all caught colds, and their mother watched them fearfully for signs of fever. Alice learned how to make a simple cough syrup for the children, and a more powerful one for Lucas using powdered betony and caraway. Using her father's notes, she also experimented with a salve containing mustard, vinegar and honey, which Lady Weston said eased the pain in her hip.

"You are a great help to me, Alice," said Christian. "You have a gift for this work."

Alice knew it was true. She seemed to have an instinct for what might be troubling someone and what would be the best remedy to try. When she made tisanes or poultices for the family, it was gratifying to see the comfort they gained from them; and she loved the cleanliness and order of the still room. She was a servant here, but not a menial; she knew Christian respected and valued her. She settled into the routine of the work and went about it happily, sometimes singing as she chopped, ground or sieved.

Christian asked one day, "What's that you're singing? What language?"

"Oh – it's Welsh." Alice had woken that morning with the tune on her mind and it would not leave her. It was the song about the girl refusing to sell her sweetheart's shirt. She remembered singing it with Nia

as they washed clothes in a stream, and now she felt a pang of sadness that she had not seen her friend for so long, and did not know if she was well.

"It's a song about staying faithful," she said.

1645 — 1646

Fourteen

"*King's* men, or Parliament's, do you reckon?" the woman asked, leaning on her gate.

Alice, on her way back from the draper's shop, had paused near the turning to Weston Hall to gaze across the fields at a line of horsemen riding by. Sunlight flashed on their weapons and harness.

"I don't know," she said. "They all look the same."

And yet… She glanced at them again. There was something about the orderly way this group rode that made her think they might be Parliament men; and when a faint sound of singing was carried towards her on the wind she knew she was right. The song had the plodding simplicity of a hymn. Perhaps these were soldiers from the New Model Army – the new Parliamentarian force they had all been hearing about: professional soldiers, godly men, who believed in the righteousness of their cause and sang hymns as they marched along.

"There have been troops all around, these last few days," the woman said. "They say the armies will soon be on the move again."

Her words stirred a restlessness that had been growing in Alice. Much as she loved Weston Hall, she knew she could not stay there much longer. It was late April. The king's army would move on, and Nia would go with it. Alice missed Nia, the closest friend she had ever had. She missed their easy-going companionship, the songs and laughter, being together in the same daily struggle for survival. The long march, with its pleasures and hardships, had forged a stronger bond between them than she could feel for Joan or Bess at the Hall. And Christian, though in many ways a friend, was a member of the gentry, and Alice was her servant; their relationship could never truly be one of equals. Nia must be near her time now, Alice knew; and she remembered how sadly they had parted, and the promise she had made to her friend that she would be there with her when the child was born.

Alice had told Christian and the maids about Nia. But Nia was not the only reason she needed to return to the army. There was also Robin. These days the thought of Robin aroused in her a mixture of grief, resignation and anger – but mostly anger. For all he knew, she thought bitterly, she was nearly seven months gone with child, her shame visible to everyone; prey to the gossip of the villagers and with no one to protect her. She had long since ceased to meet the army carrier when it arrived at the King's Arms, or to hope that Robin would appear,

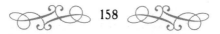

asking for her, at Weston Hall, dazzling the other girls with his dark, handsome looks. She knew the most likely reason why he had not come lay in the purse full of coins she still carried under her skirts: he had paid her off and abandoned her. The money was to assuage his guilt at leaving her with child. That was what Lady Weston and Mistress Florey and Christian and the maids all believed, and no doubt they were right. But she could never be certain. The country was at war; there was plague in Oxford; disease and danger were all around. She could not forget the baker's lad she had once been fond of, back at Tor Farm, how hurt she'd felt when he no longer sought her out; and then how she'd heard he had fallen ill and died of a fever. She could be wronging Robin. I have to know, she thought; I have to find out, be sure.

She took the turning that led back to the Hall. On the fringes of Weston's woodland she found violets growing, and gathered a posy and tucked it into the neck of her gown. Christian had said they might go out collecting flowers and leaves tomorrow, if the weather was fine, as it promised to be. The air smelt sweet and summery, and lifted her spirits.

She was up early next morning, so early that Bess and Joan were still slumbering on the bakehouse mattresses. She dressed in a gown of fine blue wool, a cast-off of Christian's that she liked for its graceful shape and the low neckline that made her feel womanly.

Last night's fire was cold in the kitchen grate. A cat

uncurled itself from the hearth, stretched, and came to rub hopefully against her leg.

"Not now, puss," she said. "Talk to Mistress Florey when she comes in."

She went into the pantry and poured herself a cup of milk, then relented and gave some to the cat before joining Christian in the still room.

"It's going to be a perfect day." Christian prepared two flat baskets, lining them with clean linen, tied in place. Alice remembered her father explaining how much care should be taken to ensure that the flowers and leaves were not bruised or tangled.

They waited until the sun was high enough to have dried up the dew.

"We'll start with the meadow at the edge of the woods," said Christian, "and work our way down to the brook."

They stepped outside, into the cool, bright morning. Bess was in the yard, tossing grain to the hens, calling each bird by name. She bobbed a curtsey as Christian passed. Alice could hear movements from within the stables: a soft knocking on wood, a whinny, rustlings of straw. The distant clamour of geese sounded from the home farm.

At the top end of the meadow, near the woodland, were primroses and violets. They gathered leaves and flowers, laying them carefully on the linen. Christian took several whole primroses, root as well as flower. The root would make a decoction for the coughs and colds that still plagued the household; and the flowers were used in remedies and could also be crystallized to decorate cakes.

As the sun rose higher they grew warm. The work was tiring, despite its seeming delicacy, for they had to dig and clamber about in woodland and through the long grass of the meadow.

"We'll go down towards the brook," said Christian. "I want to cut some willow bark. It eases pain and brings down a fever – but you would know that, I'm sure?"

Alice did. But she did not remember everything her father had taught her. It was so long ago, and she'd had only occasional need for such knowledge since. Christian, however, had been reading William Newcombe's book, taking notes from it to add to her own collection of remedies, and their discussions had rekindled Alice's interest.

By the water they found yellow flag, not yet in flower. Willows shaded the bank, and Christian set to work with her knife, taking only a little bark from the smaller branches on each tree. They were distracted by the sight of a mother duck followed by a flotilla of fluffy brown and yellow ducklings. One duckling was left behind, paddling hard to catch up, and cheeping.

They both watched a moment, listening to the duckling, willing it on. Another sound was carried on the breeze: a distant whinny. It came again, louder.

Christian glanced back at the house. "That sounds like Capel. What's got into him?"

Then they heard barking, and shouts – men's voices, but not Tom's, nor old Tobias's. This was someone

shouting orders. Alice felt a stab of alarm, and saw her own fear reflected in Christian's face.

"Come!" said Christian.

She began walking back up the sloping field, and Alice followed. As the house came into view they saw movement: horses, men — more men than lived at Weston Hall. These were soldiers. They could tell that from the harsh commands even before they caught a glimpse of helmets, buff coats, the glint of a sword. Alice and Christian started to run, catching up their long skirts and stumbling over the uneven ground. They arrived, breathless, in the yard, to see soldiers all around, the stable doors open, horses being led out. Tom was trying to block the way to the stalls, and Lady Weston stood protesting.

"These are my own horses! They are not trained for war. You cannot leave us here without a horse!" She held on to Amor's bridle while the dogs barked and snapped at the soldiers' boots.

Their leader was a stern-faced young man with a fair moustache. "The horses are requisitioned by Parliament," he said. "We will pay you for any we take. But we need more. We understood that you had officers from the king's army quartered here?"

"You were misinformed," said Lady Weston. "We have no soldiers here, and no garrison to protect us. There was sickness, and the officers were sent elsewhere."

"Then we will see to it that you keep some of your animals…"

Alice heard no more, because Christian said, "Alice,

take my basket and yours, and put them safely in the still room." She added in a low voice, "And find out what's happening in the kitchen. They are sure to be in search of food."

Alice nodded, and hurried indoors. The back door led into the passage between the kitchen and hall. In the kitchen, to her left, she heard voices raised in argument – Mistress Florey's, Joan's, and a man's – and was about to go in there, when she caught a glimpse of movement in the hall. Two soldiers were rough-handling something. She heard cracking sounds.

She rushed in. "What are you doing?"

For answer the nearest man pulled down a painting from the wall, flung it to the floor and trampled it. He turned on Alice, snarling ugly words like "malignants", "papists" and "idolatrous".

"No! Leave it!" Alice put down her baskets on the table and ran to defend the painting. It was of Mary Magdalene and Mary the mother of Jesus at the entrance to Christ's tomb, and had been hanging there ever since she came to Weston, and probably for long before. She threw herself at the man, who held her off easily with one hand. The frame snapped under his boots and she saw a split appear in the canvas.

"Idolatry and superstition," he said. "It should be burnt, along with the others." He looked at her with disgust. "And you, mistress, in your wanton gown, should be brought to repentance."

Alice stepped back, momentarily shocked and frightened by this attack. But the other man was on the

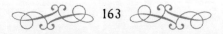

stairs. He had pulled down two more religious paintings and now he tossed them over the banisters.

"Stop! You can't do this! Get out of here!" she shouted, goaded into fury again.

They ignored her, broke up the paintings and carried them out into the front yard.

Alice ran back to the stables. Their leader was still there, negotiating with Lady Weston. In her distress Alice forgot all deference to her employer, and pushed between them. "Captain! Your men are all over the house, pulling down paintings and destroying them—"

"Paintings?" Lady Weston looked alarmed.

"The Magdalene," said Alice, "and two others, on the stairs—"

"The trappings of popery are banned—" the officer began, but Alice interrupted him.

"Not here, surely? Not in the house!" She felt outrage that this house, which had taken her in and sheltered her, should be violated by such men. "This is Lady Weston's home! Her family have lived here since Queen Elizabeth's time. She has been good to me. I won't let you destroy her home. *You* are responsible for those men. Get them out of there!"

He looked taken aback at her outburst. But before he could respond, there was a crash of breaking glass, and fragments flew from one of the chapel windows and scattered in shards across the stones.

The horses shied. Christian, who had been showered with glass, screamed and staggered, blood springing on her arms and face. Lady Weston ran to help her.

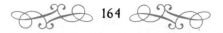

The officer leapt into action. He raced towards the chapel, where more sounds of destruction could be heard. As he ran inside Alice heard shouting, argument and remonstrance. She found that she was shaking. She turned to Christian, now the centre of a concerned group.

"These are small cuts only," Lady Weston said. She was picking fragments of glass out of Christian's hair and clothes. "But you must change this gown, Kit, and have it well shaken out."

"We have a salve for the cuts," said Alice. "I'll take care of her, my lady."

Lady Weston looked almost as white as Christian. She laid a hand on Alice's shoulder. "Dear child, what a champion I have in you! But I believe that fellow will put a stop to this rampage. He seems one to go by the rule. Can you walk, Kit? We'll go inside. Tom, you'd best come too. That bruise is swelling."

Alice saw that young Tom had a blackening bruise on his cheek and forehead – his reward for the struggle he had put up to save the horses.

She dealt with Christian first, upstairs in her chamber, unlacing her dress and helping her to step out of it and lay it aside to be checked for fragments of glass. She washed the many small cuts on Christian's hands, wrists, neck and the side of her face, and applied the salve – one they had made together only last week.

The cuts stood out on Christian's fair skin. When she was dressed again in a fresh gown, the two of them went downstairs to the hall, where Lady Weston, her

chaplain and most of the servants were assembled. At the same moment, the leader of the raiders came in from the courtyard. He bowed briefly to Lady Weston and said, "Madam, I have put a stop to the destruction of your chapel, but the altar rail – which I must remind you is forbidden by Act of Parliament – the altar rail is broken up, and some of the coloured windows smashed." He looked at Christian. "I am sorry for the hurt to the lady. But, madam, if I may speak plainly, you would be wise to be more conformist in your religious observance in these times."

"You think so, sir?" said Lady Weston. "Well, I too will speak plainly and tell you that I am a woman alone here and unprotected, with only old men, women and children, and no garrison. It is my duty to care for my people and look to their needs, both physical and spiritual—"

"Their spiritual needs might be better served if they were allowed to approach the altar," said the officer. "However" – he glanced at Alice – "I have called my men off. We have not come here to terrify women. We expected soldiers – cavalry." He drew out a purse. "Madam, I will pay you for the horses we are taking. We do not prey upon the country as our enemies do."

He stepped forward and offered the purse to Lady Weston, but she waved it aside. "Give it to my housekeeper."

At that the man flushed red, and Alice almost felt sorry for him. Mistress Denham came forward. He gave the purse to her, bowed to Lady Weston, and left.

"Arrogant pup," said Lady Weston. "They say that half the officers in the New Model Army are not even gentlemen, but shopkeepers and artisans."

She spoke dismissively, but Alice saw that she was trembling. Everyone was shaken. Bess was sobbing, and even Mistress Florey looked distressed.

"The paintings," Christian lamented.

And Tobias Fairthorne said, "Three horses they've taken, my lady, and another two from the farm."

"They went through the kitchen – stripped it bare," said Mistress Florey. "Four big hams, and a cheese just yesterday brought from the farm…"

But it was the chapel that concerned Lady Weston most. She went out to see the damage, and Alice and Christian followed soon after. They found Lady Weston kneeling in her pew with destruction all around her. The altar rail was ripped out and smashed in the nave. Jagged holes showed in two of the stained glass windows. All the paintings had been pulled down and trampled, and the carvings of saints and angels hacked with swords.

It was some time before Lady Weston stood up. When she did, she said, "This can be restored, most of it. And the king will triumph over the rebels. He must. These people cannot be allowed to prevail."

But she seemed to have aged, Alice thought, in the space of a few hours; and she felt for her, with the house and its people to care for, and her husband in prison.

Alice went to attend to Tom Pether's bruises, and then helped to put the kitchen and hall to rights. In the hall she found her basket knocked to the floor, the leaves

and blossoms, so carefully gathered, trampled by soldiers' boots. While she was picking them up, a boy came from the village with news that the king's troops quartered there had also been attacked and horses taken.

"So – it all begins again," said Mistress Florey.

Fifteen

Two weeks later they woke to the sound of drums. The drumming was all around, all over Copsey and the surrounding hamlets, no doubt sounding also in Oxford and Wallingford and Faringdon and Kidlington, all the places where the king's troops were quartered, calling them to march.

Alice said to Christian, "I must go."

She was already prepared, her few possessions packed in the hessian bag. She remembered the drums that had brought Robin to her at Tor Farm, and those that had beaten as she left to take her chance in life with him. It was going to be much harder to leave Weston Hall. She knew now what a harsh life she was returning to – this time without love to sustain her. She would miss all the comforts of Weston: the good food, warm fires, and comfortable beds, as well as the people who had cared for her. Most of all she would

miss Christian and their work in the still room. And yet her position at the Hall was not as permanent as she had at first believed it could be. The raid had brought home to them all how insecure their lives were. Lady Weston now employed two grooms for her three remaining horses. Either Tom or old Tobias would have to go, and if the house suffered many more such blows other servants would leave. There would certainly be no need for such luxuries as a still-room maid. And Christian might marry, as Lady Weston hoped. If she did, Alice would have no place at Weston.

These thoughts must have been in both Christian's and Lady Weston's minds, yet they were reluctant to let Alice go, alone and unprotected.

Lady Weston summoned her and said, "Alice, I fear you are reckless. The proper place for a young girl is at home. You are the daughter of a respectable man who was valued in his community, and your uncle is a yeoman of some standing. You should consider your position, your prospects. These Welshwomen may be worthy in their own way, and loyal, but they are not the manner of people you should keep company with. If it were in my power, I would prevent you from going."

Alice had no answer to this, and stood silent.

"And yet," Lady Weston admitted, "I admired your boldness when you stood up to that young Roundhead captain! I would not have you less courageous, child, but I hope you will learn wisdom. Promise me you will come back, if you have need?"

"I will," said Alice. "Thank you, my lady."

Now that the day had come, Alice found that she was not afraid, and did not doubt for one moment that she could find her way back to Weston Hall if necessary. She was determined to fulfil her promise to Nia, and eager to see her friend again. In her pack she carried food and beer for the journey and a small parcel of herbs, salves and other remedies that Christian had put together.

"God be with you," said Christian, and kissed her.

And then Alice set off alone.

As she entered the village she was caught in the crush of soldiers, dragoons and wagons heading east on the Oxford road. Troops were on the move from Faringdon and all the villages around where they had been quartered, and she knew her friends must be somewhere among them. But it would be impossible to find anyone here. She was obliged to begin walking at once, following the flow of people and wagons towards Oxford. Oxford! At last! She remembered how only a few months ago she'd had such dreams of going there with Robin to be married.

"Hey, pretty! Ride with us?" Two carters were grinning down at her. She usually ignored such calls, but from up there she would be able to see. She grasped the hand that reached down for her and climbed into the wagon.

"I'm looking for my husband," she said. She had already decided on an imaginary husband as her best protection on the march.

There were bales of clothing on board: soldiers' shirts and jackets – new issue.

"For pressed men?" she asked.

"Yes, and regulars. All new for the start of the campaigning season."

The driver swore at someone in the road. The cart jolted, and Alice staggered. But from here she had a better view, over the heads of those marching. She looked at the coats as they moved along. The regiment she was seeking wore blue, but so did many others. It was the colours – the regimental flags – that were distinctive. Here and there, flags showed, but mostly furled. She saw none that she recognized.

She sat down on one of the bales. The younger man, the one who was not driving, came and sat beside her, a little too close. "Lost your husband, have you? Got separated?"

She edged away. "He'll be looking out for me."

Ahead of them now she saw the massive earthworks of Oxford with their raw new embankments, and, inside, the ancient spires and the castle on its high hill. She had expected that they would go into the city, but instead they turned aside before they reached it and began moving slowly north-west. More soldiers, both foot and cavalry, joined them, and at last everything came to a halt. It was only then that Alice, staring anxiously around, saw a flag that looked as if it might be the one, some way off, near a line of trees.

"Over there!" she said. She thanked the carters, and allowed herself to be lifted down.

Now she had become part of the mass of people, and it was impossible to see the flag. She could only head out

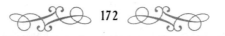

in the direction she had noted. The entire army seemed to be assembling here. She passed farriers, blacksmiths, a surgeon's wagon, another laden with barrels of water. More wagons were being unloaded of bread, beer, tents, uniforms. Bales of stockings, white, red or blue coats, and knitted caps, were piled in one wagon; another was full of boots and water bottles and snapsacks. Officers in charge shouted orders. Clerks with lists went to and fro.

Alice focused on the line of trees she had seen from the cart and moved towards it, determinedly cutting a path through the crowds. Once, she became caught in the midst of a herd of cattle and a drover swore at her to get out of the way. Slowly she drew closer to the trees. She had found the regiment, but for a long time she wandered about, searching, jostled by soldiers, seeing nothing and no one she knew. And then, suddenly, she was among women, and there were faces she recognized, and familiar wagons – and Mistress Erlam's voice!

She stumbled towards her old friend over the churned-up ground. "Mistress Erlam!"

"Alice! Welcome back, wench! You look well! I've just been talking to your little Welsh friend."

"Nia?"

"That's the one." Mistress Erlam gestured with her arms, holding them out roundly in front of her. "Huge. Any day now. Pity it didn't come early. Lord knows how she'll travel, poor girl."

Alice glanced about eagerly. "Where is she?"

"They're all over that way. See the red-headed girl?"

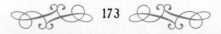

"Rhian? Yes!" Alice hurried towards them.

Rhian saw her and shouted, *"Lisi! Hei! Bronwen, Nia, dyma Lisi!"*

And then they were all around her, hugging, crying, questioning. Alice felt tears spring to her eyes as she clung to Nia and joked about the belly coming between them.

"Oh, Nia, I've missed you!" she said.

And Nia asked, "Your child? You weren't...?"

"I've much to tell you," said Alice. "Not now."

Now, she simply wanted to enjoy being with them again. Yet even as she embraced the three of them, she was aware, with a feeling of disloyalty, of their grimy skin and dirty clothes, and found herself recoiling slightly from their sour smell.

They noticed the difference too.

"You've been somewhere good, Lisi," said Nia. "You smell of soap and roses. And this gown! Take off your cloak; let me see!"

The gown was the blue one Christian had given to Alice. It was a little mended but made of fine, soft wool – clearly a lady's garment. The girls stroked and admired it.

"Beautiful," said Bronwen. "But too good for this field."

Perhaps it was the dress that made Rhian ask, "Are you married, Lisi?"

"No." She looked from one to another of them. "I did not come here with Robin."

Rhian's eyes widened.

"Tell us while we cook," said Bronwen. "Before the men come."

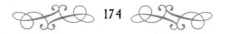

They had already collected branches from the nearby woodland. Bronwen got the fire started with her tinderbox while the others began cutting up meat and chopping herbs and onions.

"Now, Lisi…" said Nia.

And Alice told them everything that had happened to her since they were separated in November: about Copsey, and the inn, Robin, the loss of her baby, and the kind treatment she'd had at Weston Hall.

"Oh!" Nia was almost in tears. "To be all alone in such trouble! If only we'd been together."

Bronwen was furious, shocked by Robin's behaviour. "He *left* you?" she exclaimed. "How *could* he? When you were carrying his child?"

"He said he'd come back. But he never did. I suppose he was tired of me." She found that a hard thing to admit, after the love they'd shared. "But, Bronwen, I don't *know*. Perhaps something prevented him. You've not seen him, I suppose?"

"No. Not yet. But he should have got word to you, no matter what."

"Perhaps he couldn't," said Alice. "Perhaps…"

The possibility that Robin might be dead hung, unspoken, in the air between them.

"He will have come here today," said Bronwen, "if he is coming at all."

"Yes." Alice could suddenly hardly breathe at the thought that he might be near, that she might soon see him again. Her heart was in confusion, full of anger, fear and bewilderment. She would not know what to feel

until she knew why he had left her.

"You were lucky to be taken in at that big house," Nia said later, when they were alone together. "And they asked you to stay on?"

"Yes. But I wanted to see *you*. I missed you. I wanted to be with you when your baby was born."

Nia's eyes glittered again with tears. She could never hide her feelings. She said, "It won't be long. I've been getting pains already."

"And are you well? Happy?"

"I'm frightened," said Nia. "Happy, yes, but afraid of what is to come. I'm glad you're here, Lisi – very glad."

Alice feared that too much confidence was being placed in her, but then she remembered how, at Weston Hall, she had seemed to have an instinct for healing. She said, "I've brought some remedies with me – dried raspberry leaves and some other things that Mistress Christian recommended. So I can make you tisanes to ease your labour. And there's this…"

She reached into her pocket and brought out a tiny linen drawstring bag. Inside it was a stone: oval, polished smooth, its colour red, streaked with veins of grey. She put it in Nia's hand. "Shake it."

Nia did so, and the stone rattled. Her eyes widened. "What's in there?"

"Another stone, I believe. It grows inside – a stone within a stone. It's called an eagle stone. Mistress Christian gave it to me. She said it can prevent miscarriage, and will also ensure an easier birth if it's placed on the thigh during labour."

She watched as Nia examined the stone. Nia's hands were small and squarish, with short fingers. The stone fitted comfortably into her palm.

Alice said, "Christian told me her cousin, Lady Grace, used such a stone during each of her labours, and her pain was always much eased."

"I can feel the power in it," said Nia, curling her fingers around the stone. "The lady was good to give it to you. It must be very rare and costly."

Alice saw that the eagle stone was already having a good effect on Nia. She wondered, briefly, if it could be like her father's dried turtle, a mere talisman; but the stone had been tried with success by other women, and Christian had assured her of its virtues. She certainly intended to use it herself if she ever had need.

"Have you been taking raspberry leaf tea, as I told you?" she asked.

"I have, but it's all gone now." Nia kept turning the stone around, looking at it, and shaking it. It had a pleasing rattle. She passed it back to Alice. "Keep this safe."

"I will. And I'll make some raspberry leaf tea. You can drink it now."

She rummaged in her pack, glad to be doing this. It took her mind off Robin, the thought of whom was unsettling. But later, when Bryn, Edryd and Gethin and the other Welshmen began to arrive, she found she was heart in mouth, half expecting to look up and see Robin strolling towards her with his long, easy stride and his warm smile, coming to fetch her as if nothing had happened. She joined her Welsh friends at their evening

meal, all the time alert and watching for him, but he never came.

He has left me, she thought. Or he is dead.

The evening was light. They sat singing and telling jokes and stories around the campfire. Alice understood little. Even the bit of Welsh she had learned last year seemed to have deserted her. She felt cut off, lonely and out of place, and began to regret that she had ever left Weston Hall. Perhaps, she thought, once Nia has had her baby, I should go back there.

Nia noticed, and touched her arm. "I'm happy to see you again, Lisi. We all are."

Alice nodded, grateful. Nia's sympathy made her want to cry. She wished she could take Nia to Weston with her for the birth. Her friend would be better cared for there. But when she spoke this thought aloud Nia said, "Oh, no! I wouldn't be easy in that grand house! And I'd never leave Bryn."

Dusk fell, and they went to their billets. Her friends were in a large barn, and Bryn found Alice a space near by. Alice curled up, using her pack as a pillow and wrapping her cloak around her. Despite Bryn's kindness, she felt wide awake and vulnerable. Some of the Welshmen had already noticed that she was alone, and she was aware of them watching her. When they spoke and smiled together, glancing her way, she felt afraid, not knowing what they said, whether they might be making lewd comments about her.

In the morning the drums called them all to their quarters, the colours were raised, and they marched.

They were heading north-west, and as Alice followed she knew she was moving further and further away from Weston Hall and any possibility of returning there. In a few hours they reached their destination: a town on a hilltop, at a junction of many roads. Alice had seen its name on a milestone: Stow-on-the-Wold. Other forces were already assembled there, and she heard later that they had been joined by Prince Rupert's army.

Everyone is here now, she thought. And if Robin is still in the king's army, he will be here, or I'll get news of him. But even though the Welsh soldiers came early to find their womenfolk, Robin did not appear. Alice began to realize that she might never find out what had happened, that perhaps it was better to forget him. She had learned valuable skills from Christian Aubrey – enough, she believed, to find work and support herself. She would not go looking for Robin.

But then, as she and the other women were starting up the cooking fires, she saw Gethin, Rhian's husband, approach and speak to his wife. The two of them glanced across at her.

"What is it?" she asked, scrambling to her feet.

Rhian came over. "Gethin's seen your man – Robin."

Alice felt her heart begin to pound.

"Over there, by those wagons." Rhian pointed. "You'll catch him if you go now."

Alice hesitated. "I … I don't know… I think perhaps…"

"Go on!" said Rhian, giving her a little push. "I'll do the fire."

The others were listening now, and joined in.

"You go, Alice! Make him answer some questions!" urged Bronwen.

And Nia said, "You'll have no peace otherwise."

That was true. Alice moved away from the fire, towards the place Rhian had pointed out. Her mouth felt dry, and she was trembling. She half hoped that Gethin had been mistaken, or that Robin would be gone, that she need not confront him.

But he was there. She came upon him – upright and handsome as ever – standing with his two friends, Will and Jacob. They were talking animatedly. The sight of Robin's once-loved profile made her catch her breath. She almost turned and ran, but Will had seen her. His manner at once became guarded, and Robin, sensing some change, turned round.

"Alice." He did not smile, and he looked both surprised and wary.

Will and Jacob tactfully moved away.

Robin said, "Alice, I didn't expect… There was no child, then?"

"There was. It died." She did not try to soften the news. "I miscarried."

"I am sorry. Sorry to hear it."

"Are you? You did not come to enquire after me. Robin, I waited. All winter. I waited so long. You never came to the inn, or to Weston Hall. Why didn't you come back for me? Why did you desert me?"

Her voice had risen, and others were beginning to stare. He touched her then, for the first time: took her

by the upper arm and led her away to a more private place between two of the wagons.

"I was not able to come," he said. "I left you money—"

"Money!" she exclaimed. "I wanted *you*, not your money. I woke up and found you gone: no address, nothing. And the girls, Sib and Nell; they were cruel to me and said you'd found someone else, and then" – despite her determination, her voice broke – "the baby…"

"Shh, shh." He patted her shoulder, looking around uneasily. "I am sorry. There was nothing I could do."

"But you said you'd come back! I believed we'd be married. You promised, Robin."

His gaze slid away from her. She saw he wanted nothing more than to be gone. "I'm sorry, Alice," he repeated. "Sorry about the child, and your troubles. You have enough money?"

"It's not the money. You said you'd marry me."

"I never said that! I said I'd see about it." He would not look at her. "The truth is I can't marry you."

"Can't?"

"Alice, I'm already married."

She stepped back, stunned, the breath knocked out of her. She thought at first that he meant he had found another girl and married her that winter, but then he continued, speaking hurriedly. "I had to go home. My wife was with child, expected to be brought to bed around Christmastide…"

His wife. His wife who had been with child. She must

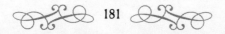

have been already more than five months gone with child when Alice and Robin met at Tor Farm. He'd spent the previous winter with his wife, made love to her, made her pregnant, then gone off on campaign and found Alice, desperate to get away from home, foolish enough to trust him.

Alice breathed in to steady herself. All her dreams of love were shattered, revealed as a sham. He had never loved her. She was nothing to him. She felt hollow.

"I thought you'd guess," he said, with a trace of irritation. "I meant you to guess, when I left you."

Why had she never guessed? She was such a fool! But he'd been so loving all those weeks; and besides, he was very young to be married. No doubt that was why none of her friends had thought of it either.

"Do you love her?" she asked faintly. "Did you always love her, and not me?"

"Of course I loved you!" he replied with warmth, looking at her reproachfully. "I was married young. Eighteen. Susan, my wife, is a neighbour's daughter. When she found she was with child our fathers made sure we were married. You know I work for my father; he gave us a cottage, saw to everything."

Alice remembered how he had told her his parents were indulgent. Yes, they would arrange everything. But – a thought struck her. He'd been married three, maybe four years. So this child, the one he went home for…

"It's your *second* child," she said.

"Yes. There are two now."

Married, and with two children. Alice had been

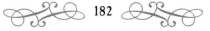

simply a girl to pass the time with while he was on campaign; and when she became a nuisance he had left her.

"You betrayed me," she said.

He looked hurt. "I never asked you to come with me! You threw yourself at me, begged me to take you. What was I to do?"

"You could have told me the truth."

"I didn't have the heart."

"You didn't have the courage."

"Alice," he coaxed. "Let's not quarrel. Can't we kiss and be friends?" He tried to draw her towards him, but she sprang away.

"Don't touch me! Keep your hands for your wife!"

And she turned her back on him and left.

"You're well rid of him," said Nia.

And Rhian said, "Who'd have thought it, though? He seemed so fond of you."

"Perhaps he was, in his way," said Bronwen.

"What will you do?" asked Nia. "Will you want to go home?"

"To Tor Farm? Never. And there is no real home for me at Weston Hall, even if I could get there." She realized now that Lady Weston had been right: it would not be safe to travel alone, especially in this time of war. Tomorrow the army was heading further north-west. She could not imagine moving against that tide. And Nia's baby would be born any day now. "I'll stay with you," she said. "If you'll have me."

"You know we will."

That night, lying awake in a shared shelter, with people snuffling, snoring and whispering all around her, Alice thought back over her time with Robin and saw how she had deceived herself. It was she who had asked to go with him; she who spoke of love and marriage. He'd made no promises, ever. He was merely passing through. All he had wanted was a few nights of love on Dartmoor; he'd never intended to take her with him. No wonder he had been so uneasy as the army drew ever closer to Oxford, to his home. He must have been wondering, all that time, what to do about her. And that letter, the one he'd hidden away: that was probably from his wife, telling him how she missed him, filling him with guilt towards both women.

A thought came to her then, and she told Nia in the morning.

"I've still got most of the money he gave me. I ought to give it back." Her pride, she felt, would not allow her to keep it. She said passionately, "I'll *throw* it back at him!"

"I'd hold on to it, Lisi," said Nia. "You don't want to go throwing money about. You might need it."

Over the next few days, Nia and the others watched over Alice, sympathized and advised. She knew from the looks on people's faces that word of her confrontation with Robin must have spread quickly. A few of the young unattached Welsh soldiers now smiled and, she felt, regarded her speculatively. Well, she could do worse.

 184

They were good-hearted boys, and handsome, some of them. But she didn't want another man, not yet. She was too hurt, too shamed. She felt like an injured animal that wants only to hide away and lick its wounds.

Sixteen

The cries and groans woke Alice towards dawn. Nia! She was up instantly, aware of doors opening and closing, footsteps up and down the stairs, women's voices. They had known that Nia was near her time and had managed to get a room in a house where a good woman lived: a widow, well used to helping women in childbirth.

Nia was already on a bed with a clean sheet under her, the eagle stone tied to her left thigh. The window was closed and herbs had been burnt in the room to ward off infection.

"Lisi!" gasped Nia. She struggled up on her elbows and arched her body in pain. Candles shone near by, illuminating the slick of sweat on her forehead.

Alice went to help her. "Don't be frightened," she said. "Lie down. That's right. Raise your knees."

Bronwen came in, and the two of them rearranged the pillows behind Nia's head and tried to soothe her.

Alice winced as a cry broke from Nia; it was hard to see her friend in pain. She took a stool and sat beside her, stroking the damp hair back from her face.

The widow and Rhian appeared with more candles, hot water, soap, cloths, a ball of twine and a knife.

"Now, now," the widow said to Nia, "you must let go of this fear. It'll tighten you up so that the child can't come easily. Will you drink some of this? Your friend has made it for you." She passed the cup of raspberry leaf tea to Alice. "Does she understand a word I say? I've had nothing but Welsh from her since it started."

"She understands," said Alice. She held the cup to Nia's lips. "Sip this, Nia. It'll help ease the birth."

Nia sipped obediently. Then her teeth clamped shut and she groaned as another pain began. Alice held her hand.

"I'm glad Bryn's not here, fretting," said Bronwen.

All the men were absent, camped in the field outside a great house near by. The house was garrisoned for Parliament, and the Royalists' siege had already continued all day and half the night. The women could hear the roar of cannon fire and distant cries of men and horses, and smell the smoke, even in this closed room.

What a time and place to give birth, Alice thought. No wonder Nia was frightened.

The widow promised Nia there was nothing to be afraid of. "Babies come when they will," she said. "And all is going well. Your pains are coming closer together now. We must pray it won't be long."

But the labour was slow. Alice continued to talk to

Nia and murmur encouragement as the hours went by. She felt she was doing nothing, but the widow assured her that the three of them were essential.

"Friends and sisters are what she needs most," she said.

While Bronwen helped the widow, Rhian hovered anxiously.

"Sit down," Alice advised her. "Talk to Nia about home. Talk in Welsh."

For a long time, nothing seemed to be happening except the relentless pains that frightened and exhausted Nia. The day grew light, and Alice could see sunshine seeping in through the gaps in the curtain. The sounds of battle continued, and so did Nia's struggle. She looked very tired.

But by midday all had changed. The pains were coming fast, and Nia gasped and cried out and gripped Alice's hand fiercely. She became incoherent, and her ability to understand English deserted her. Bronwen translated the widow's instructions as she ordered Nia to push, or to hold back.

"The head is coming," the woman said. "Wait, wench. Wait. Now push."

Nia roared – a deep, desperate, groaning roar – and Alice saw the baby slither out, purplish, slippery, streaked with blood and mucus. She cried out herself, and her eyes flooded with tears.

"A girl," the widow said with satisfaction. She held the baby head-down and its first cry broke the air. "A healthy girl." She wiped away some of the blood and put

the baby on the bed. When the cord stopped pulsating she tied twine around it in two places, then passed the knife through a candle flame and cut between them. She laid the baby on Nia's breast.

Nia's hair was stuck to her forehead in damp strands. She lay breathing gently, her hands on the baby's back. *"Merch,"* she said faintly. *"Fy merch i. Diolch yn fawr."* And she smiled.

"What's that she says?" the widow asked.

"She gives thanks to you for her daughter," said Bronwen.

"Ah. Tell her the afterbirth will come soon."

The afterbirth came easily; and then the widow took the baby from Nia, washed her carefully in warm water, bandaged the navel, and wrapped her in clean swaddling clothes, criss-crossing the strips of soft linen over and around her tiny body till it resembled a cocoon with only her head free. "There!" she said. "Wrap her like that and it'll keep her contented and make sure her limbs grow straight." She passed her to Alice. "Will you hold her while I wash your friend?"

Alice was already in love with the baby. She held her carefully, adoringly, gazing down at the little crumpled face, the unfocused slate-coloured eyes. It seemed a miracle that this child had been born safely in a stranger's house, with the sounds of battle all around. She said to the woman, "You are very good. Thank you for helping us."

"We are all sisters at a time like this," the widow said. "It's the same for everyone, rich or poor, English or

foreigner. There, my dear" – she spoke to Nia – "you'll be more comfortable now."

Alice placed the swaddled baby in Nia's arms. "What will you call her?"

"Elen," said Nia. She was speaking English quite readily now. "It's my mam's name, and I always said I'd call my first girl after her." She kissed the baby's head. "Your *nain* will be so proud to see you, little one, when we go home. And your da will! Oh, I hope this siege ends soon!"

"The longer it goes on," said Bronwen, "the longer you can rest."

"I know. But I want to see Bryn!"

Bryn did not come, but that afternoon a succession of women called, mostly the Welsh wives: Ffion, Marged, Heulwen, and a few others Alice had got to know. They sat around gossiping, admiring the baby, advising Nia and drinking spiced ale.

It was the following day that the siege of the great house – Hawkesley, it was called – came to a noisy end. They heard cannon fire and distant shouting, and then silence, and knew the besiegers had either broken through or given up. Alice went to find out what was happening, and heard that the house had been captured and the soldiers had gone in to plunder and take prisoners.

Bryn arrived an hour or so later. He had known the day before yesterday that Nia's labour was about to begin, and now he had left the others to seize what they could in the way of spoils while he hurried back to her.

Alice met him in the village, where she had gone to buy food, and gave him the news.

"You have a daughter, born yesterday, in the afternoon."

Joy and anxiety mingled in his face. "And Nia? My Nia?"

"She is well, and longs to see you." It felt good to be the bearer of such happy news.

She walked back to the house with Bryn, but could not keep up with his eager stride, and urged him, laughing, to go ahead of her. When she arrived with her basket of bread and herbs the widow was alone in the kitchen.

"They're all upstairs," she said, "jabbering in their own language, and your friend like a little queen holding court."

Alice thought best to stay below and help the widow prepare supper.

"I never imagined to have so many strangers coming and going under my roof, all foreigners," the woman went on. "You too, with your West Country talk, near as strange as the Welsh."

But Alice knew that she did not mind at all, despite the inconvenience, and would be telling her neighbours all about it when the army moved on. She busied herself chopping leeks. Soon the woman would ask her how she came to be with the army, and she did not want to have to explain that.

She was spared further questioning when the sound of an explosion shook the building. Both of them rushed

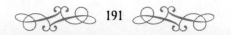

outside. They saw flames leaping up into the clear sky of evening, and among them, showing above the trees, the ruined roof and chimneys of Hawkesley House. Distant cries and screams carried on the smoky wind. Neighbours were looking out all around, and Bryn and his sisters came down from the upper room.

"Well, that's Hawkesley gone," the widow said sadly. "I was a servant there, way back. It was a fair house."

"But in rebel hands," said Bryn. "It was bound to be destroyed. That's war."

The woman sighed. "I wish it might end! And you, young man: what will you do, with your wife and child to care for?"

Bronwen and Rhian had the same question for Bryn. Later that evening the three of them talked of going home.

"This year," said Bryn. "When this campaign is ended. And who knows? Perhaps the war will be over by summer."

The next day they left the widow's house and moved on with the army. Nia bought a wicker cradle for Elen and rode in one of the covered wagons, protected by sacks full of cloth. The weather had not been as wet as last autumn, so the roads were tolerable, and the first day's journey, from Bromsgrove to Himley, was not overlong. Even so, Bryn was concerned that Nia would be jolted and perhaps injured, but she dismissed his fears.

"Back home we've all seen women working in the fields a day or two after childbirth," she said. "I'll come to no harm."

There was room for one other in the wagon, and the girls took turns to keep Nia company. Alice loved being allowed to hold the baby, and she and Nia chattered together, and giggled, and sang lullabies, as the army made its slow progress around the Midlands. Elen suckled often, and seemed contented, and while Nia was feeding the child Alice occupied herself with hemming soft linen cloths for her.

It was early in the campaigning season, and the soldiers were not as hungry and short of supplies as they had been when Alice joined them last year. Flocks of sheep and herds of cattle were being driven along in the train, and the traders who sold all kinds of necessities to the soldiers had their carts and wagons newly stocked.

"It's a good life, this," Nia said. "Good pay, good company. Better than the life we had in Wales. We toiled like beasts there, for a pittance."

"But you'll want to go home now you have the child?"

"Yes. When Bryn has his pay. There's plunder too. He missed that at Hawkesley House, hurrying back to me. But there will be more chances."

She spoke matter-of-factly, assuming her husband's right to the spoils of war. And Alice supposed it *was* his right, since the generals allowed it when a house or town was surrendered to them. All the same, she could not help thinking of the people who were attacked and robbed of their money and household goods, and the terror they must feel as the victorious army burst upon them.

"What we want, Bryn and I," Nia said, "is a little patch of land of our own. A smallholding. That's our dream." She looked searchingly at Alice. "And what's yours, Lisi? What do you most want?"

This was something Alice had deliberately not been thinking about. She knew now that she would not marry Robin. Would she slide into becoming a soldiers' drab, as Bronwen had said abandoned or widowed women often did? No, she thought, I'll never let that happen. I'll work, take care of the wounded, make myself useful around the baggage train. But when the war is over – what then?

"What I most want," she said, "is a home. A real home, where I belong. It's what I've always wanted, ever since my father died."

And love, she thought. A lover. A husband. A good man, like Bryn.

On fine days she put on the boys' clothes Mistress Erlam had given her and went out with the other women to forage for green herbs to cook: young nettles, dandelion leaves, shepherd's purse, chickweed, and the weed they called fat hen. All went into the pottages the women made each night. She also looked for healing herbs, and cut some willow bark in the way Christian had shown her. From the traders she bought a small pestle and mortar, a bowl, some pots with stoppers, a fine sieve, oil and goose fat. When they were camped for a day or more she made salves and ointments for wounds, expecting that there were sure to be some injuries soon. She also laid in a stock of linen strips to make bandages.

She bought a large basket to keep her supplies in, and stored it on the Erlams' wagon. There were a few other, older women attached to the regiment who also cared for the sick, so in order not to antagonize them she was deferential and only helped when asked.

It was around Whitsuntide that she saw Robin again. Nearly three weeks had passed since they parted, and she had stayed near her Welsh friends and tried to avoid him. That day she was buying from one of the grocers' wagons when she saw him, a little way off, talking to a girl – a pretty girl, tall and slim-waisted, a trader's daughter, she guessed. Robin, in his easy, graceful way, was leaning on the wagon and smiling as he talked, and the girl glanced shyly down and then up at him, clearly captivated.

Alice could not take her eyes off them. She knew that look of Robin's well; it had been turned on her so often. She wanted to warn the dark, pretty girl, to shout to her, "Leave him! He's a scoundrel!"

She returned to her friends, thinking back over her time with Robin. The sight of little Elen made her remember the baby she had lost before it even had a soul. Perhaps that was as well, she thought now, since he never would have married her.

"You're quiet today," Nia said. She had recovered her strength, and sometimes walked, sometimes rode on the wagon. She was busy now adding herbs to a pottage, the baby beside her in her wicker cradle.

"I saw Robin," Alice said, "with another girl."

"Oh, so that's the trouble!" Nia turned to her in sympathy. "Well, he'll deceive her, poor girl, as he did

you. Think yourself lucky to be rid of him."

"I do! But – oh, I did love him so much! And I built such dreams around him. Now I don't know where my life is going, or what plans I should make."

She thought again about Weston Hall, how much she had enjoyed working with herbs and remedies. That's what I want to do, she thought. Perhaps I could earn enough to support myself once this war is over. I could sell herbs in the marketplace, or find someone – a wise woman? – to take me on as her assistant.

But Nia, down to earth as ever, said, "What you need is another man – someone better. And I'm sure you'll find one before long." She smiled, and added teasingly, "Sergeant Llewellyn, perhaps? Rhian says she saw him taking notice of you the other day."

"What?" Alice laughed, despite herself. Sergeant Llewellyn, who drilled the Welsh troops, was all side whiskers and bellowing voice.

"He's a yeoman in a fair way of business, back in Dolgellau, so they say."

"Never!" said Alice. And they laughed.

"Well, you'll probably see little enough of any of the troops soon," said Nia. "Bryn says there's a rumour of an assault on Leicester. The city is in rebel hands."

Leicester. Alice had heard of that place, though she was unsure of where it was, or indeed where *they* were – they had travelled around so much since leaving Oxford. But the next day's march brought them to Loughborough. They were quartered in the outskirts of the town, and Alice was sure that Bryn must be right

about a coming assault: she sensed an undercurrent of excitement among the troops that had not been there before.

In the morning they marched towards Leicester, and set up their leaguer outside the city walls.

Seventeen

$\mathcal{A}$ sudden burst of cannon fire shook the makeshift shelters where the women were camped. Alice put her hands over her ears; the sound was huge, unbearable. Smoke from the guns billowed up and hid their view of the city wall and the battery where the six cannon had been installed.

Nia, who was feeding Elen, jolted the child as she cried out, "Oh, God save us, it's starting! They'll be going in! Oh God, keep our men safe!"

Elen, jerked from the breast, began to wail.

"Shush, shush," murmured Nia contritely, and the baby latched on again, gulping. "Now you'll have hiccups, won't you, *cariad*? And it'll be my fault."

All morning they had been on edge, hearing rumours that trumpeters were going to and fro between Prince Rupert and the burgesses of the city, the prince demanding surrender and the city wanting time to parley.

This cannon fire, Alice realized, must be the prince's answer.

The bombardment continued all afternoon. The noise was deafening and relentless, and smoke began to fill every part of the camp, causing everyone to cough. Nia tried to tie a gauze strip loosely across Elen's nose and mouth, but the baby would have none of it, her face turning red with distress.

Alice thought how frustrated the child must feel, unable to wave her arms in protest. But most of the time she was a contented baby, and would lie in her cradle, rocked by her mother's foot, or be carried in a cloth sling on Nia's back. Keeping her clean and dry had been a problem on the march, since they moved every day and her cloths could not easily be laundered. Nia used absorbent moss when she could find it. Last night she had washed some linen and today had strung it on twine between the shelters. Already it was flecked with smuts from the smoky wind.

"She's dirty," said Nia, wrinkling her nose, then smiling at the baby.

She gathered dry cloths from the line, laid Elen down in the shelter and began to unwrap her. It was now late afternoon, the sun still high in the summer sky, though masked by smoke blowing across the camp. Changing the baby was troublesome with all the swaddling to undo and rewind, and it was impossible for Nia to do it often enough. Elen smelt, and had a red rash on her buttocks and thighs. Nia tutted as she washed and dried her, and dabbed on some soothing ointment that Alice had made.

"Let her get the air on it awhile," Alice suggested, and Nia agreed.

The truth was, they all liked to look at Elen and watch her move. She jiggled her arms and legs rhythmically, and seemed happy to be free. Alice offered a finger to her, and Elen grasped it in her tiny fist. Her grip was surprisingly strong.

A thick billow of smoke engulfed them, and Nia cried out, "Oh, it's all over the washing!" She ran to rescue her linen.

"Let me do the swaddling?" Alice asked. She began wrapping the baby as she had seen Nia do it, one side and then the other, criss-crossing down the body, talking to the child as she went.

The guns stopped firing, and the sudden silence seemed loud. Into it came a roar of voices – cheers and shouts.

"They must have breached the wall," said Bronwen. "They'll be going in soon." She chewed her lip. She was anxious. They all knew that their people – the attackers, on open ground – were easy targets for those hidden behind the defences.

Alice remembered that musketeers were often first in the firing line. Robin would be part of this assault, when it began. She pushed the image away. Let his wife and that trader's daughter fear for him, she thought; I won't.

There was quiet now around the walls, but it was a purposeful lull, full of planning and activity. As the smoke started to clear they could see movements of men around the battery and all across the field. Rhian went

to investigate, and reported back that the defenders were filling in the breach and bringing up cannon.

The men did not return for food. The women knew this meant the assault would happen soon. They ate together and went early to their beds. Alice shared Nia's shelter, the baby lying between them. All three fell quickly asleep.

They woke to the pounding of cannon fire. It was black night. The flimsy shelter shook. Elen stirred and began to wail, and Nia lifted her up and tried to soothe her. Guns were firing from both sides of the wall, lighting up the sky with flashes of fire. For a while Alice and Nia sat stunned as the huge explosions filled the night with terror. When the roar subsided, Alice could hear the sharp crack of musket fire and, despite herself, she pictured Robin, his face soot-smudged, the lighted slow match dangling from his fingers as he raised his gun to fire. Her friends' husbands were pikemen; they would go in later, if the defenders were pushed back.

Behind the walls, the citizens must have filled the breach with whatever they could find. In daylight they might have picked off their enemies, but now, in total darkness, the king's forces had the upper hand while the defenders faced an onrushing wave of firepower. The attack was so close that the women could hear shouts and screams and the cries of the wounded.

The camp came alive with activity. All around, fires and lanterns were relit and people were moving about. Everyone was waiting, tense and expectant, for the outcome – which could surely only be a victory for

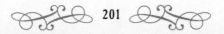

the king? The source of the firing changed. It began to come mostly from another part of the wall, further away. Perhaps a second breach was being made, or a gate stormed? Nia was in an agony of fear for Bryn. Rhian and Bronwen came out, Rhian fussing over her half-grown cat, which was wide-eyed and sharp-clawed with terror. They all stayed together, drinking warm beer and talking to keep their spirits up. Bronwen sat puffing on Edryd's long-stemmed tobacco pipe. She passed it around, but when it reached Alice she coughed and her eyes stung, and she gave it hastily to Rhian.

The breakthrough came about an hour later. The guns stopped firing and they heard a roar of voices and an occasional musket shot. Someone with a lantern swinging from a pole walked through the camp shouting that the city had fallen to the king.

No one expected to see their men yet unless they had been wounded; the soldiers would have gone in to plunder the city. But a large number of injured men were brought into the camp, and there was talk of many dead. Bronwen went to check on the wounded, and reported back to her group that no one they knew was there. Alice took her basket of salves and bandages and went with Bronwen to help the women who were dealing with minor injuries. For several hours they washed and bandaged or smeared salve on wounds. Distant sounds of shouting and screaming reached them. Alice knew this must be only the echo of the hell on earth of butchery, rape and robbery that was taking place in the city. It filled her with unease, particularly when she and Bronwen returned to the shelter and the Welsh girls continued to smoke and to speculate calmly on the booty their men might expect to find.

"I hope Bryn might think to take some linen, if he sees any," said Nia. "Though coin would do as well, and it's easier to carry."

"Don't you pity the people they steal from?" Alice asked. "The women, especially?"

Bronwen looked reproachful. "It's not stealing; it's war. They would do the same to us – except we have nothing in our homes to steal."

Nia agreed. "It's our right as victors. God knows, our men have given enough to this war! I only hope Bryn is there, and not lying dead in the breach."

It was a huge relief to all of them when, towards dawn, Bryn and Gethin stumbled into the camp, followed by Edryd and other friends in search of their wives. They were all drunk, and smeared with blood and dirt. Bryn kissed Nia, and poured a purseful of silver into her lap.

She gazed at him, wide-eyed. "There must be fifty shillings or more here, Bryn! That's more than three months' pay! Where did you get it?"

"From a merchant's house we broke into. Everyone's got money. So many fine houses! So much gold and silver! It was like shaking apples off a tree. Put it away, love. Put it in your pocket and hide it."

They spoke in Welsh, and it was only later, when the men had fallen asleep, that Nia told Alice what they had said. The Welshwomen exclaimed softly together over

their good fortune, and found safe places to stow away the money.

"I never saw such wealth before," Nia said to Alice. "I thought we were rich when Bryn joined the army! Back home he'd been lucky to earn six groats a week. The army pay more than doubled that. I reckon a lot of the men will desert now with their plunder and head for home. If it wasn't for me and the child, Bryn might do the same."

Alice was left with confused feelings. Her instinct was to celebrate with her friends and join in with their certainty that their men had earned this prize; and yet she could not help thinking of those who had been pillaged. Were they truly the enemy? Had they had any say at all in their city's defiance of Prince Rupert?

Before long the drums roused everyone to move into Leicester. The infantry were to be quartered there for the night. As they entered the sacked city, where Prince Rupert's black colours now flew from the battery, Alice began to tremble with shock at what she glimpsed through the smoke: corpses; wrecked and blackened buildings; people scurrying in panic, or huddled, weeping, in doorways. Her horror mounted as they went further in. Most of the dead – many of them piled in the gateway and around the battery – were soldiers from both sides. Many more of their own men lay dead in the streets.

But not all those slain were soldiers.

She turned to Nia, appalled. "These are ordinary people: shopkeepers, women!"

She saw that the citizens had tried to defend their

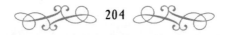

homes and had been killed for it. They came upon the body of a man sprawled in the street, his shirt bloody, great wounds on his neck and arms as if he had been hacked at with a sword. He wore no coat or breeches; they had been stolen from his corpse. Alice had seen cruel sights before: public hangings, people pelted with rubbish and stones in the stocks, or whipped at the cart's tail; but never violence on this scale, meted out to innocent people.

Bonfires were burning in the streets, and furniture, storage chests and empty wine casks lay scattered where the victorious soldiers had picked them over and moved on. Refugees – whole families with children, babes in arms, dogs and even pigs – were stumbling through the smoke towards the gates. Some of them panicked and ran when they saw the soldiers – running from *us*, Alice realized, overcome with shame. A woman burst out of a doorway and screamed in a frenzy, "You have killed my husband! My children have no father. How shall we live? Tell me that? How shall we live?" Alice could not bear to meet her eyes.

More dead lay in the side streets, and a man's body hung limp from an inn sign. The living scuttled away into cellars and alleyways as the soldiers came through.

Alice looked at her friends, at Edryd, Bryn and Gethin. Had they been part of this? Kind, gentle Bryn? Shy Gethin? Edryd? It was hard to believe. And yet they had come back to camp drunk, laden with stolen money, and she did not know whether the dried blood on their faces and arms came from enemy soldiers or from some

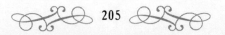

hapless citizen. She was relieved to see that the other women seemed shocked, and even the men appeared surprised at the devastation, as if they had woken from a dream, as if the night's work had been undertaken while they were in some altered condition.

Their quarters for the night, along with a dozen or so others of the Welsh soldiers, were in a stocking-frame knitter's home workshop – a tall narrow house in a poor part of the city. They tramped in while the distressed family – a husband, wife and four children – watched from their kitchen. The wife cried out, "They have dragged out the frames and burned them in the street! Our neighbours' too! Those frames were our livelihood, but they burned them. And for what?"

"You are rebels," one of the officers retorted. "All of you, in this city. You are lucky not to be locked up."

"We might as well be!"

The husband tried to hush his wife, but she would not be silenced. She turned on Alice and the Welsh girls and howled at them, "You worthless leaguer whores! Coming here with your brats into my home!"

The husband exclaimed, "Wife! Wife!" and the younger children – two little boys – began to cry.

"Get us beer, woman," the officer said, "and look to your own brats."

But the family had no beer, and no food. It had all been looted, and their small hoard of earnings stolen from its hiding place in the chimney breast. All this Alice heard from the weeping woman as some of the soldiers went out to forage for beer. The Welsh girls had brought

food, but Alice could not eat. She wanted to share her food with the family, but two of the soldiers drove them out into their own cellar, and shut the door on them.

The house was full of soldiers. Alice felt little safer from them than the stocking-frame worker's family did. They were full of drink, and fights threatened to break out over nothing. She stayed close to her three friends, and they took some beer and escaped to the upper room where they were to spend the night. This was a room that ran the whole width and depth of the house and had tall windows to let in light for the knitting. Yarn and half-finished stockings were scattered about, and broken wood littered the floor. One of the shutters had been smashed when the looters threw the wrecked frames out of the window into the street.

"*Why* did they do this?" she said. "There was no sense in it. No need. Did they go insane?"

"I think people do go mad sometimes, when they get together in groups," said Bronwen. "Especially after a battle, when they've seen comrades killed, and when there's strong drink." She shuddered. "Oh, I shall be glad when we leave this place!"

And Alice, standing at the open window, looked down and saw soldiers swaggering along the street, some in stolen hats and jerkins, bullying, swearing, shouting abuse: downtrodden foot soldiers, glorying in their moment of power. A woman answered back, and one of them struck her in the face with a musket butt. Somewhere across the way a child was crying, "Mammy! Mammy!" over and over again.

Alice sat down on the floor and put her hands over her ears. Her voice shook as she said, "I wish we had not come here. I wish I had never seen this."

Eighteen

"*You'll* get aches in your bones," Bronwen warned.

Alice didn't care. She lay on her back on the damp grass, gazing up at a blue sky full of high white castles of cloud – a welcome sight after yesterday's heavy rain. Far, far up she could hear larks singing. The wind was strong here on the hill, but lying down she could not feel the force of it. This place reminded her of the tor above her uncle's farm. Borough Hill, it was called: a hill fort, built in ancient times, with banks and ditches to repel invaders. The king's army had fortified it further with higher banks and batteries and a palisade, and were constantly scouring the countryside around for food and horses. The officers had set up their tents; the soldiers had built neat rows of huts; and over here, where she lay, the camp followers had created their own more easy-going space. Laundry flapped from tent poles, and Alice could hear Nia and Bryn playing with their daughter.

Bronwen was mending clothes and Rhian teasing her cat with a length of thread. Lower down, on the hillside, the Cavaliers' horses grazed contentedly.

It was mid-June, almost midsummer. Alice knew this, despite the lack of almanacs, because of the length of the days and the plants she found: pink and purple clover, yellow trefoil and plantain in the valley; harebells on these high slopes.

This was a world away from Leicester, where they had stayed for three grim nights before abruptly moving on to one rendezvous after another. Whatever alarm had occasioned these movements, they came to nothing, and the troops did not travel far but installed themselves on this hill, where they had been now for a week. Edryd said they had been awaiting the return of a convoy of horse from Oxford. Regardless of the reason, Alice thought she would be quite happy to stay here, poised in time. It was a fortress, but there seemed at this moment to be no war. Everyone was at ease. She sat up, half blinded after gazing so long at the bright sky, then rose and brushed mud from her skirt. "Bronwen, I must do like you and mend some clothes."

She ducked into her shelter, and had her hand on a torn shift, when a drum began to beat – a sudden, urgent tattoo – and she heard an eruption of loud voices and shouted orders. She darted out. Everyone was on their feet and staring, startled. Bryn hastened away; Nia snatched up the baby. Soldiers were running to their stations, the Cavaliers hurrying down the hillside after their horses.

There was no sign of any attacker. But the gates were manned; everyone was being drawn inside. Clearly there had been an alarm.

By evening the entire army, with all its wagons, ordnance and animals, was inside the fort, and the men stood to their arms all night. In the morning they prepared to march. As they filed down the hill and out onto the road, Alice looked back and saw dragoons riding across the camp, firing the huts. The fires leapt up one after another, and the smoke of their burning blew on the wind as the column moved off.

They lodged that night in villages around a town called Harborough. It was a night full of unease. Something was afoot; some alarm kept them all close and ready to move.

"The enemy must be near," said Nia. "We're getting ready to fight." She gave a nervous smile. "Perhaps it'll be the one to end this war? They say all is going well for the king. Perhaps we'll soon be home."

Later the drums roused them from sleep. In total darkness they began to move and gather together – like an army of ghosts, Alice thought. By morning they were all at the rendezvous outside the town. News flew around that the enemy was close; that some of their own scouts had been captured the evening before; that both armies were gathering. They were to march and prepare to fight.

Alice caught a brief glimpse, in the distance, of the princes and generals riding at the head of the army with the cavalry, of sun glinting on armour, of the ensigns

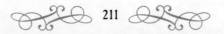

holding aloft the colours. The infantry followed – the musketeers and pikemen – then the forty or so carts and wagons of the artillery and provisions, with all their gunners, carters and farriers. It was much later that the wagons and coaches of the baggage train began to move. They made their ponderous way down narrow muddy roads where the wheels often got caught in ruts or toppled into ditches and had to be hauled free.

Once Rhian exclaimed, "Look!" and pointed, and Alice saw a band of horsemen – Parliament's, they must be – on the hillside near by. A tingle of excitement and fear ran through her.

They began to see more movements of enemy horse. Far ahead of them stretched their own army, occasionally visible – furled colours, a thicket of pikes – but more often hidden by hedgerows or farm buildings.

The women never heard the fighting begin; the baggage train was too far behind, struggling for an hour or more down the rutted roads and with the army out of sight behind higher ground. The wagons jolted and rattled, the carters swore, the dragoons shouted orders, and their noise drowned out any more distant sound.

Nia had the baby in a sling on her back. She was well recovered from the birth now and able to walk most of the time. The women were talking about what they would do when the war was over – for they had all of them begun to believe that the king would soon have victory, and none of them wanted to return to the poverty they had known before.

"It'll be good to go home with money in our

pockets," said Nia. "And a child! We've enjoyed these times – they've been good, and comradely – but Bryn wants to settle, be a bit more independent than before. If we could get the tenancy of a small farm…"

She chattered on, and Alice guessed it was partly to overcome her fear; for surely she must be afraid for Bryn, who was perhaps already in the thick of battle?

Rhian was more direct. "I wish I was with child! I do, truly. If Gethin dies, I'll have nothing."

Bronwen said, "Now, Rhian, now."

And Nia asked, "What will *you* do, Lisi? Will you go back to that great house where you stayed over winter? But no – how would you get there, alone? I wish you'd come to Wales with us. We've been such friends. I'd miss you. Why not come with us?"

"I might," said Alice. It was a possibility she had not considered before. When she left Dartmoor she had thought of nothing beyond her love for Robin and her need to escape, not realizing how difficult life would be for a young woman without a man to protect her. Certainly it would be unwise to travel alone, and in any case she did not relish the thought of returning to Weston Hall and admitting what a fool she had been over Robin. It would be good to go to Wales in company with her friends, to begin a new life. She'd learn to speak Welsh, get work at an inn or a tradesman's house, perhaps even an apothecary's, be an aunt of sorts to her darling Elen…

"I'd like that," she said. "To come with you. Will I find work there, do you think?"

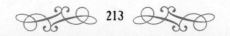

"Certainly you will," said Bronwen. "You'll find a husband too, I'm sure, before long."

"*We'll* find you someone," Nia agreed. "A nice Welsh boy."

"Oh! I've had enough of love."

Nia rolled her eyes. "She's seventeen and she's had enough of love!"

They were laughing together and teasing Alice, when Rhian said, "We're stopping!"

They saw that the baggage wagons at the head of the column – the sumpter wagons that carried the royal wealth and clothing – had turned off the road. Behind these, other wagons began to form a circle. A stream of lesser conveyances still blocked the road. The women, seeing everything slowing to a stop, stepped aside into the field.

With a sigh of relief Nia sat down on a tussock of grass, took Elen from her sling and untied the neck ribbon of her shift. Alice looked up, and was startled to see several horsemen burst into view and gallop across the road in front of them. She heard shouting, shots, a cry of "Road's blocked!" Still the carters struggled to get more of the heavy wagons into the field. Another group of riders came through, then many more; and suddenly there was alarm, the carters left the wagons in the road and the dragoons made ready their muskets.

"Back to the wagons! Take cover!"

The sergeant's bellow caused Nia to scramble to her feet, the baby clutched to her breast.

"Women! Off the field! Take cover!"

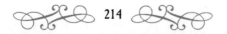

"Nia! Alice! Come!" Bronwen and Rhian were crouched beside a wagon's back wheel. Some women climbed inside the wagons; most hid around and beneath them. The sergeant shouted orders to the musketeers to make ready.

Alice's heart was pounding. She saw the baggage train guards run to man the swivel guns on the main wagons, the defenders race to their stations; and then the fighting erupted all around them: crack of muskets, flash of fire, horses and men in a confusion of smoke and screams. It seemed that the battlefield was on the move and they were now part of it.

The women huddled closer together. More crawled under the wagons as the shot flew. Their own cavalry were in retreat, turning to fire their pistols at their pursuers as they fled past the wagons, across the road and the rough field, and away in the direction they had come from that morning. Near the sumpter wagons some of them regrouped to make a stand, firing at the oncoming enemy horsemen. Alice saw several Cavaliers fall. The rest fled, pursued by the rebels.

The Welshwomen all began murmuring – prayers, Alice guessed – in their own language. Everyone looked terrified. They could hear, now, another great din of battle – shouts and screams and gunfire – coming from beyond the ridge less than a mile away, where their men, the foot soldiers, must be fighting. When a sudden silence fell, it was more frightening than the sounds of battle.

Alice held her breath. A volley of shots rang out. Nia

cried, *"Duw!"* and clutched her child tighter. Moments later men came pouring over the brow of the ridge – cavalry in flight, musketeers flinging themselves down for cover in the circle of wagons. Alice, crouched next to Nia, heard her friend, still speaking Welsh, sobbing out Bryn's name and the name of God. All the women were crying and wailing. Alice shook with fear. This was utter defeat.

And now came a new terror: the victorious foot soldiers of the rebel army. They raced towards the baggage train with a great roar of anticipation. As they fired, the swivel guns thundered in reply, followed by volleys of shot from all around as the guards and musketeers returned fire.

But the enemy advanced. Through the smoke Alice saw them, running, shouting, towards the sumpter wagons of the king and court. A defender fell dead almost at Alice's feet. Another pitched from the side of a cart. Screams and gunfire burst out all around.

"Get back! Get back!"

A guard urged the women to leave the circle of wagons and move further away. They ran, a great flock of women, sobbing in fear, to crouch and hide among the carts and wagons still strung out along the road.

The guards were fighting hand to hand now, musket butts wielded like clubs, swords stabbing. But they were overwhelmed as more and more rebel foot came on. Alice saw their own dragoons and musketeers fall, one after another, the wagons' curtains ripped apart, the bales and boxes dragged out. One wagon was still full of

women, wealthy whores who clung to their possessions. A strong-looking, yellow-haired woman set about the enemy with a stool, but they hauled her out, and her companions with her, forcibly stripped them of their fine gowns and shoes, and left them barefoot and screeching in their shifts. They flung out everything from the wagon: velvets, silks, jewel caskets, bag after bag of coin.

Then one of them turned on the women. "Whores! Harlots! You are an offence to God!"

The yellow-haired woman cursed him.

He drew his sword and slashed her across the face.

Alice gasped. The woman shrieked, her hands over her face, bright blood streaming between her fingers and staining her white shift. As if at a signal, the soldiers turned on the other women before they could flee and sliced their faces in the same way, slitting their noses and thus marking them as whores. The women, blinded by blood and fear, stumbled and screamed for help.

And suddenly Alice realized what was to come. The soldiers, fired up by blood, turned towards the huddled horde of less wealthy women – the wives, widows and drabs cowering in and around the provisions wagons. They advanced with drawn swords, and their threats were terrifying.

"This nest of vermin…" "…filthy army of whores…" "…clean them out…"

"Run!" someone cried. *"Run!"*

Alice, Bronwen, Rhian, Nia: all got to their feet – Nia with the baby gripped in her arms – and fled across the road into a field, part of a tide of frantic women, crying,

sobbing, gasping, tripping on their skirts, stumbling and falling on the uneven, marshy ground.

The soldiers pursued and quickly surrounded and corralled them. Alice could scarcely breathe for terror. She darted first one way, then another. There was no escape. As the soldiers closed in, the Welshwomen around her called on God, fell to their knees and cried out for mercy in their own language.

"Yn y enw Duw, arbeda ni!"

"Trugaredd!"

"Duw! Arbeda ni! Trugaredd! Trugaredd!"

Their foreign speech was like a spark to gunpowder. With a howl of hatred the soldiers drew their swords and moved in. Ffion and Heulwen, still begging to be spared, were slashed to a cry of "Irish! Papists!" Then, to her horror, Alice saw a soldier strike Ffion again and run her through with his sword. For an instant Ffion stood still. Then all the colour fled from her face, blood gushed forth, drenching her gown, and she crumpled to the ground. Heulwen was felled with a great blow to the neck.

"Oh God – oh God," Alice sobbed.

Now the soldiers set about their work with righteous glee, striking left and right, damning all the women as Irish whores. Alice heard terrible screams, saw women cut down, caught the panic as they all tried to run and were penned in by the cordon of soldiers. Some drew their own knives and slashed at their attackers before they were killed.

Alice had run with her friends; but now, in the

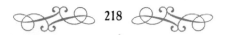

tumult, they were torn apart. Bronwen and Rhian had disappeared. She saw, briefly, Nia's small sturdy figure stumbling over the tussocky grass, hunched over the child in her arms; then saw a soldier cut her down – a butcher's blow that felled her instantly, so that she pitched forward onto her face. Alice felt such terror that her body seemed to dissolve like water, and she feared she would fall and die of fear; and yet, with some deeper instinct, she moved to save herself. As the swords hacked and the screaming women fell around her, she dropped down and tried to hide under a corpse; but she slipped and plunged into a hidden ditch, landing in a few inches of muddy water. There she lay still, covered in the other woman's blood.

For a long time – hours, it seemed – she dared not move. Her feet and hips were in water, and she felt her skirts grow cold and wet, their weight dragging. At first her upper body lay on the edge of the ditch, one arm flung out, the hand showing above the top. Slowly, inch by inch, she drew it in, terrified at every small move that she would be seen, dragged out and killed. With her hand down to shoulder level, she let her whole body slip deeper into the ditch. She could hear the soldiers moving around, finishing off those wounded who still cried out. She prayed that if they came near they would see the blood on her and take her for a corpse.

In her mind's eye she saw, again and again, Nia stumbling across the field; the sword coming down; her friend pitching forward with Elen beneath her. The mother's instinct had been to run bent over her child, to

protect her. Alice, reliving those moments, remembered where in the field Nia had fallen, but she did not dare go to her. She heard the soldiers rounding up those they had not killed and sending them away under guard. These, she guessed, were also marked on the face as whores, for their screams and howls of pain overlaid any groans that the dying women in the field might be making.

Now she heard sounds of plunder. From the whoops of delight, crashing sounds and cheers, she realized several wagons had been overturned, their contents shared out or fought over. The rebel soldiers must have been hungry; she heard them exclaiming at the contents of the provisions wagons, and wondered about the Erlams, what had become of them. She remembered too that her own belongings – her spare linen, her winter cloak, the basket containing her salves and ointments and her father's book – were in the Erlams' wagon.

Most of all she thought about Elen.

She waited hours, till the sun began to sink and there were no more voices – nothing but a faint rattling gasp from a woman close by; and that soon ceased.

At last she moved.

Her feet felt like rocks, her shoes were saturated, and the sodden weight of her long skirts threatened to pull her back into the ditch. She struggled out, eyes darting, heart beating fast. She saw no soldiers. But all around lay the bodies of women, heaped one upon another – all the Welshwomen who had come with their husbands or lovers, the women she had marched with and cooked and sung and talked with, all these weeks. There must

have been a hundred of them dead in the field.

And among them were her friends.

She kept low to the ground, knowing there would be enemy guards on the sumpter wagons, if not in the road. She found Rhian first, drawn by her red-gold hair, all puddled now with blood. She lay face up, her blue eyes wide and blank. Near by was Bronwen, one arm stretched out as if to try to reach her sister. Already flies were beginning to settle on their bodies. Alice crouched beside them. She closed their eyes, and smoothed their skirts that the soldiers had rumpled, not to rape but to steal the pockets hidden beneath – pockets that they would have guessed were full of silver looted from the sack of Leicester.

A flicker of movement startled her: soldiers, horsemen, advancing along the ridge. And there were more in the lane leading to this place. She had to be quick. She remembered where she had seen Nia, and crawled there, pausing often, so as not to attract attention.

Nia lay where she had fallen, the ground beside her dark with blood. Alice didn't want to turn her over, to see her dead face, but she knew she must. Her flesh was still warm. She pushed, and rolled Nia over, revealing the body of Elen, face up, eyes closed.

Fear gripped Alice. Had the baby suffocated? She snatched her up, hugged her to her heart. "Oh, Elen, sweeting, don't die! Don't die!" Tears rolled down her cheeks and wet the baby's face; and Elen sneezed, a little *"tiss!"* like a cat, and began to cry.

"Elen!" Alice gazed in joy at the small cross face.

But the wailing might bring soldiers. She licked her finger clean and put it in the baby's mouth, and even in that moment of danger she felt pleasure and hope at the instant vigorous suck.

She paused briefly, to make sure no one had heard Elen's cry. Then she turned to the body of her friend. Nia was beyond help, her dead eyes staring up at the sky.

"I've got your baby here, safe, Nia," she whispered. "I'll keep her and take care of her for you. I promise."

The child's wrappings were wet, and she was hungry. In the Erlams' wagon, as well as Alice's belongings, was Nia's stock of baby cloths and swaddling bands. The wagon was still on the road. But now Alice could see that there were indeed enemy guards over there, two of them sitting on one of the carts, smoking their clay pipes. She could not go there. She had to leave this place of slaughter as quickly as possible, and find help.

There was a farmhouse close by; she'd noticed it as they came down the road. But it was too near for safety, and the people might be hostile. There might even be soldiers inside. Better to head for the village she could see less than half a mile away along the road to the west.

She took her finger out of Elen's mouth, muffled the baby's cries against her chest, and hid behind some furze bushes, well clear of the baggage train. From there she crept from one hiding place to another until she drew close to the nearest houses.

It was then, as she looked at the row of cottages and wondered which one to approach, that the full weight

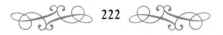

of her promise to her dead friend struck home. Elen had been soothed by the jogging movement of the walk into a fretful sleep. But she was only a month old. If she were to survive she would need a woman's milk for a year. She was hungry now, and Alice had no milk. Her most urgent need was to find someone who had.

Nineteen

The woman spoke from behind her closed door. "We've nothing worth stealing."

"Please!" Alice called. "There are no soldiers with me. I need help. I have a baby."

This was the third house she had tried. At the first one she had heard the bar dropped across the door inside, a dog growling. At the second a man had come from behind the house with a pitchfork and told her to be gone. People were afraid. To find that the common fields around your village have become a battlefield, that thousands of soldiers are on the loose, must be alarming, she realized.

She tried again. "Please!" By this time Elen was screaming.

The door opened a crack to reveal the wary face of an old woman.

Alice stepped forward. "The baby — she's hungry. I'm looking for a wet nurse."

"None here." The woman seemed nervous.

A man's voice came from within. "Who is it?"

"A soldier's woman."

"Shut the door on her."

"I must find a wet nurse," Alice repeated. She put her hand on the door.

"The forge," the woman said. She pointed the way. "The blacksmith's wife has a baby, born in January."

"Thank you!"

The door closed, and was swiftly bolted from within. But now Alice felt hopeful. The forge was a short distance away, on this eastern edge of the village. She hurried towards it, aware that dusk was approaching. The beauty of the evening astonished her: the light still gold on the hilltops, the fields in shadow, the whistle and chirrup of roosting birds filling the oak trees on the green. And yet, only half a mile from here, the slaughtered women lay in their blood.

The blacksmith's wife came to the door with her shift untied, a baby at her breast, another small child peeping out from behind her skirts. She was a fair, plump woman with a pleasant face. Alice knew she was Elen's only chance. She held out the wailing baby.

"For the love of God, can you help me? She needs milk. I can't feed her."

The woman stared. She looked shocked, and Alice realized that she and Elen, bloodied from the battlefield, must be a startling sight.

"Her mother is dead. She has not fed for hours."

The woman's face softened. She stepped back from

the door. "Come in," she said. Her own child was dropping back from the breast, replete. She eased him off, rubbed his back till he burped, then laid him in a cradle. She sat down and rocked it with her foot as she took the child from Alice and put her to the other breast. "Sit down," she said, indicating the settle by the fire. "You look half dead."

Alice obeyed, feeling the strength drain out of her now that she no longer had to struggle.

"Are you hurt? There's blood on you."

"It's not mine." She tried to tell the woman about the killings in the field, but the words would not come. "Dead," was all she could say. "The baby's mother – dead." She found she was shaking, and could not stop.

"There's beer in the jug there. And bread on the table."

"Thank you." Alice sipped some beer, but could not eat.

"You're alone?" the woman asked.

"Yes. Please – may we stay here tonight?"

For the first time the woman looked doubtful. "If my husband agrees. He's gone out over the fields towards Naseby, to see what's come of the fight."

"I can pay."

The woman nodded. "We have room. I'll speak to him." She turned her attention to Elen. After a few hiccuping cries Elen had begun to suck strongly, as if the woman were her own mother. Faithless creature, thought Alice. She felt a pang of grief for Nia that stabbed like a knife in her heart. But it was for the best, she knew, that

the child was too young to grieve.

Later the woman brought clean linen, and Alice washed and wrapped the baby. The blacksmith came in soon after. His wife explained, and Alice repeated her offer to pay. His eyes, suspicious under heavy brows, looked her up and down.

"Camp follower?" he asked.

She nodded. She was too tired to justify herself. Let him think her a whore if he wished.

He turned to his wife. "There are many dead in the field, and on the ridge, and all along the line of the hedges over by Sulby."

"The girl says there were women killed. In the king's baggage train."

"I never saw that. Didn't go near the train; it's guarded by soldiers. I walked straight down over the fields." He jerked his head towards the closed door to an adjoining room. "How's he?"

"I don't know." There was an edge of irritation to her voice. "Haven't had time to look." She gave Elen back to Alice. "There. Rub her back. That's right."

The man frowned. "She won't take away my son's milk?"

"There's plenty of milk. And nursing will make it come more."

"I won't stay long," said Alice. "But tonight? If I could…?" She felt in her pocket and brought out some coins, thinking that it was as well she had taken Nia's advice and not thrown Robin's money back at him.

The man looked at the coins, and she knew he

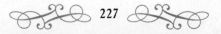

thought it was her earnings as a whore. But the woman said, "She can sleep here tonight, husband, can't she? For the child's sake." She turned to Alice. "Where will you go from here?"

Alice thought about this for the first time. Elen was motherless – but where was Bryn? The army had seemed to be in retreat. The King must surely have been defeated, perhaps even killed. She ought to find Bryn, but how? He was probably dead. Alone, with the baby, she could never search for him. Nor ever go to Wales with her friends, as they'd planned. There was only one place she could think of now. "How far is Copsey?" she asked.

"Copsey?"

"Weston Hall at Copsey. It's on the road between Faringdon and Oxford."

"I'd say it's sixty miles to Oxford," the man said.

Sixty miles. And she had no milk.

"She can't travel sixty miles with a baby, and two armies roaming the countryside," said the woman.

"We'll talk about it in the morning."

There was a small room above, next to their own bedchamber. The woman aired the bed by whisking a pan of hot coals over it. She found a basket for the baby and lined it with fleece and cotton.

"We'll put the baby next to *my* bed," she said. "I'll feed her when she wakes in the night." She paused in the doorway. "Hannah, my name is. Hannah Barford."

Alice thanked her, giving her own name.

She went early to her bed, and lay awake for a long

while. She had felt reluctant to part with Elen, even for a night, and missed the feel of the baby in her arms. The events of the day forced themselves again and again into her mind, vivid and relentless. The yellow-haired whore with blood streaming between her fingers. The colour fleeing from Ffion's face. Nia stumbling across the field. The sword coming down. She tried to shut out the images but they would not leave her. She tossed restlessly in the narrow bed.

After the blacksmith and his wife came upstairs she heard a murmur of voices going on for some time and guessed they were talking about her – wondering, no doubt, how long they would be troubled with her.

Sixty miles to Copsey. And her friends lying dead and unburied in the field.

Oh, Nia, she thought, you wanted so much to go home! We would all have gone to Wales together, you and me, and Rhian and Bronwen, and the men, and little Elen. The awfulness of being the only one left seemed too much to bear, but she could not cry. She was beyond tears.

She slept at last, but woke, screaming, from a dream of mutilated faces. The woman – Hannah – came in to calm her, to tell her not to be afraid; it was a nightmare. Alice was sweat-soaked and shaking, bewildered in the strange room.

"Go to sleep now," Hannah said. Her hand on Alice's shoulder was kind. "The baby's sleeping. I've fed her."

Alice was afraid to sleep again, but exhaustion overcame her at last and she slept until early morning,

when sounds from outside roused her. She looked out to see Master Barford starting the fire in his forge. His little daughter stood watching the red flames grow. From downstairs Alice heard a baby – Hannah's – squealing, and the woman's voice, then a door opening and shutting.

She washed in the bowl of water Hannah had provided and put her sweat-stained linen back on. She took her comb from her pocket and struggled with the tangles in her hair. Her comb was now almost her only possession – that and the eagle stone she kept in a pouch on a thong around her neck. She pictured her hessian bag, her clean linen, her basket of salves, in the Erlams' wagon. And saw again the field full of dead.

When will they bury them? she wondered. They'd be stiff now. Perhaps it was done already. And she felt horror at the thought that her friends might have been tumbled together into a pit dug by soldiers, unloved, unblessed.

She went downstairs. The two babies lay side by side, one in his cradle, the other in her basket. The yard door opened, and Hannah Barford came in with a bucket of water, her daughter beside her, chattering about the blacksmith's fire. "Hot. Dadda's fire, hot. Mustn't touch…" She fell silent when she saw Alice.

Hannah smiled. "Prudence, say good morning to Alice." She shunted her daughter forward.

But the child darted away and went to study the two babies. "Matty," she said, rocking her brother rather too vigorously. She considered Elen. *"Babba."*

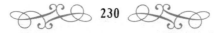

"This is Elen," said Alice, lifting up Nia's baby. It felt good to hold her again. "Can you say Elen?"

Prudence ran and clung to her mother.

Hannah had been watching Alice. "You are very young," she said.

"I'm seventeen."

"Don't you have a family? This house near Oxford – is it your home?"

"No. But I worked there last winter. They would take me in, I believe, if I can find my way there."

"My husband says you can stay here awhile. Best to wait till the armies are gone; then we'll see how you might travel. Till then – there is a way you could help *me*."

"Yes! I will." Alice imagined washing and cooking.

But Hannah looked towards the closed inner door. She lowered her voice. "There's a soldier – a dragoon – in there, in the parlour. He's sorely wounded; mortally wounded, we believe. His comrades brought him here across the field on his horse after the battle; asked us to care for him until he died. He's lost a lot of blood. My husband prised a pistol ball from his thigh and he has a sword cut in his shoulder. I thought to find him dead this morning, but he clings to life. Could you sit with him, Alice? Talk to him, give him sips of beer? He's as comfortable as I could make him – oh, there was so much blood, and we'd to bring down an old mattress from the loft, and no time to air it – but I don't want Prue to see him, and I can't leave the children alone. I look in on him when I can. But it seems an unchristian

231

thing to let him lie there alone, facing death. Would you sit with him?"

"Yes. Of course," said Alice, though there was nothing she wanted to do less. The thought of more death filled her with despair. "I'll go to him now."

"Oh, have a bite to eat first." Hannah set meat, bread and beer on the table, and Alice was surprised to find herself hungry after all.

"There's a flagon of beer for him in there," Hannah said afterwards, "and a wash bowl and some clean linen cloths. We fetch water from the well in the yard."

He was lucky to be brought here, to these people, Alice thought. We were both lucky.

"This village," she asked, "what's it called?"

"Sibbertoft," said Hannah.

Sibbertoft. It sounded gentle. Not a name for a place of death.

She braced herself and opened the door to the parlour.

Twenty

It was dark in the room, and stuffy. Although Hannah had evidently been burning herbs to purify the air, nothing could mask the smell of blood.

Alice steeled herself to look at the man on the bed. He lay as if asleep, his body covered by a blanket, his face so white she felt sure he must have died, as Hannah had predicted. She sat down on the stool at his left side, watched the blanket where it lay over his chest, and was relieved to see a faint, steady movement. She studied his face. He was young, with fairish hair hanging dirty and tangled, a moustache, a few days' pale stubble on his jaw. His skin was pitted with gunpowder. An ordinary-looking young man, were it not that he was perhaps mortally wounded and already close to death.

Near by were his belongings: a bulky buff coat of tan leather; a helmet; big leather gauntlets; a sword and musket lying against the wall; and on the floor, near her

feet, a jumble of belt, leather flask, bandolier, various bags and pouches. On top lay a Bible and some printed papers. She glanced at these. Some were newsbooks and pamphlets. One seemed to be a hymn sheet.

He was one of the other side, she felt sure. The hymn sheet in particular suggested it. She supposed she should hate him because of what had happened to her friends, but she found she felt nothing at the sight of this man but sadness and a profound pity at the waste of his life.

She could see part of the bandaging on his left shoulder. It bore a dark, dried bloodstain. The other wound, she had been told, was in the thigh: a pistol shot. A cavalryman must have caused that injury, since only they had pistols.

She touched the man's forehead gently. His eyelids flickered. "My name is Alice," she said. "Mistress Barford asked me to sit with you. Is there anything you need?"

"Drink…" The word was a whisper.

She poured a little beer into the tankard. He was lying slightly propped against a pillow, but even with her help he managed only a few sips before he fell back, exhausted.

Alice glanced at the Bible. "Would you like me to read to you?" she asked.

He gave the faintest of nods. "Thank you."

She picked up the Bible. Its leather binding was scuffed with use and it fell open at several much-studied passages. She glanced at the flyleaf and saw his name written there: *Jeremiah Banks*. Jeremiah: he was the son of Puritans, then, for sure. She wondered what text to

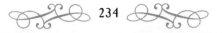

choose, what would be appropriate, and fell back on something familiar that would be easy for her to read without stumbling:

> "The Lord is my shepherd; I shall not want.
> He maketh me to lie down in green pastures:
> He leadeth me beside the still waters.
> He restoreth my soul: He leadeth me in the
>   paths of righteousness for His name's sake.
> Yea, though I walk through the valley of the
>   shadow of death, I will fear no evil..."

He listened, or she supposed he did. His eyes remained closed.

She read on, and when she stopped he said, on a faint breath, "We've met before."

He was rambling. She hoped it was not the first sign of fever. "No," she said. "You're thinking of someone else."

Most of that day she sat with him. From time to time she gave him more sips of beer, but when she suggested food he seemed too tired. He slept for hours, his breathing so shallow that sometimes she wondered if he would ever wake again. Once, while he slept, she drew the blanket away and looked at his injuries. Both wounds – in the left shoulder and right thigh – had been bound in clean linen which was now soaked with blood. But the blood had dried; it did not seem to be flowing, at least while he lay still. She wondered whether any salve or poultice had been applied, whether anything should

235

be done now, or whether the wounds were best left alone.

In the late afternoon she helped Hannah change his bandages. He came more fully, and painfully, awake then, for they had to turn him onto his injured right side so that they could prise the stuck linen away from the wound just below his left shoulder.

Alice flinched at the sight of the great slicing cut, but Hannah said, "It heals well. The bleeding has almost stopped."

They bandaged the arm again, rolled him gently onto his back, and attended to the thigh wound. This still oozed blood. It was less extensive, but deep, and Alice knew that such a wound could do much damage.

They left him resting and went into the kitchen.

Alice said, "I've been watching him. I believe he may live, if the wounds don't fester."

Hannah nodded agreement. "He has clung to life for a full day now. Does he drink?"

"Not much. He's very weak. I think he has almost no blood in him."

"Some red wine would do him good."

"To replace the lost blood. Yes."

"And perhaps a thin broth, made with meat stock."

She left Alice with the children and went to the inn on the green, returning with a flagon of wine. Its dark red colour made Alice feel sure it would be wholesome for the injured soldier.

Elen, meanwhile, was thriving on Hannah's milk. Alice changed the baby and swaddled her again, all the

time talking to her and getting smiles in return. She was determined to do as much for Elen as possible, for she had a jealous fear that if they stayed here long, the baby would come to love Hannah, and not her.

Not that she intended to stay any longer than necessary. When Master Barford came in for his supper, her easy relationship with Hannah changed and the air became charged with mistrust. The blacksmith had been persuaded, out of Christian charity, to take her under his roof, but it was clear that he regarded her as a woman of dubious morals who might corrupt his wife and daughter. He avoided speaking directly to her, and she could only listen as he told his wife what he had been hearing from his customers during the day about movements of the troops. It seemed that hundreds – maybe thousands – of Royalist prisoners were being sent to London under guard; but General Fairfax was believed to be leading the Parliamentarian army towards Leicester. Alice thought with pity of the people of Leicester, who had already suffered so much under Prince Rupert's assault.

After supper Master Barford went out to see what he could find on the battlefield. Alice had told Hannah earlier about the possessions she had left in the Erlams' wagon, but she did not dare ask the blacksmith to search for them. And she would not go out herself; she knew people would be stripping the corpses. She ventured only as far as the field edge at the back of the forge. From there she could see wagons, some overturned, and distant figures moving about. There were more men walking the field tracks

237

north-east of the village, and she noticed circlings of crows over the highest ground.

Master Barford returned with a pair of pistols, spurs and other horse trappings, and a man's gold ring that Hannah took and examined.

"Anything worth having has gone," he told his wife. "I reckon General Fairfax's army have taken most of the wagons with them. The villagers are coming out now, same as me, to look around. Some have gone up Hellcombe, towards Wadborough." He sighed, passing a hand across his face. "Lord, there are some sights! The corpses…"

In desperation Alice turned to him. "My friends … the women?"

He looked at her with a reluctant compassion. "There were soldiers left behind to bury the dead. I saw them filling in a pit near where the baggage train was attacked."

Alice tried not to think of the pit, but the image forced itself into her mind: the tumbled bodies, purplish-white, stripped of any saleable clothes. Her friends were gone. But what of Bryn? What of Gethin and Edryd? Were they prisoners now, or were they too among the dead, buried in another pit a few fields away from their wives? And Robin? She hadn't thought of him until now. Surely Robin would somehow have escaped the slaughter?

Hannah had made the promised broth, and added some of the red wine to it. Alice fed it to the soldier with a spoon. He seemed better already, less hollow-faced, his eyes more alert.

* * *

That night Alice was tired and fell asleep quickly; but once again, towards dawn, she woke from a nightmare to the sound of her own screams. From the next room she heard Prudence begin to cry, and her mother soothing her. When Hannah appeared, Alice was sitting trembling on the bed.

"I'm sorry," she said.

"It's not your fault." Hannah yawned. "Your baby's awake. I'll feed her."

Alice was afraid to fall asleep again. "I'll go down and see how the soldier is."

They never referred to the man by his name, though Alice had told Hannah she had found it on the flyleaf of his Bible. It was as if by not naming him they would be less unhappy if all their efforts failed and he died.

Alice washed and dressed, then went downstairs, feeling her way in the dark. In the kitchen several cats woke and pressed around her ankles. She knelt and stroked them, soothed by their warm furriness.

The embers of last night's fire still glowed. She lit a candle from it, and opened the door to the parlour. He was awake. She saw the gleam of his eyes in the candlelight.

"Good morning." She set the candle down. "How do you feel?"

"Grateful. To you, and these good people, and to God."

"Your voice is stronger."

He grimaced. "But the pain keeps me awake. You are up early."

"I don't want to sleep. I have nightmares." And before he could ask her why and perhaps provoke her into a grief-stricken response, she said, "There is more broth in the kitchen. I'll fetch you some."

"Mistress Alice – wait! Could you open the shutters? I've not seen daylight since I was brought in here."

Alice hesitated. "A sickroom should be warm and dark…" But she knew that the main reason Hannah had closed up the room was because she had thought this was to be a death chamber.

She crossed the room and drew back the shutters. The window faced east, overlooking the road where the baggage train had been attacked. The glass panes were small and greenish-coloured and distorted the view, but they let in the growing daylight.

When she brought the broth, he got her to help him sit up; and he wanted to feed himself, so she poured the broth into a tankard that he could hold in his right hand.

"Are you right-handed?" she asked.

"Yes. For which I thank God. I fear I may always have pain in the left shoulder."

"What is your trade?"

"I'm a carpenter. Or was about to be, before this war. Tell me, have you heard anything of how the fight went?"

"I believe it was a victory for your side." She could not keep the bitterness out of her voice. The news clearly pleased and heartened him, and that offended her still more.

He saw this, and said, puzzled, "I see that my side is not yours? But I thought Master Barford was for Parliament."

"I am not one of Master Barford's family."

"No. Your voice…"

He gave her the empty tankard and she set it down. Sunlight was now streaming into the room; she could feel it on her face. When she turned back to him she saw that he was looking at her intently.

"I was not mistaken," he said. "We *have* met before. You are the girl from the house we raided near Oxford. Weston House, was it?"

"Weston Hall," said Alice. She knew him now. The officious young captain – so upright and proud he'd looked then! And she remembered how she had pushed between him and Lady Weston and demanded that he keep his men in order. She felt a flush rise in her face.

"I recognized your voice first," he said. "That West Country burr." A smile twitched his lips and he imitated her reading: *"'The Lord is my shepherd…'"*

Alice, embarrassed, was seized with a desire to laugh. And then she thought of Nia only a few hours buried, and herself here with their enemy, and the shock of it all overwhelmed her and she began to sob.

He looked instantly contrite. "Please forgive me," he said. "I meant no mockery of you."

She wiped her eyes, gulping. "It's not you. My friends – my friends were…" But she could not bring herself to tell him.

"Please forgive me," he repeated.

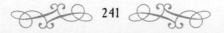 241

"There is no need."

He sighed, suddenly weary, and leaned back, white-faced, on the pillows. "What I don't understand," he said, "is how you come to be here, so far from Oxford."

Alice rose and began gathering up the crockery to take out to the kitchen. "You're tired," she said. "I'll tell you another time."

The fact was, she was not at all eager to tell him. At the moment, he probably imagined her to be Lady Weston's innocent young maidservant. If he knew the truth he would despise her, as Master Barford did, and she would lose his respect.

Twenty-one

Alice took over from Hannah the task of changing the soldier's bandages each afternoon. She also made him tisanes from herbs that she gathered in the Barfords' small garden. The wounds were healing well, with no sign of infection; his appetite had improved; and he became concerned about washing and changing his linen.

"In my pack," he said, reaching awkwardly towards it, "there's a shirt, cleaner than this one."

She found it; and at his request she helped him to wash, comb his tangled hair, and put on the clean, crumpled shirt.

He smiled. "Thank you."

"You look better."

He looked more as she remembered him from Weston Hall, except that now he was bearded with a growth of untrimmed fair hair. His eyes, which had been dull, were blue and had recovered their brightness.

She felt pleased – with herself for her care; and with him for responding so well to it.

There was no longer any need for her to watch over him continuously, so she would leave him with a tankard of beer within reach, and a small pile of his belongings – books, pamphlets and letters – on the bed beside him, and go and help Hannah or play with Elen. Often when she came back she found him reading his Bible. Sometimes he asked her for news.

In those first few days after the battle the village was full of news and speculation: what people had seen, what they'd heard or witnessed in Clipston or Naseby or Marston Trussell. Those who had connections to the army reported that a great Parliamentarian victory had been gained: the king's entire army of foot was destroyed, his cavalry dispersed, hundreds killed and nearly five thousand men taken prisoner. Ammunition and cannon had been captured, and all the contents of the Royalist baggage train. It was even rumoured that a box containing the king's private correspondence had been found on one of the wagons. People who had been out soon after the battle talked of seeing bodies – heaps of them – on the field near Naseby, along the road to Sibbertoft, around the baggage train, and on across country towards Harborough.

"All along by Hellcombe they lay," Master Barford reported. "They were in retreat, those Cavaliers, but they fought every step of the way. Wadborough Hill's where the bodies lay thickest; where they made their last stand."

Alice looked out towards Wadborough, only a few miles away to the north-east. So that was where it had ended, that last great fight she'd been so terrifyingly caught up in.

"What of the king?" Hannah asked. "And the princes?"

"Fled. No doubt they'll re-form. But if you ask me, Cromwell's the man of the future."

Master Barford, as blacksmith, was well placed to gather news. He would come in for his supper and relay it first to his wife; and then, since Jeremiah Banks was now recovered enough to talk, he would spend time with him in the evening. Alice heard, from behind the closed door, their voices rising and falling, and occasional bursts of laughter.

"They'll be talking horses, if I know my man," said Hannah. "Horses and horse management, and equipment."

Alice thought the blacksmith's conversation would tire her patient, and was perversely annoyed, when she went in to check on him before retiring to bed, to find him cheerful and invigorated.

The next day, when she brought him one of her herbal drinks, she asked him about his own part in the fighting, and he told her what he remembered. He described how, on that morning, he had seen the front line of the king's army ranged along the ridge opposite – a sight of beauty, gallantry and terror: the colours rippling, the sunlight glinting on armour and weapons, the forest of pikes; how he had watched

Prince Rupert's cavalry begin to move: a trot, a canter, a gallop, a charge; how he and his comrades had raced into position to be ready to fire. He spoke of the difficult, uneven terrain, the furze bushes and rabbit holes, the confusion of battle. In the general melee he had been wounded in the shoulder, but ignored it and fought on till the Royalist foot began to surrender. Then he joined in the pursuit of the Cavaliers as they fled north. Near Sibbertoft he had been thrown from his horse by a pistol shot in the thigh.

He was innocent of the attack on the baggage train, Alice realized. Indeed, he seemed unaware that it had taken place.

"My friends found me later, close to death, and lifted me onto my horse and brought me here." He took a sip of the drink she had given him and pulled a face. "What's this?"

"Nettle tea. Drink it!" she said sternly, with a smile. She had found nettles growing near by and knew the tea would strengthen him and restore the blood. But in truth he seemed to have a strength of his own that needed little help.

She saw letters lying on the bed, and asked him about his family.

"I have a mother and two sisters," he said. "My home is in Hertford."

He showed her where the town was in his pocketbook of maps, and she leaned with him over the small, densely printed pages. The maps, with their tracery of roads and pictured hills, fascinated her, and she longed to

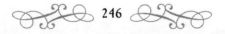

study them more, to see all the places she had travelled through, to see Wales.

"Do your sisters live at home?" she asked.

"Priscilla does. My elder sister, Phoebe, is married and has her own home at Ware. But her husband is a soldier, in the king's army—"

"The king's?" Alice was surprised.

"Yes. I believe he was at Naseby fight, though I did not encounter him – and I'm glad of that, for I like him well, though this war has torn our two households apart. He could have been taken prisoner, or even killed. I shall be relieved when I can get news of him. And I must write to my mother and Priscilla." He looked at her. "She's about your age, Priscilla. Eighteen?"

"I'm seventeen." And nothing like your sister, Alice thought. She imagined Priscilla Banks, innocent and well protected, her fair head bent over a prayer book.

"And you?" she asked. "What age are you? Are you an apprentice?" She knew that some of the Parliamentarian regiments were full of London apprentices, unruly and violent, who brought terror to the countryside. This young man was not of that sort.

But he said, "Yes, I was apprenticed to a carpenter in Willesden, and was near the end of my term, when I enlisted for Parliament. I'm twenty-three, and should have been working as a journeyman by now had it not been for this war. I never thought it would go on for so long, nor grow so bitter."

Alice admitted, "I don't know what it's all about."

He laughed, shortly. "It's about our arrogant, devious

king, and his Catholic wife; about the will of Parliament, of the people, and their right to be heard. It's about God's purpose—" He stopped. "I'm sorry. Tell me about you. You sit with me, and read, and listen to me talking about myself, but you still haven't told me how you came to be here."

Alice took a breath. "I came with the king's army," she said. "Following the baggage train." She spoke defiantly, watching his face, challenging him – and caught the slight, shocked widening of his eyes.

He was silent for so long that she thought he would not speak to her again; but he recovered himself, and said, "Then … you left the service of Lady Weston?"

"I was never in her service. I stayed at Weston Hall over the winter, when the soldiers were in their winter quarters. I was already with the army."

She found that her heart was beating fast. Why should I care? she thought. What does it matter what he thinks of me?

"Last year," she continued, "I ran away from home with a soldier. I thought he loved me, that we'd be married; but – oh, you know the old story, the one in all the ballads – he already had a wife."

He stared and was silent again. Then he sighed, whether in sympathy or despair at her wickedness she could not tell. "He abandoned you?"

"Yes. But my friends in the train – the wives of Welsh pikemen – did not. I stayed with them, and we came here, to this battleground…" She had begun to tremble. "Captain Banks, do you know what your righteous,

248

hymn-singing, God-fearing comrades did to the women in the baggage train?"

He said faintly, as if he did not want to hear, "What did they do?" And when she told him, he groaned and pulled back as if he had been struck. "Your friends…?"

"All dead. But I escaped. And I saved Elen." She left him and went out to the kitchen, and lifted the baby from her basket and carried her into the parlour.

Now he was astonished and confused. "You have a child!"

"She's not mine. Her mother – my friend – was murdered. I came to this house to find a wet nurse."

"Mistress Barford. Of course… But what will you do now? Will you stay in this village?"

"Oh, no." She would not stay here, where her friends had died, and where she would probably always be known as the Cavaliers' whore. "I'll go back to Weston Hall. I believe they will give me work as a maidservant."

"And the baby?"

"I'll take her with me."

"You can't travel so far alone, with a baby!"

"We must trust in God to care for us."

Twenty-two

The next time she saw him he was standing up. His teeth were clenched, and the bandage on his thigh, below the rolled-up edge of his breeches, was stained with fresh blood. He limped forward – and grabbed at the windowsill for support.

"What are you doing?"

She rushed to his side, put an arm about his waist and tried to lead him back towards the bed. It was the first time she had seen him on his feet since their encounter at Weston Hall. He was of middle height, strongly built, with a determined vigour about him that had probably saved his life.

"No!" he exclaimed. "I won't lie down there again." But he rested his arm on her shoulder and allowed himself to be lowered onto the stool, where he sat scowling with impatience. "I want to move," he said. "I want to look out – to open the window."

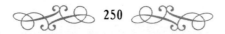

"You have made the wound bleed again." She frowned, wishing she had more knowledge. "Perhaps it should have been stitched. I must ask Hannah—"

"Not now!" He caught her arm. "Open the window – please? Let me see where I am."

"I suppose it can do no harm." She crossed the room and pushed open the window.

Warm summer air flowed in, and a scent of hay, wonderfully fragrant after the foul air of the sickroom. The view was of rough pasture and distant wooded hills. Over to the right was the road where the baggage wagons had halted. She saw, with relief, that the few remaining wagons had been removed. But somewhere near by must be the burial pit.

He was on his feet again, limping towards her.

"Oh!" she cried, exasperated.

"I want to see! That's the Clipston road, isn't it? So Naseby must be over there, to the right…"

"You're not thinking of leaving? Not yet?" She spoke lightly, for of course she had no reason to hold him back. She had always known he would leave, that both of them would go their different ways. But now, suddenly, it was upon them, and she realized how afraid she was of the long, lonely journey she herself must soon make. For the moment, the two of them were together in a place where both their lives seemed suspended in time. She was not yet prepared for change.

But he was restless.

"I must leave as soon as I can." He gazed out, drinking in the long view like a caged bird on the brink of freedom.

 251

"Where will you go?"

"I don't know. I'll need to find my regiment."

Alice looked again at the bloodstained bandage. "You'll travel nowhere yet," she said. "*Please* sit down."

"Bring the stool, then. I'll sit here. The air won't hurt me."

Alice wasn't sure about that, but she brought the stool and he sat obediently.

"How big is this village?" he asked.

"Middling."

"Do they get newsbooks here, from London?"

"I don't know."

Alice had not been out much, no further than the yard and garden or field edge, helping Hannah around the forge. The nightmares still troubled her, and since she had found shelter here she had become afraid to venture out. And yet, she thought, I must prepare myself for leaving. The Barfords will have no need of me here once this man is on his feet and his wounds healed.

"I'll ask Master Barford," she said. "Most likely the inn has them, or the parsonage."

Later, in the kitchen, Hannah asked, "How is he?"

"Up and bothersome and asking for newsbooks."

"Oh! He's on the mend, then."

"Yes. But, Hannah, he's moving about, and that thigh wound is bleeding again."

They looked at it in the afternoon.

The place where the pistol ball had entered was an ugly, purplish area, surrounded by dark red bruising.

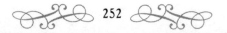

There was a trickle of fresh blood, but it was slowing now that he lay still.

"There's no pus," said Hannah. "That's good."

The two of them discussed what to do. Wash it? Smear on comfrey ointment? Try to stitch it? Send to Harborough for a doctor?

"No," said their patient. "None of those. Let it be. It will heal of itself."

Alice guessed he was right. "But only if you rest," she said.

She and Hannah re-bandaged the wound in clean linen, and then attended to the shoulder injury. Alice looked at his exposed shoulder and upper arm, and remembered the weight of that arm on her own shoulder when he had limped across the room. She caught his eye and immediately glanced away. She wondered what he thought of her. She had shocked him with her revelation about how she came to be here. He treated her with the same courtesy as before and always seemed glad of her company – but a godly young man of his sort must surely despise her now?

"We'll move him out of that sickroom," said Hannah.

Jeremiah was now allowed to spend his days in the kitchen, on condition that he did not attempt to walk about too much. He sat by the fireside, writing letters, or reading his Bible, or studying the pocketbook of maps that he had shown to Alice. He told them he had bought the book earlier that year, and he seemed very taken with it. Hannah trimmed his beard for him, and lent him

253

a clean shirt of her husband's while they washed both of his. He ate with the family, and grew stronger, "and a better colour", Hannah said approvingly.

She found some old, softened linen and gave it to Alice to make gowns for Elen, ready for the time when she was no longer in swaddling bands. "You could start freeing her arms already," she said.

She helped Alice to cut out simple shapes for the garments, and Alice sewed with fine small stitches. It was the kind of work she enjoyed, and she was especially happy to be doing it for Elen since she could not give the baby a mother's milk.

"When I've finished the gowns," she told Hannah, "I must leave you." The armies were gone, and Jeremiah would soon be on his way. "It's summer," she said. "There won't be a better time to travel."

"You'll take Elen?"

"Of course!"

"You'll have to find wet nurses along the road, and another when you reach that house near Oxford. You know, Alice, I fear for the little one. I've spoken to my husband about this, and he's agreed that if you can pay me the money in advance you could leave her with me until she's weaned. Come back for her next year if you want to keep her; or, if you don't, we could take her to the orphanage at Northampton. What do you think?"

"No!" Alice's response was immediate. "No, not the orphanage. Thank you, I am grateful, but…"

She remembered kneeling beside Nia's body, holding the baby and promising, "I'll keep her and take care of

her." She *couldn't* leave her. And yet, she asked herself, wouldn't it be more caring to leave Elen here? But it was a long way to Copsey, and there was no knowing what might prevent her from returning, or prevent Hannah from looking after the baby. Elen could end up in the orphanage in spite of everything.

Above all, there was Alice's instinctive feeling.

"I can't bear to be parted from her!" she said. "I can't do it!" And tears sprang to her eyes.

"There now," said Hannah, "no need to cry. You must do as you will. And I can help you. I'll show you how to make pap for her, in case you can't find a wet nurse. You steep barley bread in water and then boil it in milk. It makes an excellent substitute. You can take some with you and perhaps make more along the way."

Alice began to feel calmer. "Thank you," she said. "I'd be glad to learn."

Jeremiah Banks had been writing while this exchange took place. He said nothing at the time, but later, when Hannah had taken Prudence out to help her feed the hens, he said, "Mistress Alice, I must leave soon, like you. We could travel together. I could accompany you as far as Weston Hall and then go on from there to find my regiment. What do you think?"

Alice felt as if a huge burden had been lifted from her. She had been so afraid of travelling alone. The baby's welfare – her very survival – was an immense responsibility, and she knew she would need to travel as quickly as possible, and to ask for help and accept rides from people who might not be trustworthy. She feared

the many soldiers and ruffians now at large on the roads; the assumptions that would be made about her as a lone woman; the risks of robbery and rape. Jeremiah's presence would protect her from all that. And to go with him, to stay with him a little longer, to have more time with him… That, too, she realized, was what she wanted.

But… "Is Weston Hall on your way?" she asked.

"I think so. The word is that the army is heading west now, to relieve Taunton."

"But I fear I will be a burden to you – slow you down."

"It is no matter to me. I'd be more worried to think of you alone on the roads."

"But Elen—"

"Elen comes too."

"But—"

"No more buts!" he exclaimed. "I have a horse. I'll see if I can hire one for you. Can you ride?"

"Only a market horse – an old, steady creature."

"I'll find you a placid one. It will save many hours if we ride, and that will be safer for the baby. We could be there in three days. So, will you travel with me?"

She looked at him, met his concerned, serious gaze. "Yes. I will. Thank you."

The quietness of her response belied her feelings. She wanted to go with him, and it was not only because she was afraid of travelling alone. He was going out of his way for her, and it was a generous gesture – so generous that she wondered if he too had mixed motives; if, in spite of everything, he might be as reluctant to part as she was.

Twenty-three

"*If* I go anywhere these days," the widow said, "I go astride, like a man." She laughed, showing gappy teeth.

She had brought out the pillion, covered in dirt and cobwebs, from the back of a shed: a wooden frame with a padded leather seat, and a footrest hanging from one side. She brushed grit and mouse droppings from the seat. "It'll clean up, good as new."

And it would be cheaper and easier than hiring a second horse, Alice knew. Horses were hard to come by, with the armies needing a constant supply; and Jeremiah Banks, hearing that a neighbour in Sibbertoft had a pillion she might sell, had taken Alice to see it. Alice had never ridden pillion before, though she had seen wives travelling that way with their husbands.

Jeremiah looked it over. "It'll fix on securely," he said. "And if you carry the child in a sling..."

The widow winked at Alice. "Oh, you'll be safe

enough, lass, as long as you grab on tight to your man!"

Alice avoided meeting Jeremiah's eye. She knew the woman must have her own ideas about their relationship: the Parliamentarian dragoon and the leaguer whore from the king's defeated army. Even though she had scarcely stepped out of doors since her arrival, gossip about her would have been all around the village, and no one would have had much good to say of her. Well, she needn't care; she'd be away from here for ever tomorrow morning.

Jeremiah paid three shillings for the pillion. Alice wanted to say, "I'll pay," but thought he might be offended. She had paid Hannah for the wet-nursing; and Jeremiah, his injuries healed, had paid the couple for their care of him and his horse. Everything was settled now for the journey. Hannah had helped Alice construct a sling for Elen out of strong unbleached linen so that the baby could be carried close to her body while they were riding. She had also found her a piece of oiled canvas to put over herself and Elen if it rained.

Next morning, when all was ready, Jeremiah and Alice both thanked the Barfords for their care. Alice felt sad parting from Hannah, who had been so kind and generous to her. They hugged each other, and Hannah said, "God go with you, and the child."

Then Jeremiah mounted his horse, and Master Barford helped Alice up into the pillion seat behind him. The pillion was awkward, for she had to sit as if on a side saddle with her legs twisted away from her body. She clung tightly, as the old woman had advised,

to Jeremiah's buff coat, the baby pressed between them – Alice having decided that despite this inconvenience she would prefer to have Elen where she could see her, rather than on her back.

They took the road to Naseby, which meant passing the place where the women had been killed. Alice had walked out there the evening before, to the field where she had once felt she could never bear to go again. She had knelt on the trampled ground and prayed for the souls of Nia, Bronwen and Rhian, and all the women who had died there. Now she was glad to be riding quickly past and on, across the battlefield, to the village of Naseby, and beyond.

Elen had been grizzling when they left the forge, but the jogging movement of the horse and her closeness to Alice soothed her, and she soon fell asleep. Jeremiah called back, "Are you comfortable there?" and Alice said, "Yes," though she was not. But no travel was ever comfortable, and riding was better than most, and quicker. Gradually Alice settled into the rhythm, and watched the countryside in all its midsummer sweetness unfold on either side. She did not know where they were, and was gladder than ever that she was travelling with someone who did, and need not be constantly asking the way and begging lifts from strangers.

The day was a Thursday, and in several of the villages they passed through it was market day. The roads were busy with country people: farmers' wives on horseback with panniers of goods, carters driving wagons, a few lone travellers walking. Sometimes there were groups

of soldiers from one side or the other. Jeremiah told Alice that some of those from the New Model Army were probably rounding up deserters. There would be thousands of deserters after such a victory, he said, laden with loot from the king's wagons. He had no wish to encounter even his own people on this journey, and if he caught sight of them in time he turned his horse aside down a lane to avoid confrontation.

But on one occasion they could not avoid being stopped by a Parliamentarian patrol. Jeremiah told them he had been wounded at Naseby and had since been given leave to take his wife and child to her parents' home near Oxford before rejoining his regiment.

After they had gone he laughed in relief, and said, "God forgive me for lying! But I must have done it well. I was afraid they'd ask to see my pass."

"Are you absent without permission?"

"I was left for dead, so need no permission! But it's always dangerous to be on the roads alone. I could be hanged as a spy or a deserter before they finish questioning me."

At midday he brought them to a meadow at the edge of a little wood. A stream flowed through it, and there was a fallen log on which they could sit and eat. He helped Alice down and led the horse to the stream to drink. Alice untied the sling and laid Elen on the canvas rain cover. Freed of her burden, she stood and stretched.

Jeremiah smiled at her. "How do you feel?"

"Bent sideways! But I don't complain," she added

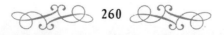

hastily. "Do your wounds trouble you?"

"Not much."

Alice sat down with the baby. Under Hannah's direction she had made pap for the journey, and now she tried to persuade Elen to suck it from the pewter bottle. Elen cried. She didn't like the bottle, and instead Alice dipped her finger in the stuff and let the baby suck from that. It wasn't much, but she hoped it might keep her contented until they could find another wet nurse.

When she had finished, and laid the child down, Jeremiah came and sat beside her and they ate the bread and cheese Hannah had packed for them. It was a pleasant place they had found, the meadow full of clover and buttercups, the stream glinting with sparkles of sunlight. Alice glanced sidelong at Jeremiah, at his profile, his hands, the line of fair stubble along his jaw. She found herself wanting to reach out and take his hand. In the sickroom at Sibbertoft she had touched him often, and without shame, and had been so close to him for so long that she had felt as if she knew him. But he had been in her power then; now he was free.

He caught her gaze on him and she looked quickly away. Near by, his horse cropped grass with a soft tearing sound.

"Does he have a name?" she asked.

"The horse? No. I don't give them names any more. My last two were shot under me."

She felt the weight of sadness and danger behind this remark. "You were fighting in the north?" she asked.

"Yes, and then Oxford, and up to Naseby. But you're

as likely to be killed in a skirmish – running into an enemy patrol on the road – as in a battle. I lost a friend – a good friend – in just such an exchange of fire outside an inn. So sudden they came on us! And nothing lost or gained by it. Except a man's life." He began packing things away. "We'd best ride hard while we can, and stop early this evening. It may take some time to find a wet nurse. Besides, you'll be tired. You're not used to riding."

Alice nodded agreement. Elen probably hadn't taken much. The sooner they found a wet nurse the better. She lifted the baby and asked Jeremiah to help her fasten the sling in place.

He tied the knots, and paused with his hands on her shoulders. "What was her name," he asked, "the baby's mother?"

"Nia," said Alice. She felt intensely aware of his hands.

He checked that the sling was secure, and said, "She had a loyal friend in you."

Then he helped her onto the pillion and swung up in front of her. His back, in the thick hide coat, was broad and protective, like a bastion.

They stopped only once in the afternoon, to buy a London newsbook from a pedlar. Jeremiah pushed it into his snapsack to read later, and rode on, anxious to cover as many miles as possible.

That evening they were lucky to find an inn where the landlord's wife had recently had a child. She was shocked to see how young Elen was, and travelling

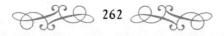

without mother or nurse. Alice explained to her that they were going only as far as Oxfordshire, and left Jeremiah to arrange food and beds for the night with the landlord. While they were talking, a noisy throng of soldiers came in, calling for beer and spreading themselves around, to the annoyance of other customers. Alice felt their eyes on her. She handed over the fretful baby to the woman and was glad to follow Jeremiah and the landlord, who led the way upstairs.

The landlord explained that the room was close to that of himself and his wife – "Just a step across this landing if you need to bring the baby to her in the night." He pushed open the door to reveal a simple room with a washstand, a small table, two chairs, and only one bed. "You'll want to eat in your chamber, I expect," he said. "Those soldiers look like trouble. I'll bring yours first. We have a mutton stew, and some pies and fresh bread…"

He left – and the two of them looked at the bed.

"I'm sorry," said Jeremiah. He had reddened. "I was anxious to be settled, to get you away from the soldiers, and of course the landlord assumed…" He seemed suddenly younger, wrong-footed and unsure of himself. "I don't know whether they have another room – or perhaps a loft, or barn; I could sleep there—"

"Captain Banks—" began Alice.

"Sergeant," he corrected her. "But please – call me Jem."

Jem. It sounded too familiar, especially in the intimacy of this private room. She spoke it quickly and

rushed on. "Jem, I would rather you stayed here with me. I'd feel safer if we were in the same room." She added awkwardly, "I would not have come away with you if I did not trust you."

He looked relieved, but still concerned. "I'll sleep on the floor—"

"No…"

"Alice – may I call you Alice? – I have my blanket and coat. I've slept in open fields in winter."

"And I've slept in barns, surrounded by soldiers."

He appeared shocked for a moment, then laughed.

He threw down his snapsack and took off the buff coat, and looked around. "The room will do well enough. And perhaps you are right: we may both be safer together."

A serving woman arrived with food and drink and set it on the table for them. He regarded it gratefully. "Let's eat."

While they were eating, another maid brought Elen back. "Fed and winded, but she wasn't happy, mistress says: cried a lot. They don't like change, do they?" She regarded the two of them curiously. "Her mother died, I suppose?"

"Yes."

After she had gone, Jeremiah said, "We had better think of a story. We are husband and wife—"

"And she is our niece – my dead sister's child."

"And I have permission to take the two of you to a place of safety – to your parents' home near Oxford. Only you had better leave the talking to me. You don't

sound like an Oxfordshire girl."

Alice rocked the baby in her arms until she fell asleep, then laid her down gently on the bed. Jeremiah watched her and said, "My sister Phoebe has a new baby. I have not seen him yet." He smiled. "They all look much the same to me."

"But not to their mothers! You are lucky to have a family – sisters, a mother – living."

"Yes, I am." She felt his concerned gaze on her. "Do you have no wish to go home? To your uncle's farm?"

"The farm was never a home."

She told him about her childhood in Bideford, and the shock of her removal to Dartmoor. He listened attentively, and she found she could even tell him about her uncle's behaviour towards her. But both of them avoided the subject of Robin, and she could not bring herself to mention the baby she had lost.

His own home life had been happier than hers, his parents strict but kind. "Much Bible-reading and soul-searching," he said. "They taught us to avoid luxury and, most of all, indolence. We worked hard. My father was a tailor. He was at work till the day he died. And he set me up with my apprenticeship."

"Will you go back to that, when the war is over?"

"I hope so. I write to my master regularly. He understood that I wanted to join the army; said he would have joined himself if he'd been younger. We were all of us fired up for the defence of London. We helped dig the trenches around the city walls, and cheered when the trained bands defeated the Cavalier army at Turnham

Green. All the apprentices were joining up."

Elen woke and cried while they were talking, and Alice walked about the room with her, singing a Welsh lullaby she had learnt from Nia. Jeremiah reached into his pack and took out the newsbook he had bought earlier, on the road. He sat reading it, but Alice was aware that he was distracted by her – as she was by him.

When the baby had settled she put her down again and went to lean on the back of Jeremiah's chair. "Is there news of that fight at Naseby?" she asked.

"Yes." He looked guarded, though she could not think why. "It tells how the king's army was utterly routed, most of his infantry taken prisoner, at least four thousand of them, and many of his horse. Ordnance too." He read out:

> "...there was many of the Wagons laden with rich plunder, and others with Arms and Ammunition, about 50 loads of Muskets, Pikes, Powder, Match and Bullets, abundance of Trunks, which the Souldiers soone emptied...

"And so on."

He went to close the page, but she caught it and said, "No! Wait! Let me see. There's more."

"No more—"

"There is! Let me see."

He gave it up reluctantly. "Don't read this, Alice. Please."

"Why not?"

She felt more than ever determined, and read, following the print with her finger:

> ...which the Souldiers soone emptied, as they did the Waggons that carried the middle sort of Ammunition Whoores ... full of money and rich apparell, there being at least 1500 of that tribe, the gentler sort in Coaches ... and the common rabble of common vermin on foot, 500 of them at least being taken and kept within guard, until order was taken to dispose of them ... many of these were Irish women, of cruel countenances, some of them were cut by our Souldiers when they tooke them...

The common rabble. Common vermin. Dispose of them. It made them sound like rats. The scene came back to her in all its horror: the screaming women cut down around her, wives, mothers, lovers, whores – brave, hardy, defenceless women, all of them. The common vermin.

In her fury she crumpled the newsbook and threw it on the floor.

Jeremiah stood up. "Alice…"

"How dare they call them vermin?" she exploded. "They were my friends – good women, good to me. They came with the army to be with their men, to cook and care for them; to suffer with them, if need be; but not to die like that, stripped and thrown into a pit, and then – then to be counted as naught, called vermin…"

"Hush! Hush, Alice!" His arms went around her, and she realized she was shouting and tears were rolling down her face, and that Elen had woken again and begun to cry.

He pressed her face against his shoulder. "I told you not to read it."

"Who writes these evil things?" she asked, her voice muffled by his shirt.

"A gentleman wrote this, one who supports Parliament, and who reported what happened." He let go of her and said gently, "You'd better quieten the child. Don't get us thrown out."

She lifted up Elen and paced back and forth with her.

"The week before the fight," Jeremiah said, "there was a rumour going around among our men that a thousand Irishwomen followed the king's army, armed with long knives. I think the soldiers believed they had come upon these women and must wipe them out."

"Some of the women *were* Irish," said Alice. "That was no reason to kill them."

"But you know how people feel about the Irish, how they fear them, since the massacres of the settlers over there. These old hatreds build up. Oh, I don't seek to make excuses for them... And I hope the killers will be punished – though I fear they will not."

Elen had stopped crying as soon as Alice picked her up and began walking with her again. Jeremiah watched them. "Will you try to find her father?" he asked.

Alice was startled. "He must surely be dead? Master Barford said the bodies lay in heaps on the field."

"But it says there" – he indicated the crumpled pamphlet on the floor – "that most of the foot surrendered and were taken prisoner. It's more likely that he was one of them."

"So I might find him? What will happen to the prisoners?"

"They'll have been taken to London and paraded through the streets. As for the future, most may be persuaded to change sides. Others will remain in prison. If you tell me his name and company, I may be able to find out for you."

"He was in Sir John Agnew's regiment, but I knew him only as Bryn." Alice realized then that she was faced with a great gulf of ignorance about her Welsh friends. She had no surname for any of them. Nor could she remember ever being told the name of their village in Wales.

If Bryn is alive, she thought, he'll get to hear about what happened to the women. How will he ever bear it?

"I should try and find him," she said, "to tell him his daughter is alive – that he hasn't lost everything."

"It won't be easy, without a name."

Jeremiah got out his blanket and prepared to sleep on the floor, leaving the bed to Alice and the baby. She saw that his wounds were paining him, but he made no complaint. Despite having slept in barns and outhouses full of other people, Alice felt strangely shy in this small room. Jeremiah had stripped to shirt and breeches and rolled himself up in his blanket, turning away from her.

She changed Elen's wet linen, then took off her gown and stays and got into the bed in her shift with the baby beside her. She kept a small candle alight in a dish near by.

Elen woke, hungry, in the night, and Alice scooped her up quickly and carried her out onto the landing and knocked on the couple's door. To her relief the woman came at once and took the baby from her.

"My own little one is wakeful," she whispered. "I wasn't asleep. Go back. I'll bring her to you."

But when Elen returned she would not settle. She cried and fretted, and Alice walked up and down with her, shushing and murmuring. Elen's eyelids drooped, but as soon as Alice laid her down she began crying again.

Jeremiah woke and sat up. "Is she sick?"

"No." Alice sank down wearily on the bed. "I think she is missing Hannah." I should have left her with Hannah, she thought, guiltily. She's not happy. And I don't know who I will find for her at Copsey.

"Don't get cold." He took a blanket and wrapped it around her shoulders, and sat down next to her.

All that could be seen of the swaddled baby was a red furious face, contorted with misery. Alice jogged her. "Shh, shh…" She hoped no one was in a room near by.

"I suppose they improve as they get older," he said.

Alice laughed and yawned at the same time. "Oh, I hope so!"

"Alice, if you can't find her father, or you find that he is dead, what will you do? Will you give her to an

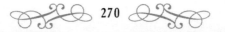

orphanage, as Mistress Barford suggested?"

"No." Alice held the baby against her heart. Elen's cries had subsided. Her eyes closed again, and the lashes lay wet and dark on her cheeks. "No. I couldn't do that. I'll keep her myself."

"People will think she is your bastard."

Alice lifted her head and looked him in the eye. "I may not have a bastard child," she said, "but I should have done. So if people think ill of me, they have good reason." And she told him, then, about the child she had lost after Robin left her at Copsey.

His expression, in the guttering candlelight, was unreadable. Now, she thought, he will condemn me; for it was common knowledge that a woman could only conceive if she was willing and eager, and the thought of her that way with Robin would surely disgust him.

But Jeremiah simply said, "He was a base man, and unworthy of you."

Twenty-four

$\mathcal{B}oth$ Alice and Jeremiah were tired the next morning. Elen had kept them awake much of the night, but now, as they came down to pay for their lodging and the wet-nursing, she lay deeply asleep, well fed and peaceful. The innkeeper's wife had given Alice fresh pap for the journey, but Alice guessed Elen would not like it. The longer she sleeps now, the better, she thought.

The day was misty, with a fine drizzle that was wetter than it looked; coming from the south-west, it drove relentlessly into their faces as they rode. Alice, with the canvas tied around herself and Elen, kept her gaze on Jeremiah's back and ignored the passing countryside. They did not talk much, for it was difficult to hear each other's voices against the hoof beats, the creaking of the pillion and the hiss of rain.

Alice was dozing when the sound of a musket shot jolted her into wakefulness. The horse reared

and half turned, unsteadying her, and she clung, terrified, to Jeremiah as men burst from the bushes: wild, desperate-looking men, armed with muskets and swords.

Jeremiah shouted, "Alice! Hold on!" He drew his sword, dug in his spurs and charged straight at their attackers. Alice screamed as she was hurled backwards. The pillion jolted and bounced, and she feared she would slide sideways off the galloping horse.

It lasted only a moment. The men scattered. Jeremiah reined in the horse, throwing Alice forward again. He leaped down, raised his musket and fired one shot. She heard a shout, but no one fell. There were three men, all ragged, two of them barefoot. They threw themselves down out of sight behind some ramshackle farm buildings.

Jeremiah lowered his musket and turned to Alice. "Is the pillion secure?"

"Yes."

"Good. Hold fast."

He mounted again and they rode hard for a mile or more, till they came to an inn on the outskirts of a village. There, at last, he reined in the horse, dismounted, and reached to help Alice down.

He was breathing heavily. "The baby?"

"She's safe. She cried at first." Her own voice was shaking. "She was not as frightened as I was."

"I know. I'm sorry." He looked contrite. "I had to act instantly. A charge on horseback always terrifies the enemy. They could have shot me, but their instinct was to run. I gambled on that. If I'd shown any hesitation

they would have been all around us, like wolves."

"They looked as desperate as wolves – so ragged and gaunt."

"They were deserters – from the king's army, I'd guess, though it's hard to tell. Those who don't get home often turn robber."

"Your musket... You fired so quickly!" She remembered Robin's musket drill, the slow-burning match.

"It's a flintlock. A good weapon." There was pride in his voice. "London-made."

He led the horse to the stable yard, and they went into the inn and bought beer and a dish of beef and onions with bread.

"Those deserters must be starving," said Alice.

"Don't waste any pity on them. If they'd caught us they would have killed and stripped us and taken all our goods."

Alice shuddered at the thought of what could so easily have been their fate.

"They should be hunted down and hanged," Jeremiah said; and later she heard him giving the landlord information about where they had been attacked and where the robbers had their hideout.

The incident had made it a sombre day, and in the late afternoon their attempts to find a wet nurse were unsuccessful. The sun was low in the sky and Elen was crying with hunger when at last they were directed to a cottage where the daughter had recently given birth to a bastard child and would no doubt be glad of the money.

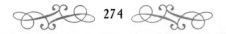

The cottage was well kept enough, but the disgraced daughter was a surly, slatternly girl who looked as if she would like to murder both infants. Her mother, after securing payment in advance, offered Alice and Jeremiah a low-ceilinged attic room with straw to sleep on, and a box to use as a cradle.

Alice had already handed the frantic Elen to the girl for feeding.

"I don't like it," she said to Jeremiah when the woman had gone. "The girl is dirty and vicious-looking, and everyone knows a mother's nature goes into her milk and passes to the baby."

"Not in one night, surely," he said. "This one night the girl may save her from starvation."

"I suppose so. But I wish – oh, I don't know! I hope all will be well when we reach Weston Hall. I'll need to find someone permanent in Copsey. A good, motherly woman."

"Your friends will help you. And if we set off early tomorrow we should arrive in good time."

"Where are we now?"

"Just north of Oxford." He rummaged for his book of maps, and found the page. "It's not marked, but about here, I think."

She smiled. "You get much pleasure as well as instruction from that book."

"I do."

"I too had a book I loved: a book of herbs and remedies that my father wrote over the years. It was the only thing of his I owned."

"And you lost it?"

"Yes. After the battle. It was in my pack, on the wagon. I lost my best gown too – a fine blue wool that Mistress Christian gave me."

"I remember it," he said.

"But – how?"

"You were wearing it when I led my men to Weston Hall."

She looked at him in surprise. She'd had no idea he had taken so much note of her that day, but the realization pleased her.

"No doubt you thought me a bold, uncivil girl," she said, "despite my fine gown."

He regarded her gravely. "I thought you bold, yes – valiant – in defence of your lady. I admired you."

"Admired me?"

She wanted him to say more, but they were interrupted by the girl shouting from below that Alice could fetch Elen now. She left him and went down, then carefully carried the almost-sleeping baby back up the ladder to the loft.

Jeremiah had made himself a bed in the straw and was already lying down. He had left his blanket for Alice. She was so tired that she slept in her clothes, not even bothering to remove her stays. And Elen, despite Alice's disapproval of the slatternly girl, slept until the early hours of the morning, when she woke Alice with a resounding wail.

In the grey light before dawn Alice took the child down again. The girl lay snoring – like a sow, Alice

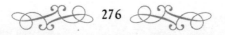

thought crossly – and had to be prodded and pushed into wakefulness. She stayed and watched the girl in case she fell asleep and left Elen hungry. Back in the loft, she removed the baby's wrappings. Elen was dirty and sore, and the woman had not left them any water for washing. Alice took a linen cloth and used some of the beer from her leather flask to clean the baby. By the time she began swaddling her again Elen was thoroughly awake and crying. Alice rocked her in her arms, her own head drooping with tiredness, and longed for some relief from the burden she had taken on.

At last she put the child down, asleep. By now it was light, and birds were rustling and twittering in the thatch. She crawled under her blanket, and looked across at Jeremiah, who had not stirred throughout. He lay facing her, breathing steadily, his face defenceless in sleep. They were so close that their breath mingled.

I want to kiss him, she thought. I'd like to wake him with a kiss.

But she lay still. And soon he opened his eyes and looked into hers, and she saw the realization of where he was come back to him.

"Alice," he said, and smiled.

"I was watching you sleep."

Could he see from her face what she had been thinking? Did he have the same wish? For a moment she thought he did – but then he drew away and sat up, saying, "How is the child? Has that surly wench's milk turned her into a monster?"

"Don't tease me!"

"Why not? I always tease my sisters."

"I'm not your sister."

"No," he said. "You are not."

He rose quickly, and began gathering up his possessions. "No water for washing." He looked around, disgruntled.

"I washed Elen's bottom with beer."

He started to laugh. "You did what?"

"Well, there was nothing else to hand! It was only small beer…"

That made him laugh more. "A waste of good beer!" he said, and ducked his head under the low ceiling and went downstairs to ask for water. When it came, he told her, "You wash first. I'll use your water." He grinned and jerked his head towards Elen. "*She* goes last!"

Alice giggled. "I won't be changing her again. Not till we get to Weston Hall."

At the thought of Weston Hall her light-hearted mood left her. She'd wanted to go back there; it had seemed almost like home to her. But now it meant parting from Jem. He had deliberately turned his back and was reading his Bible. She washed briefly, splashing her face, then untied the neck ribbon of her shift to reach a bit further. Anything more could wait till their journey was over.

They were out early, Elen asleep in the sling, rocked by the now familiar movement. It was a clear day, and these were roads Jeremiah knew. In the afternoon they found themselves on the road from Oxford to Faringdon, and

then Alice saw the inn – the King's Arms at Copsey – and the turning that led through the woods to Weston Hall.

She felt a sudden misgiving. Would they have her back? As before, she was arriving uninvited, in need of help. And what would they think of her bringing with her the man who had caused them so much pain in the spring?

The woods were in full leaf now, the violets gone, and in their place the verges were thick with elderflower and wild roses. In the distance she glimpsed the warm golden stone of the house. A peaceful scene – but as they approached she heard the unmistakable sound of a musket being cocked.

Oh God! she thought. The house is taken! And fear washed through her.

Jeremiah dismounted and raised his hands as a man stepped out of the tree cover with his weapon at the ready. Another appeared behind him.

"I come as a friend – alone," said Jeremiah.

The musket shook in the defender's hands. Alice saw then that he was Tobias Fairthorne, and the other was Tom Pether.

"Tobias! It's me, Alice!" she cried, and at the same moment, Tom recognized her and called out her name.

They both lowered their weapons, though they watched Jeremiah nervously.

"I am here only as escort," he said, and with their permission he reached up and lifted Alice down. "Tell your mistress I have brought Alice Newcombe back."

* * *

Elen absorbed all the attention at first. Anne Florey was sent running to the home farm to fetch a woman they knew of who would be able to feed her. Mistress Florey brought a soft woollen shawl and prepared a makeshift cradle. Bess asked, "May I hold her?" And Alice was only too willing to surrender Elen for a while to the care of others.

Christian came in from the dairy, wiping her hands on her apron. She looked more like a maidservant than a lady. At sight of her Alice was suddenly overwhelmed with emotion. "Oh, Mistress Christian!" she exclaimed. "I'm so glad to see you!"

And Christian, looking equally shaken, seized Alice's hands. "We heard such news of the king's defeat at Naseby, and the women killed! And I feared—" She stopped and stared at Jeremiah, and Alice wondered whether she recognized him.

"Sergeant Banks brought me here," she said, "with my friend's child. I had nowhere else to go. I'd like – oh, I hope! – to come back and work for you, if Lady Weston agrees. Will you have me, Mistress Christian? I need to find work, to pay for the care of Nia's baby."

"Your friend is dead?"

"Yes. Killed in the field by the Parliament troops."

"Oh, Alice, I'm sorry. It was a wicked deed. We read about it in the newsbooks." She turned to Jeremiah. "Nevertheless I must thank you, Sergeant Banks, for bringing Alice back to us. Mistress Florey, give the travellers some food; and Tom, see that the sergeant's horse is fed and groomed. I'll go and tell Lady Weston."

Alice and Jeremiah were given bread, cheese, cold venison and beer, and they sat at the kitchen table eating while everyone else ran around after the baby and marvelled at her survival. Jeremiah was hungry, and at first he concentrated on the food. Afterwards it seemed to Alice that he could not make up his mind what to say or do. He would look at her, and then away, then back at her again. And Alice, who did not want to part from him, could think of nothing to say either. She could see that the servants were wary of him – this Parliamentarian dragoon, an enemy, in their midst – and she saw them casting glances at the two of them and knew everyone was wondering what their relationship might be. Embarrassed by their scrutiny, she gazed around the kitchen and saw signs of damage she had not noticed at first: initials gouged into the big work table, a broken chair, the rim of the bread crock chipped and a great crack running down its length.

She was relieved when Christian returned, looking pleased.

"Lady Weston will speak to you later, Alice. She is much reduced in spirits these days. The war has dealt her cruel blows. But she bade me tell you that you are welcome to stay if you will turn your hand to whatever work is needed."

"I will, indeed," Alice promised.

The woman from the farm arrived soon after to feed the baby; and at the same moment, Jeremiah rose and thanked Mistress Florey for the food and said he must be on his way.

"I'll go and see to my horse," he said.

Alice jumped up. It was so sudden, this parting! She was not ready for it. She stammered, "Oh! I must thank you, sir ... my gratitude for all your help..." Her words sounded to her ridiculously formal. They could not express what she felt.

But Jeremiah replied equally formally that he was glad all had turned out well. He left for the stables; and Alice was obliged to greet the woman, who was a dairymaid at the farm and had lost a child, and who settled down at once to feed Elen. Alice talked to the dairymaid for a while, but her mind was all on Jeremiah. Would he wait for her? How long would it take him to saddle up?

As soon as she could, she excused herself and left. She ran to the stables, desperate with anxiety that he might be gone already. But he was still there, talking to old Tobias, who withdrew at sight of her.

She saw Jeremiah's face light up, and felt her heart leap in response. So he *did* want to see her; she had not been too bold in running after him.

But she stopped short. "Jem! I..." She could not say what she felt.

And he said nothing, but stepped forward and took her in his arms and kissed her. She kissed him back, and felt his arms grip tighter and hold her hard against him. They clung together. His stubbly beard scratched her face, and a buckle on some strap he wore pressed painfully against her chest, but she didn't care. She would not let go, because she knew that when she did he would ride away from this place and she might never see him again.

"I was afraid you wouldn't come out," he said at last. "I couldn't talk to you in there, with all those people. You'll be safe here, won't you? It's what you wanted?"

"I'll be safe. But you? Will you go to Taunton now?"

He nodded. "I'll head that way, and see what news I can find."

"Oh, Jem, take care!" The thought of him travelling alone filled her with dread. She remembered the deserters they had met on the road. The war was everywhere: any hedge might hide an ambush; any village might hold angry inhabitants looking for a scapegoat. A lone soldier was always at risk.

"Don't fear," he said. "I'll write to you when I can. And I'll come back, I promise, if … if I may?"

"Of course you may!" she said. She saw the relief in his eyes.

"You know my regiment and company, don't you? And you know my mother lives in Hertford, in Fore Street. Send word to me if you should move away from here, if anything should happen. Alice" – his voice cracked – "don't let me lose you."

She nodded, unable to speak.

They hugged each other hard, and kissed again; and then he mounted his horse, and she stood and watched him ride down the road until he was gone from her sight.

Twenty-five

"Has this child been baptized?" asked Lady Weston.

And when Alice said no, Elen had not, she insisted that it be done that very week.

Alice wondered what Nia's wish would have been. Many people were against infant baptism. She was certain that little Prudence Barford had not been baptized, and that Jem's family would be against the practice. But Elen was hers now, if anyone's, and she had no objection; indeed, she liked the idea of bringing the child into the family of God in the Weston family chapel.

Of more immediate concern, however, was the need to find a wet nurse. The dairymaid at the farm, who had no living child of her own, was not willing. Christian made enquiries in the village and found a more suitable woman, Jane Edginton, the wife of a baker, respected and liked in the community. She had several children and

could take Elen to live with her until she was weaned, in about a year.

A year. It seemed such a long time ahead, and the care of this child such a big task to have taken on. Lady Weston made it clear to Alice that she thought it unnecessary.

"The baby is the child of peasants," she said. "She cannot aspire to anything more than servitude. When she is weaned you should take her to an orphanage. There is one of good repute in Oxford. She will be well cared for and put out to work as a maidservant at twelve or thirteen, when she is old enough to earn her own living."

Mistress Florey agreed. "Don't shackle yourself with a child, wench. Folk will say she's yours. You're young, and without her you might pass for a maiden."

But Alice knew she would never let Elen go to an orphanage. And Jem – the only man whose opinion she cared about – already knew she was not a maiden.

Because the child had been brought to her house, Lady Weston felt a responsibility for her soul, and she took charge of the baptism. The ceremony was held in the family chapel, now cleared of rubble and roughly repaired. The broken windows were still boarded up, but the altar was back behind its rail, and candlelight softened the damage to the walls.

Alice, as the baby's adoptive mother, carried her in. She was proud of Elen's appearance, having used some lace that Christian had given her to embellish one of the plain baby gowns she had made at Sibbertoft. Elen waved

her tiny limbs and darted bright glances around, until the priest sprinkled cold holy water on her and made her scream. Her godfather was Richard Edginton, her godmothers Jane Edginton and Bess, whose name was Elizabeth Akers. The child was entered in the register simply as *Elen, adopted daughter of Alice Newcombe*.

Alice visited Elen at least twice a week at the Edgintons' house in the village. Christian had chosen well. Jane Edginton was calm and capable, and Alice knew that her temperament would pass to Elen. The Edgintons were kindly people, and their own three children – John, Kate and the baby, Mary – were well cared for. Jane helped her husband in the shop, and the smells of baking bread, of cinnamon and honey, surrounded Elen at all times; as did a fine powdering of flour, which could be seen on her clothes and hair. Alice thought it was the flour dust that made Elen's hair appear lighter, but Jane said no: the very dark newborn hair had rubbed off and been replaced by a fuzz of chestnut brown. Nia's colour, Alice remembered.

The baby was Alice's, and no one forgot it. Whenever she called, Jane would say, "Here's your mam come to see you!" and give the child to Alice to hold. But Alice was now free of the day-to-day care of Elen, and that was a huge relief. She was able to work and not be constantly concerned about the baby. She soon found there was much to be done. The kitchen maid Joan had left, and Lady Weston had not replaced her. Tom was to go as gamekeeper's boy to a neighbouring estate; and Mistress

Denham had also gone, and Christian had taken over her duties as housekeeper. It was clear that all was not well at Weston Hall. Christian told Alice that the house had been pillaged twice since Alice had left in May: once by Fairfax's men and earlier by their own side, men from the king's army, who took all the remaining horses except Amor, ate all the stock of meat and cheese, and sat in the kitchen drinking great quantities of wine and beer, quarrelling among themselves, and taking pot-shots at the pans and ladles on the walls. They had also invaded the home farm and tied up the farmer and threatened him with hanging till he revealed where he had hidden his savings. His wife had been so terrified that she lost her wits, and it was feared she might never be entirely well again.

But this was not all the trouble that had come upon the family. Lady Weston's daughter Grace Bramford was there, with her three children, and Alice was shocked when she saw her. Lady Grace had lost weight; she was pale and there were shadows under her eyes. Even the little boys seemed subdued.

Alice soon heard the story. Bramford Hall, where Grace lived with her husband and children, had been garrisoned for the king, and came under siege by Parliament. Those defending the house were greatly outnumbered by the rebels, and when the enemy asked for the house to be given up to Parliament, Colonel Bramford surrendered. There was no dishonour, Christian insisted to Alice, in surrendering under such circumstances – but the colonel's superior officers thought otherwise. They believed that

he had been influenced by fear for his wife and young family, and so had given up the house too readily when he might have fought on. He was brought to trial, sentenced to death for cowardice, and shot.

"Lady Grace is overcome with grief," said Christian. "I fear for her if she will not rally. She says her life is ruined: she is homeless, her husband lost to her, and her sons will always have the shame of their father's execution staining their honour. It has brought down her mother's spirits, as you might imagine." She shook her head. "Lady Weston has many troubles. She is not long returned from London, visiting her husband in prison. She found him in poor health and ill-attended. Now she is writing letters to the authorities and to Parliamentarian gentlemen, former friends of the family, in hope of getting him released."

Alice felt all the more grateful that Lady Weston had been willing to take her in at such a time. But Christian said Lady Weston would always keep a promise, and she had promised Alice a place here if she needed it. Christian had also convinced Lady Weston that Alice would be useful, with Joan and the former housekeeper gone.

"But we won't be making sweet waters for banquets," she said. "Our work will be in running the house and preparing remedies." She sighed. "Lord knows, the news is bad enough!"

And so it was – for the king. News reached them through the church and inn, and they also read both the Royalist and London newsbooks – the truth, Christian

suspected, lying somewhere in the middle. They heard, as the summer went by, that General Fairfax was still in the West Country, fighting Lord Goring's forces, and had taken two thousand prisoners.

Jem will be part of all this, Alice thought. And though she had once seen Jem's side as the enemy, she could not help but be glad at the news as the towns fell one after another to Parliament, for she longed for the war to be over, for Jem to return.

But she had to keep such thoughts to herself, since the Weston family were loyal to the king and in despair at the ongoing tally of defeats. Even the publication of the king's private correspondence, captured at Naseby, did not shake their confidence in his cause. Lady Weston had banned the pamphlet – entitled *The King's Cabinet Opened* – from her house; but Christian managed to get hold of a copy. It was too long and difficult for Alice to read right through, but she saw that it detailed all the king's correspondence with his wife, and with Catholic nobles in Ireland and Europe; and it revealed how he was deceiving Parliament, planning to bring in foreign armies from those countries to fight Englishmen.

Christian and Alice were shocked by the revelations, and Alice began to feel that Jem's view of the king might be right. But these thoughts too she kept to herself.

She said nothing to anyone at Weston about her feelings for Jeremiah Banks; not only because he was their enemy, but because she did not want them to think of her as a girl who, having been abandoned by one man, would fall straight into the arms of another. Indeed,

she did not want to see herself in that way, and tried hard to put thoughts of Jem out of her mind. She must be independent, she decided; earn a respectable living; support Elen; and let the future take care of itself. Jem might never return. He might forget her, now she was out of his sight. She recalled Mistress Erlam saying that injured men often imagined themselves in love with the women who tended them. It might come to nothing.

And yet she thought about him often, remembering their time together at Sibbertoft, and on the road; their close companionship on those two nights. And then that first kiss, followed so quickly by parting. Whenever the newsbooks came and she read of the war in the West Country, she could not help but imagine him there, riding along hollow lanes thick with summer foliage on either side – hedges that might hide any number of enemy musketeers.

"I'll write," he had said.

But the weeks went by and no letter came.

Christian had extended the vegetable garden at the back of Weston Hall and was now managing it almost single-handed, old Lucas Rowles, the gardener, being no longer fit for work. Alice helped her: weeding, sowing lettuce, and then, through the later summer and early autumn, harvesting beans, cabbages, onions and radishes.

"I intend to grow more vegetables next year," Christian said. "I fear we must eat like the poor in these sad times."

They struggled against slugs and rot, but Christian

 290

remained determined. There was an apple tree in the kitchen garden, and apricot trees growing espaliered against a south-facing wall, and these were producing fruit. She had already begun picking herbs to dry, and now Alice took over this work. She shook coriander seeds into a small linen bag, and gathered rue and wormwood for drying, to protect the household against moths; she cut lavender for the same purpose, and also for a remedy against headaches. The black seeds of poppies were caught in a bag and dried, and Mistress Florey and Bess picked marjoram, thyme and dandelion leaves for use in the kitchen.

Alice made calming herbal mixtures for Lady Grace and a salve for Bessy's hands, which were so chapped and sore she could not work. The salve was Alice's own invention. Christian used it to soothe her scratched hands after gardening, and Lady Weston asked for some to keep her hands soft for the great quantity of sewing and embroidery she always did. Alice enjoyed experimenting with remedies and having the space and equipment to do so. The drying cupboard for herbs was put to good use as she and Christian harvested what they grew in the garden or found in the woods and meadows near by. All these tasks, along with helping Mistress Florey in the kitchen and the maids in the dairy, kept Alice too busy to pine for Jem.

The course of the war continued to favour Parliament. Prince Rupert surrendered Bristol. City after city fell. And then, one day, Alice found Christian shocked and distressed at news of the fall of Basing House – that great Royalist stronghold in Hampshire where, it was said,

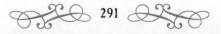 291

every window had carried the message *Aimez Loyaute* scratched in the glass with a diamond.

"All is lost," said Christian, scanning the printed report. "The greatest people of the kingdom turned out, stripped naked; everything dragged from the house, smashed, or looted; the house burned to the ground – oh, and people trapped in the cellars who cried in vain for help!"

She passed the pamphlet to Alice. It told of a ferocious assault. Cromwell had raised a huge force against the great house, and many soldiers had been killed on both sides.

There seemed no end to the horror. I must not hope, Alice told herself. I must expect nothing.

It was November when at last a letter came for her.

Christian, as housekeeper, was the one who received and delivered the household's mail. That day she came into the kitchen carrying a bundle of letters and handed Alice a small package.

Alice felt her heart give a jump. It *had* to be from Jem! Who else would write to her? She stared at the rain-smudged handwriting, and became aware of everyone watching. I can't open it here, she thought.

Christian touched her arm. "Go to the still room, Alice. I must take these letters upstairs to Lady Weston."

Alone in that quiet place, Alice untied the string on the package, broke the wax seal, and opened it. Inside the paper, wrapped in news-sheets, was a small book, bound

in soft brown leather, very pleasing to handle. The pages were blank. It was a notebook or journal. A book for me to write in, she thought; and she stroked its cover.

Two pages of writing accompanied it. She unfolded the letter, and glanced quickly at the last page, which ended: *Your faithful friend, Jeremiah Banks.* The date at the top was August, but this had been crossed out and replaced with a September date. Clearly the letter had been written over several weeks, and then had taken many more weeks to reach Weston Hall.

He wrote:

> *Alice,*
> *Forgive me for this long delay in writing to you. Never believe it was because I had forgotten you. Indeed, I think of you constantly and pray for this campaign to be over so that I may see you again and we may come to know one another better.*
>
> *I had trouble at first to find my regiment, for all is confusion here in the west and there was danger of being taken prisoner by the enemy, but I was reunited with them some weeks ago. My comrades, who had thought me dead at Naseby, were overjoyed to see me, though I was grieved to hear that one of the men who carried me to safety was killed soon after. The fighting here is fierce. We have taken Bridgwater and Bath. Bridgwater was a sorry business – half the town left in flames from our cannon before they would surrender. Where we are now, I don't know, only*

that we marched a weary way to get here and are
mired in dirt.

Here there was a break, and she realized he had been interrupted and then come back to the letter much later. He wrote now of being camped outside Bristol, during the siege, and of the alarm caused by the capture of his regiment's colonel in a raid. But in the main his letter was to tell her that he thought of her often, and hoped all was well at Weston.

I have some fear for you in that malignant (your friends would say loyal) house, for I believe the king faces certain defeat. We are all assured that we do God's work, that a better government will come of this, and that we will bring it about with God's help. It seems there will be no winter halt to this campaign. We press on to the end, which surely cannot be long. Meantime, I send you this small gift. I wish I could say I had bought it for you, for I would willingly have done so; but the truth is I found it in the ruins of a shop that had been ransacked, and thought of you and the book you lost. Perhaps you can use this to make a herbal of your own.

Alice loved the book. She was still examining it when Christian returned, and could not resist showing it to her, even though she had not meant to talk about Jem.

"It is to make a herbal, to replace my father's book

that was lost," she said, adding awkwardly, "a friend sent it."

"The same friend who brought you here?" asked Christian, with a smile. "The Roundhead?"

"He's no *Roundhead*!" said Alice. "He wears his hair quite long."

"Whatever the length of his hair, he knows well enough what gift will please you."

"Did you guess?" asked Alice. "When we arrived together? Did everyone guess?"

"I'm sure they did. It was in your eyes – the way you looked at each other."

Alice sighed. "I have been determined not to talk about him. Not to think about him. In case he never wrote, never came back. And now of course I'm happy, but – oh, I'm so afraid for him! It's weeks since he sent this. Anything might have happened since." She turned in appeal to Christian. "You must all think of me as a traitor, consorting with your enemy. Lady Weston must think that."

"Nobody thinks it," said Christian. "Of course there is no love for Cromwell and Fairfax here, but as for your soldier: we are all English men and women, Alice. This war will end, and we shall learn to live together again." She smiled. "Do you have paper to write to your friend?"

"No. But I can buy some."

"Do that. And write."

Twenty-six

Before she began her letter, Alice wrote on the first page of the leather-bound book:

Alice Newcombe
Her Book

She would make a collection of her own herbal preparations, she decided; and collect the recipes of others; and she would write down her observations on the properties of various plants, and the effect on them of the phases of the moon and the movements of the stars and planets, as her father had done. She did not start writing at once, but took time to consider how best the book should be laid out. The blank pages held a promise of pleasure to come.

But she did not delay writing to Jem, though she found it difficult because she had never composed a letter

before, only brief notes of remedies or descriptions of plants. She copied his style of address, beginning simply: *Jeremiah, I thank you for your gift. Nothing could have pleased me more.* She assured him she was safe at Weston Hall, but did not mention the family's troubles and left him to imagine how distraught they were at the progress of the war. She wrote:

> *Elen has been baptized. I think you will not approve of infant baptism, but Lady Weston was pressing in the matter, and I confess I was happy to see Elen brought before God. Jane Edginton, the baker's wife, is wet nurse, and has Elen to live with her in the village. I visit often and see that the child is thriving. I love her as my daughter now, yet almost fear to do so in case Bryn should be found and come to claim her.*
>
> *Mistress Christian and I worked hard in the garden through the summer. We have fruit preserved and beans salted and laid in crocks and new supplies of herbs in the still room.*

She paused. This is women's talk, she thought; he doesn't want to hear this. She continued:

> *We read the newsbooks here and try to follow the course of the campaign. You say there will be no winter halt to the fighting, so I can only pray for this war to be over soon.*

And she ended with what was most in her mind:

It will seem a long winter if you do not come.

Afterwards, she read her letter through. It sounded somewhat stiff, she thought, not like her own voice, not quite as she had meant it to sound. But it *looked* well; she was proud of the neat, careful handwriting her father had taught her. She signed the letter exactly as Jem had: *Your faithful friend*, followed by her name; then folded and sealed it.

And then she waited. The waiting was almost harder to bear now that she had heard from him once and knew he would write again. All through late November and December she scanned the newsbooks in hopes of discovering where he might be; but, with winter closing in, there was little news. She busied herself with work: not only in the still room, but in the kitchen and dairy and around the house, dusting and sweeping, running errands for the ladies, helping the nursemaid with the little boys.

At last, a few days before Christmas, came another letter. She opened it eagerly, expecting a response to hers, but it soon became clear that he had not yet received it. He sounded anxious. Had his parcel reached her? Was she safe, and in good health? And he asked: *I hope you were not offended by anything I said in my letter?'*

Alice, distressed that he should even consider that possibility, wrote back quickly, without considering her words:

Oh, Jem, how can you even think that I would be offended? You must know how much I long to hear from you. Every time I see Christian carrying letters I silently wish, Let there be one for me! Let me hear again from Jem! I think of you every moment of the day, and pray for your safety. My letter and thanks are on their way to you, perhaps have reached you already. Forgive these hasty words; I make ready for Walt to take this to the carrier. There will be no more letters taken before Christmas...

It was a sad, reduced Christmas they had, after last year's. Lady Grace had accepted an invitation from her sister to visit, which their mother thought might cheer her, so Grace had gathered up her children and their nursemaid and gone to Buckinghamshire. The yule log burned in the hearth, but there was little festive food, and the kissing bough was reduced to a posy of ivy and mistletoe over the main door. One who passed under it in the week between Christmas and Twelfth Night was Sir Walter Clare, the elderly neighbour who had been at last year's feast.

"He comes courting me," Christian told Alice.

"But he's old!" exclaimed Alice. "Oh, I'm sorry—"

Christian laughed. "He is not so *very* old, and I am nearing thirty. He is a kind man, well thought of; a widower twice over, with grown-up children." It was clear that Christian did not love Sir Walter, but...

"Will you have him, then?" Alice asked.

"I think I may. Lady Weston wishes it."

"But won't she miss you? You run the household now; you do so much for her."

"She will, but you see, Alice, since I came of age it has been her duty to find me a husband, to see me settled, and I have thwarted her plans several times. Lady Weston is always mindful of her duty and careful of the welfare of everyone in this house. It would please her greatly to see me married."

Alice, thinking of Robin, and Jem, asked, "Did you never fall in love?"

"Yes, I did once, or thought I did, when I was much younger. He was eager to marry me, but I was unsure. He was energetic, ambitious; a diplomat, who was often abroad. We would have spent our lives travelling, setting up home for a year or two in cities all over Europe. I like to be in one place that is familiar to me. So I hesitated..."

"And he died in the war?"

"Oh, no! Nothing so sad! And it was before the war. No, he married someone else."

"But *that's* sad – for you."

"It was my own doing. And perhaps for the best. Sir Walter offers me a quiet home, a garden, a still room of my own, anything I want."

But I'd want love, Alice thought. She yearned to hear again from Jem.

Throughout January there were no letters in or out. Weston Hall was cut off by deep snow, and Lady Grace and her children were obliged to remain in

Buckinghamshire. The cold was intense. Ice froze on the windowpanes, and snow was banked up outside so high it was a struggle each morning to open the kitchen door. Bess would trudge out and smash the ice on the well, and later she would feed the chickens huddled with fluffed-up feathers in the hen house. The dogs lay by the fire, and the cats insinuated themselves in front of them, so close to the flames that sparks singed their fur. Lady Weston and her maid sat sewing with little portable heaters full of hot coals tucked under their long skirts.

Alice could not even get to the village to see Elen. She worried that the baby might take cold, or succumb to a fever. She knew that little children could fall ill and be gone in a matter of days. Each night she prayed to God to keep Elen safe. By day she worked with Christian or with Mistress Florey, making herself indispensable in every aspect of the running of the house.

"Her Ladyship'll miss you, when your Roundhead comes for you," said Bess.

The two of them were in the woodshed, tossing kindling into the big, two-handled basket.

So Bess knows, thought Alice. She didn't mind. Bessy was a simple, good-natured girl who would understand, and not think of Jeremiah as an enemy.

"Don't call him Roundhead," she begged. "His name is Jem."

Bess smiled. "Jem? I like that name. I liked the look of him. A proper man, he is, Mistress Florey says."

"Oh!" So they were all talking about her.

"Tell you something else," confided Bess. Her breath

hung in a cloud on the cold air and her dark hair sparkled with melting snow. "He's a letter-writing man, that one, isn't he? And you're clever. You can write, and read the newsbooks, like he does. So I think he's right for you; he's the one."

Alice wanted to hug her; but she only said, "Yes. I think so too."

The snow thawed, and at last Alice was able to walk to the Edgintons' house in the village.

Jane opened the door, and behind her came Elen, crawling towards them and squealing with excitement. She was wearing a little gown that Alice recognized as one she herself had made at Sibbertoft, and she looked rosy and well. A tide of relief surged through Alice. She scooped up the child into her arms.

"Oh, I've missed you, sweeting – and feared for you!" she exclaimed. She looked around the room, which was full of children – the youngest, Mary, pulling herself up with the aid of a table leg; the other two squabbling over a toy. "They are all well?"

Jane nodded. "As you see! I thank God no illness has struck this winter. Only Kate has a cough that tickles at night and frets her."

"I'll bring you a syrup for it."

Alice felt happy, full of hope. And two weeks later came the long-awaited news that the carrier from Faringdon was on his way, with mail. She met him at the King's Arms with a letter for Jem that she had been writing at intervals since Christmas: more journal than

letter, telling him of her day-to-day life and that she had begun writing up some of her remedies in the book he had given her, and that she hoped soon to show it to him. In return, the carrier handed her a bundle of letters for Weston Hall. She hurried back, anxious to help Christian sort them.

There were two for her.

"Two!" she exclaimed, snatching them up.

And Christian laughed and said, "Go and read them. Go! Now!"

Alice went out to the stables – unused these days except for Amor – found an empty stall, and snuggled down in the hay to read. She felt a glow spread through her as she saw how the first one began:

> *Dear love, Alice,*
> *I cannot tell you how much joy your letters gave me, to know you think of me and hold me in your prayers – as I do you. In this cold place where we sit out the winter I read your words often and they keep me warm. We are in quarters near Exeter, and have been for many weeks. We have surrounded the city with our forces and keep up a blockade in hope of weakening the enemy's resolve. I am here with a dozen others, lodged in a widow's house – one of the gentry of this village whose only son fought for the king and was killed at Bridgwater. She is a hard, bitter woman and keeps a cold house, but who can blame her? All the people here are resentful of us; they have been*

plundered so often these last years by one side or the other. The church has bullet holes in the door and the effigies of the dead have their faces hacked off – a reminder of our army's last passing this way.

I have friends here, but my companions are rough men for the most part. They grow restless and quarrelsome the less action we see. The weather is cruelly cold, with deep snow, and much of the time we are confined to quarters. I sit with a candle and write my journal and letters, and sometimes – often – I study my book of maps and plot my way to you.

This paper is running out and I have no more space. I'll seal it now, though I know not when I may send it.

Until then, I remain your loving friend,
Jem Banks

Alice felt very satisfied by this letter, despite Jem's discomforts. She set it down beside her in the straw to read again and savour, and turned to the second letter. This was dated mid-January and told her they were at last about to move and march on Dartmouth. But that was a month or more ago, she realized. Where was he now? Was Dartmouth taken? Please God, she thought, let him be safe.

He had found some more paper, he told her; the widow had sold it to him.

* * *

304

I have written to my mother and sisters, and to my former master – the one I was apprenticed to in Willesden. And now to you, dear love. I think of you, so far away, and pray you are well, and little Elen too.

I forgot to tell you that I heard last year from Phoebe that her husband came safe from Naseby fight, for which we all give thanks. And today we had a delivery of mail here, the first since Christmas. I had letters, very loving, from both my sisters. I hope one day you will meet my sisters, Alice. From my mother came a parcel containing a shirt and knitted stockings. She worries greatly about my health, and whether I am warm and have enough to eat. Priscilla said she was obliged to restrain Mother from sending me a cake, promising they would make one together when I came home...

How lucky he is, Alice thought, to have such an affectionate family. Even though his sister Phoebe's husband fought for the king, they all care for one another.

And she read, and reread, his words *I hope one day you will meet my sisters*. That surely meant he saw her as part of his future life?

Spring came, and with it the news that Lady Grace's home, Bramford Hall, had been slighted – burnt to the ground. Lady Grace, even more cast down, moved

restlessly between Weston Hall and her sister's home in Buckinghamshire.

"She must marry again," said Christian. "There is nothing else for a woman in her situation."

Alice wrote regularly to Jem, but heard only once from him in that time – a brief note, written at the end of a day's march:

> *I can scarce stand for weariness, but with God's help we are winning this war. Wait for me, sweetheart.*
> *Your love,*
> *J.B.'*

The paper was creased and dirty, and there was a thumbprint on one corner. Alice kissed it.

All around the country, castles and strongholds were falling to Parliament. They read of the campaign in the west and the towns taken by Fairfax's army: Dartmouth, Torrington, Launceston, Bodmin, Truro. No more letters came from Jem. He's fighting, Alice thought; marching, and fighting, and with no time to write. She refused to give way to fear, and instead tried consciously to bring his image to mind: his strong frame; the fairish hair, with a slight curl to it, that hung in twisting strands on his neck; his eyes; the shape of his face, his mouth, his hands.

In mid-April, Exeter surrendered, and by the end of the month they heard that the whole of Somerset was at last in Parliament's control, the king had gone to seek help from the Scots – and the New Model Army led by

306

Fairfax was on its way to Oxford.

"Oxford!" Alice's heart gave a leap of traitorous joy even as she realized that Lady Weston and her husband might lose their home and what was left of their fortune.

"It is the end," said Christian. "We must prepare for defeat."

A week later they all heard, from far off, the sound of drums and fifes; and then, as the victorious army drew nearer, the hymn-singing and tramp of boots and hooves and the rumble of wheels. They came marching along the road from Faringdon, passing only half a mile from the Copsey turn.

The Weston family shut their eyes and ears and hearts to this final assault and closeted themselves in their rooms. But Alice could not be contained. She begged Mistress Florey to let her go, and hurried down the lane to the village to join the throng of people moving towards the Faringdon road. All she could think about was that she might see Jem. The generals, the officers and cavalry, resplendent in their feathers and sashes – a glorious sight – held no interest for her. She stared only at the dragoons. But there were so many of them, rank on rank, riding three or four abreast, and all alike in their buff coats and helmets. She would never know him, she realized, not unless he turned aside and looked for her – and how could he do that? Even if he glanced towards the crowd, she would be hidden among so many people.

For more than two hours she stood there, knowing

she would not see him, and yet unable to bring herself to leave. She would not have moved even then, but Bess arrived, pushing through the crowd, sent by Mistress Florey to fetch her.

"He might come later!" Alice protested. "He might be a guard on the ammunition train."

Bess looked hot and tired. "There's work to be done," she said.

And Alice trudged back with her to Weston Hall in low spirits.

"You must wait," said Mistress Florey, though not unkindly. "It's a woman's lot, often enough. Get those pots scoured, then clear the table and scrub it. And when you're done, go and ask Mistress Christian if she needs you. She's not herself today. None of us are."

The siege of Oxford lasted nearly seven weeks. They seemed to Alice the longest, hardest weeks of her life. She heard nothing from Jem, and had no way of knowing whether he was alive or dead; nothing but that last brief letter which she kept always about her, in a pocket under her skirts. There were movements of troops all around, rumours that the city was on the point of surrender, and yet still the siege continued. And then, at last, on a morning in midsummer, almost a year to the day when Alice and Jem had left Sibbertoft, the news burst upon them that all was over: Oxford had capitulated, all the king's children except the Prince of Wales were prisoners, and the New Model Army had marched into the city, which was now in the hands of Parliament.

Jem will be there! thought Alice. If he is still in this world, he must be in Oxford now! And she wanted to leave the house at once and run the nine or ten miles to the city and search until she found him – for surely they would be drawn towards each other like magnets?

But all she could do was to continue to wait. Now, with release perhaps so near, the waiting had an intense, unbearable quality. Lady Weston had collapsed at the news, and Alice, feeling guilt and sympathy, made tisanes of lavender and camomile, and recommended rest – even as her own heart raced. Later that day she hurried down to the King's Arms to find out if there was any more news, any message for her, but there was nothing.

It was on the afternoon of the following day, when she was stepping out from Jane Edginton's house after visiting Elen, that she saw a horseman approaching from the direction of the Oxford road.

She stood still, uncertain. The man drew nearer. She held her breath, almost afraid to hope – and then she gave a gasp and caught up her skirts and ran to meet him.

Twenty-seven

"Alice!"

He looked bone-weary, but his face flushed with delight when he saw her. He dismounted and seemed about to seize her in his arms, when both of them remembered that they were standing in the village street, visible to everyone. But Alice thought her soul must be in her eyes as she said, "I have so hoped you would come. It's—" her voice broke. "It's been a long year…"

"Too long. And I have much to say – to ask – that I could not speak of in a letter."

People passing by had begun to glance curiously at them.

"I was on my way to the King's Arms," he said. "Shall we go there? I'll stable the horse, and then we could walk and talk – if you have time? Do they expect you at the house?"

"No. I have the afternoon free. I've been at Mistress Edginton's, visiting Elen."

"And is the child well?"

"She is very well. And may leave the Edgintons' at any time now, for Jane has weaned her." She was glad to be talking about the baby; she wanted to make sure he understood that Elen was now her daughter. "She'll be walking soon. She pulls herself up to stand, holding on to the furniture. And she begins to talk! Calls me Mamma."

After they left the inn she led him down a lane and onto a path that wound alongside a stream. There were trees growing beside the water, and moorhens cheeping and ducks delving for weeds. On the other side was common land, where a few cows grazed. He took her hand as they turned onto the path, and then his arm went round her waist, and soon they were in each other's arms, kissing and clinging to one another as if they would never let go.

They stayed locked together for a long time, then found a secluded place in the field and lay down and kissed some more and laughed as they fumbled with shirt and shift.

"Last year," he said, between kisses, "a whole year ago, wasn't it? This is what I wanted to do then! And those nights we spent together on the road, and never – oh, Alice! Shall we be married? Will you have me?"

"Yes," she said. "Yes, I will! Only…" She looked at him, still uncertain, searching his face. "There's Elen…"

"Of course there's Elen. I told you before: Elen comes too."

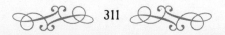

Alice felt the knot of anxiety she had been carrying loosen. "Truly?"

"Truly. She will be my daughter; take my name."

They kissed to seal the promise – and might have done more had they not become aware of a presence, a breathing, near by, and looked up to find that all the cows in the field had moved towards them and were now standing, bunched and curious, watching.

"Oh!" Alice scrambled to her feet, and Jem laughed and got up. The cows retreated, but only a few steps. Alice brushed grass from her clothes and his, and they returned to the path and walked on, laughing.

Jem took her hand and said, "I've told my mother about Elen."

"Your mother?" She looked up at him, alarmed, realizing that there was more to marriage than two people who loved each other. There were mothers, sisters, neighbourhoods.

He said, "When we were at Sibbertoft I wrote to my mother, and told her I had been nursed back to life by a sweet girl; and I told her then about the baby – your friend's baby. This spring I wrote and told her I hoped to be married, if you would agree."

"I am afraid she will not approve of me."

"She will probably say you are too young and we are in too much haste to wed."

"She will think… Jem, what else did you tell her about me?"

"As much as she needs to know. I didn't tell her anything that is private between you and me."

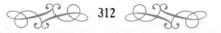

"She will find out that I was following the army."

"Alice, she knows you cared for me when I was left for dead after Naseby fight, and for that alone I am sure she loves you already. And she will come to love you more." Alice must have looked doubtful, for he added, "I do not need her permission to marry you."

They walked on, their arms around each other.

"My mother is not the problem," he said. "The problem is that now I have left the army I have no employment, no home to offer you and Elen. I have written to my former master and to acquaintances back home, and I don't doubt I shall find work, though it may take a little time." He laughed, shortly. "There should be work enough for carpenters after all the destruction of this war. But I need to go home, to Hertford. I haven't seen my mother for nearly two years. She longs to see me again. And I must find a home for us. If it hadn't been for the war I might have been my own master by now, but I shall have to start as a journeyman. We won't be rich, but I have my army pay – some of it."

"Money doesn't matter," said Alice. "Not as long as we are together, even if it's in one room."

He turned to her eagerly. "Would you marry me before I go? Not wait till I return? We need only find witnesses—"

Alice stopped still, and stared at him. It had not occurred to her until then that he meant to go home without her. She had no intention of letting him leave her here again, married or unmarried.

"Jem," she said, "let's marry at once, and go together.

Please. I can't bear to be left waiting again."

"Oh, love!" He wrapped her in his arms and kissed her and held her close. "That's what *I* wanted too, but it seemed wrong to ask it of you; not to have a home to take you to—"

"We have both lived on the road, and I have seen husbands and wives set up their shelters at night and take them down in the morning, and cook on a campfire…"

"It won't be as bad as that," he said, smiling. "Though if we have nowhere to go I promise I'll build you a shack on the common."

She laughed. "How long do you plan to stay in Copsey?"

"Only as long as need be: to marry, to bring Elen away from the wet nurse, for you to finish your term of service with Lady Weston."

"It *is* finished. I am free to leave – and I think she expects it."

Lady Weston did expect Alice to leave. However, she made it clear that a hasty marriage would not have her approval. Marriage, in her view, should always take place in church, with banns published for three Sundays beforehand. But Alice knew that Jem did not hold with church weddings; and Christian said that with people so displaced and thrown together by the war, there must be many such simple ceremonies taking place.

They were married two days later at the Edgintons' house, in a private ceremony without clergy. Jane and

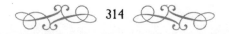

Richard Edginton were there, and Christian and Bess. Alice and Jeremiah had arranged to fetch Elen from the Edgintons' the morning after the wedding and begin their long cross-country journey to Hertfordshire; but their wedding night would be spent in Copsey, at the White Hart Inn.

Alice wore a yellow gown that had once been Lady Cecily's. It was cut rather low in the neck for an artisan's wife, but she wore it over a modest shift. She had slept with pieces of rag tied in her hair to curl it, and in the morning Bess had arranged the hair so that little ringlets showed prettily around the edge of her cap. She and Christian and Bess walked down to the Edgintons' house, which was full of the smell of baking bread and buns. Jane had made a large cherry pie, dusted with sugar, for the occasion, and it stood waiting on a plate. The jug of spiced wine carried by Bess was placed next to it. The children, including Elen, were minded by a neighbour's girl while Alice and Jem, along with Christian, Bessy, Richard and Jane, went into the quiet back room.

In that small homely space Jem took both Alice's hands in a firm grasp, and said, "I declare before God and these witnesses that I take you, Alice Newcombe, to be my lawful wedded wife, and promise to be a faithful and loving husband until death shall part us."

She repeated the vow, stumbling a little over the words, and all the time looking into his eyes, thinking, I'll always remember this day. And she felt sure that she would never regret it.

Jem, who liked to have things preserved on paper,

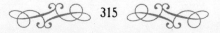

had written out their declaration and added the names of the witnesses: Jane Edginton, Richard Edginton, Christian Aubrey and Elizabeth Akers. They all signed it afterwards, Jane and Bess both marking it with a cross.

And then they drank spiced wine and ate cherry pie and all wished one another health and happiness. Alice had already said farewell to Lady Weston and had received her pay and the lady's blessing. Now she had to part with Christian, and that was hard. Although Alice was a servant and Christian a gentlewoman, they had worked together, shared knowledge and discoveries, and become friends. Alice curtseyed to Christian, but Christian exclaimed, "Oh, Alice! I wish you good fortune!" and kissed her. Bessy, quite overcome by the occasion, sobbed as she hugged Alice goodbye.

The landlord of the White Hart had left them linen towels and a scented wash-ball. On the table was a flagon of wine and two glasses, fruit, bread and cold meat. The casement was open, and mild summer air flowed into the room. Alice looked out. It was not yet dusk, but already a few stars showed in the greenish sky and a full moon hung pale above the treetops.

Jem came and stood behind her and kissed the back of her neck. "Are you hungry, love?"

"No." She smiled and turned round into his arms. "Let's eat later."

They were both shy at first, for they had not spent much time together, though they had come to know each other through their letters. Alice was afraid of

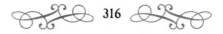

seeming too forward, but she need not have feared, for nothing she did displeased him. They lay and kissed and caressed one another, and Alice traced with her hand and then with her lips the cruel lines of his scars on shoulder and thigh. When they made love she felt not only passionate but also safe and certain in a way she had never felt with Robin. They slept, and woke, and made love again, and the food lay untouched on the table, and outside the night turned dark and silver.

1649

Epilogue

Alice had tied holly and mistletoe to a ring of bent twigs and was winding a strand of ivy around them. It was scarcely a kissing bough, for it was far too small, and she would not hang it over their threshold now that the celebration of Christmas was forbidden by Act of Parliament. This kissing knot, as she thought of it, would hang at the top of the stairs, and would be for the family alone: herself, and Jem, and their children: Elen, Daniel and the new baby, Hannah. There would also be sweetmeats for the children, and a festive pudding.

Alice knew Jem would not object to these small rituals, and guessed that many neighbours might do the same. With the banning of its celebration in churches, Christmas had vanished from the calendar, and many people felt the lack at this dark time of year, with spring far off. Soon after last Christmas, on a cold January day,

King Charles had been executed in London. A huge crowd had attended his beheading, and it was reported that as the executioner held aloft the severed head a vast sighing groan rose up from the people, and several fainted. Jem said that many who supported Parliament were unhappy at the killing of the king.

But at least it did seem that the wars were finally over. After the fall of Oxford in 1646, they had enjoyed only a year and a half of uncertain peace: a peace full of Royalist plots and uprisings and much dissent among those in power, in Parliament and in the army. There had been a mutiny less than two miles away, at Ware, and Jem and Alice, visiting Phoebe there, had seen Cromwell's forces out on the roads, and heard the shots when the ringleaders were executed.

Jem did not get involved in the debates and arguments that shook the army, and neither did he join up when war broke out again. He had become milder in his opinions. Like many of their friends and neighbours he had begun to resent the growing power of the army in the affairs of Parliament.

Alice was glad to have him safe at home with her and the children. He had his own carpenter's workshop now, on the edge of Hartham Common. The house was attached to the workshop, and Alice had space in the attic for drying herbs. She gathered herbs on the common and in Waterford marshes, and experimented and made simple remedies in the kitchen, and wrote up her findings in the book Jem had given her. The neighbours soon got to know of her skills, and came for advice, though she

made sure only to offer homely remedies, and only to her friends. There was an apothecary practising in Hertford and she had no wish to antagonize him.

As Alice fastened the ivy around the ring of twigs, Elen watched intently. She would want to make one herself; she was four and a half now, and copied everything Alice did. But the ring would be too difficult for her.

"You could help me make dumplings to go in the pottage," Alice suggested. "Dadda will come in for his dinner soon. Are your hands clean?"

Elen held up her hands for inspection. They were small and square, with short fingers – quite different from Alice's or from anyone's in Jem's family. Elen was short for her age, and sturdy, with curling dark chestnut hair. She caught at Alice's heart, for she looked more like Nia every day.

Jem had tried several times over the years to trace Elen's father. Most of the Royalist infantry were in prison, and he asked after the names Alice had given him: Bryn, Edryd, Gethin. None of them, it seemed, were uncommon names among the Welsh soldiers. But at last came a message from a man named Edryd, who told of two friends, Bryn and Gethin, who had been killed at Naseby. Alice guessed that this was the closest they would ever come to being sure that Bryn was dead.

"So you see, love, he will not come for her," Jem said.

He knew it had been a fear of Alice's that she might lose Elen to Bryn, if he was found. Alice was sad that Bryn had died, but his death meant that Elen was truly

323

hers and Jem's, as the child believed herself to be. One day, Alice thought, if she asks why she does not look like either of us, or questions me about the Welsh songs I sing, I'll tell her who her real parents were and what became of them, how they were good, honest, loving people who vanished from the earth like the dust under the generals' boots. I'll tell her who she is, and where she comes from – but not now.

Daniel, Alice's own firstborn child, was two years old, slim and fair. He was trundling around the room with a wooden dog on wheels made by his father. Hannah lay in her cradle near the hearth, sleeping through everything.

When Jem came in, dusty from the workshop, Elen ran to him and said, "We made a kissing knot and dumplings!"

He lifted and swung her up. "Did you, my wench? And shall we eat them together for dinner?"

Elen giggled. "Not the kissing knot! Silly Dadda!"

Alice held up the knot and Jem kissed Elen under it, and then Alice, and then put Elen down and scooped up Daniel; and they all laughed, and went to eat their midday dinner.

Later, when the December dusk was closing in, and Jem had gone back to the workshop and the children were quiet, Alice lit rushlights and began placing them around the room. Jem had teased her about her Christmastide greenery and the festive pudding she had made.

"A pudding in defiance of Parliament!" he had joked.

But both of them were concerned about the leaders he had once had so much faith in, and uneasy about what the future held.

"There are zealots in the army," he said, "and they wield too much power. We have too many new laws."

And yet all over the country, Alice thought, people like us are healing rifts and making peace with their neighbours; and all these small kindnesses are at work in the world.

She lit the last taper and set it on the windowsill – the one that overlooked the common. The light bloomed and shone out, challenging the dark.

About the Author

Ann Turnbull was brought up in Bexleyheath, London, but now lives in Shropshire. She has always loved reading and knew from the age of ten that she wanted to be a writer. Her numerous books for young readers include *Pigeon Summer; Deep Water; Room for a Stranger; No Friend of Mine; No Shame, No Fear,* which was shortlisted for both the Whitbread Children's Book Award and the Guardian Children's Fiction Prize; and *Forged in the Fire.*

Of *Alice in Love and War*, Ann says, "I've been fascinated by the English Civil War ever since I read *The Children of the New Forest* as a child. It was a time of enormous upheaval and confusion that caused people to move around. For many, like Alice, it changed their lives forever. I wanted to explore how these great events felt at the time to ordinary people caught up in the thick of them."

Find out more about Ann Turnbull and her
books by visiting her website at
www.annturnbull.com

It is 1662 and England is reeling from the after-effects of civil war, with its clashes of faith and culture.

Seventeen-year-old Will returns home after completing his studies to begin an apprenticeship arranged by his wealthy father.

Susanna, a young Quaker girl, leaves her family to become a servant in the same town.

Theirs is a story that speaks across the centuries, telling of love and the struggle to stay true to what is most important – in spite of parents, society and even the law.

But is the love between Will and Susanna strong enough to survive – no matter what?

Shortlisted for the Whitbread Children's Book Award and the Guardian Fiction Prize.

ANN TURNBULL

The brilliant sequel to *No Shame, No Fear.*

England, 1665–1666. Will, now a Quaker, travels to London to find work. Waiting for him in Shropshire, Susanna becomes increasingly worried; Will's letters grow fewer as the plague spreads, and the city gates are closing. Susanna sets off in search of him, but hopes of marriage fade as an even greater threat looms.

Then, one night, fire breaks out...

ANN TURNBULL